DEATH CIRCLES

A HENRY & ⌐W NOVEL

SPARTILLUS

DEATH CIRCLES

Published worldwide by Spartillus.
This edition published in 2021.

1

❀ Created with Vellum

****

Would it have been worthwhile,
To have bitten off the matter with a smile,
To have squeezed the universe into a ball
To roll it toward some overwhelming question,
To say: "I am Lazarus, come from the dead,
Come back to tell you all, I shall tell you all."

T S Eliot

PROLOGUE

'Reggie! Reggie! Oh, for god's sake, Reggie!'

Sally Aiken gave a shout of frustration, lifting her hands and dropping them, her dog's lead clinking in one fist.

'Oh, let him go,' said Vicky, ambling close by with her black miniature schnauzer at her heels. 'We're miles from anywhere. What harm can he do?'

There was a 'doof' from Sue, walking up ahead with her springer spaniel puppy, as Reggie doubled back on the stony path and randomly leapt up to lick her face. For a modestly built staffy-labrador cross he could deliver quite a punch in the midriff.

'REGGIE! You bastard!' yelled Sally. 'Stop jumping on Sue!'

She was beginning to regret coming along on this little jaunt with the dog walking crew. Normally they would all meet up first thing at the park and river path near her home, but on this warm July day they had decided to get up even earlier and drive up to the Parkway Valley trail and get away from the city. Not that Salisbury was exactly a throbbing metropolis, but sometimes it was nice to vary the routine. Trouble was, the variation seemed to have made Reggie even more excitable and jumpy. Sometimes she felt like nailing his bloody paws to the floor.

'It's fine,' said Sue, who was well used to Reggie and his antics. 'I'm obviously the most gorgeous female here. He can't help himself.'

'Nobody's more gorgeous than Luna,' said Vicky, stopping to drop a treat into her furry princess's dainty mouth.

'Yeah, but she knows it,' said Sally. 'And she's a total tart. She won't leave poor Reggie alone when she's on heat.'

'How dare you!' squeaked Vicky, clutching her throat theatrically. 'She's my precious baby!'

Further down the track the four other dog walkers in their party had paused to take in the view of Stonehenge. The distant stone circle was living up to its mysterious reputation by wearing a drifting skirt of morning mist while the sun bathed its upper reaches. It was all very picturesque and, as they traipsed along, the smell of warming grass was intoxicating. As she caught up with them, Sally decided she must come here on her own some time... for a bit of mindfulness... living in the moment and all that... She had been trying to practise mindfulness over the past few months and thought she might be able to do it much better somewhere like this than in the middle of her lounge with the washing machine banging through its final spin in the kitchen.

She wouldn't bring Reggie, of course. Unless she wanted to live in the moment of pinning him down by his neck while she attempted to free her mind.

'Impressive, isn't it?' said Kathy, stroking the head of Wilson as the stately black doodle nosed into her pocket for treats. 'Should go and see it properly, really.'

'Aye, if you don't mind paying thirty quid to stand in a queue with a bunch of whining kids and joss stick-waving druids,' pointed out Jim, looking around for Molly, his black, furry barrel of a dog, who was usually about two minutes back down their track.

'I'm not sure druids do joss sticks,' said Vicky. 'That's more hippies, isn't it?'

'Hippies, druids, I don't care, I'm not paying thirty quid to stand in line with 'em just to look at a pile of stones. What a rip-off.'

'Well, they **are** one of the seven wonders of the world, Jim,' Nicola pointed out, throwing a ball for Freddie, another mini schnauzer. 'It's not like someone scooped them up from a day trip to Hengistbury Head. They brought them all the way from Wales, apparently.'

'What the bloody hell for?' said Jim. 'Can you imagine a more pointless task?'

'Well, the jury's out on whether anyone actually **did** roll them all the way down from Wales,' said Sally, giving in to Luna's request for a biscuit. 'A lot of people round here think they were put there by aliens.'

'Aye, well a lot of people round here need their heads examining,' said Jim. As the group elder, he usually had the final word, but Sally decided to wind him up.

'I don't know...' she mused. 'They do say there are a lot of unexplained happenings... especially around here, what with all the ley lines...'

'Ley lines? Bollocks!' said Jim.

'But we're on one right now,' went on Sally, adopting a breathy, reverential tone. 'Can't you feel it? The vibrations?' She lifted her plump arms and spun slowly in the warm morning air. 'Can't you feel your chakras opening, Jim? I bet they are — I bet they're wide open.'

'Wide open, my arse!' said Jim, to much hilarity.

'Reggie!' Sally called, suddenly noticing her hellhound was out of sight. She dropped her arms and scanned the group to see if

Reggie was currently shoving his snout into someone's treat-laden pocket or trying to lick a face. Everyone was currently unmolested. She gave a light, sing-song whistle, which usually brought Reggie back, but after thirty seconds he had still not emerged.

'Oh god,' she groaned. 'The little sod is rolling in fox shite somewhere... I just know it.'

'Did you shampoo him yesterday by any chance?' asked Mark, scratching Alfie, his sandy, short-legged rescue dog, on the head. 'Nothing drives a dog to fox shite quite like giving it a bath.'

'Not this time,' said Sally. 'But I know what you mean.' She called again, and then got out the big guns — an Acme Thunderer sports whistle, which she blasted with vigour.

All the other dogs came running. They sat in a circle, waiting. Because they knew that when Reggie responded quickly to the whistle, he'd get a quality treat and they'd normally get something, too.

But Reggie did not come.

Everyone started yelling for him.

'I think he went down that way,' said Sue, waving towards the lower slopes of the grassy path which wound down to a wheat field.

'Whoa! Jim!' yelled Vicky. 'Your chakras MUST be wide open! Look at that!'

Everyone paused and stared down at the vibrant green field and the most beautiful, mathematical, perfectly executed crop circle they'd ever seen. It contained circles and arcs and triangles and must have taken HOURS to create.

'Jesus Christ!' murmured Jim, who was not a religious man.

'Wow!' Sally marvelled. 'That's so beautiful! What's that in the middle of it?' She pointed at a white shape at the centre of the circle.

Everyone shielded their eyes and peered down at the white shape. 'Is that someone lying in it?' asked Nicola.

'I bet it's a bloody druid,' said Jim. 'They get everywhere.'

'I think it is someone,' said Sally. 'Probably doing some spiritual thing. Oh shit. SHIT! REGGIE! NO!"

A dark, furry, four-legged shape was suddenly pelting across the wheat field, making directly for the person in the centre of the circle. Whatever spiritual experience they were having was about to be rudely interrupted by 30 kilos of offensive mutt. Sally blew her whistle again, fruitlessly, and began to run. The others sped up behind her but she powered ahead of them, disregarding the twinge in her ankle, which had been broken only last year, thanks to Reggie.

'REGGIE!' she bawled, watching helplessly as her dog snuffled the woman — because she was pretty sure now that it was a woman — right in the face. Any moment now he was going to start shagging her leg. Oh GOD!

But the woman was clearly very focused on whatever mantra of mindfulness she was working on because she did not react to Reggie at all. Except... perhaps she'd hissed something at him, because he suddenly backed away, tail tucked under, as Sally bore down on the scene, running through a narrow gap in the crops to avoid causing any damage.

She might ask this woman what she'd said — she could use a trick like that herself. Reggie was still edging low, in reverse, glancing back at her with what she now recognised as anxiety. His ears were flat and he was lowering himself onto his belly.

Dog whisperer! That's what the druid woman had to be. Or maybe it was the mystical energy from the crop circle. Maybe it had just walloped Reggie in the Obedience Chakra. Who knew?

It was only as she reached the edge of the circle that Sally got her first stab of anxiety. Reggie was still on his belly, a low whine emitting from his throat. She dropped to her knees beside him, smoothing down the ridge of fur that had risen along his spine.

She didn't speak but let her eyes dwell on the figure in the centre of the circle.

The resting woman was dressed in a white smock gown and white tights, fine silver slippers on her feet. Her hair was long and grey, and wild flowers were woven through it. Her hands were folded, fingers intertwined, across her waist and her eyes gazed at the sky, as if she was seeing into the great beyond. Her mouth hung open. A grasshopper leapt out of it.

Sally's heart gave a massive thud of shock. What she was looking at here wasn't someone with fully open chakras.

It was a corpse.

Detective Inspector Kate Sparrow punched Lucas Henry in the face. Hard. She felt his nose crumple under her knuckles. She drew back and drove her fist forward again with a wild cry of fury, smashing his mouth into a pulp.

He was knocked flat under her blows but she didn't stop, hammering down on top of him again and again until it was impossible to know that he'd ever had human features.

There was a polite cough. Joanna Cassidy leaned forward, elbows on knees, and scrutinised her work closely. 'Has he taken enough yet?' she asked.

Kate drew a long, juddery breath and settled back in her chair, massaging her knuckles. 'Nope,' she said. 'But it'll do for now.'

'Well, that's some pretty impressive Gestalt therapy in action,' observed Joanna. She reached across to the wooden coffee table and picked up the misshapen lump of plasticine which, until a minute ago, had been a recognisable effigy of a man. 'Although it seems almost a shame. You're going to have to make a new Lucas. There's clearly more work to do here.'

Kate nodded and grabbed a glass of water. 'Sorry about the language,' she said, aware that she'd been shouting some pretty choice obscenities as she'd pummelled her modelling clay foe to death.

'No problem,' said Joanna. 'Letting off steam is what swearing is designed for. I've heard much worse.'

Kate let out a long sigh. She did actually feel a bit better.

'How many Lucases have you made now?' asked Joanna.

Kate shrugged. 'Twenty or more. It's costing me a fortune in Hobbycraft.'

'And are you sticking pins in any of them?'

'Of course not,' said Kate, quickly. 'I'm not *insane*.'

Joanna gave her an appraising stare, both eyebrows raised.

'Well, maybe once or twice,' Kate admitted. 'Usually I prefer to take a sharp knife to him.'

'Kate, when I suggested you use plasticine as a way of easing your PTSD symptoms, I have to confess this wasn't really what I had in mind,' said Joanna, the ghost of a smile on her lips. 'And although it's clearly... refreshing... for you, I am concerned that smashing up your pretend Lucases is getting in the way of just talking about him.'

'What do you want me to say?' said Kate. 'That he's a murdering shit who took my sister from me? That he lied to me and pretended he was innocent? That it's taking every bit of self-control I have not to leave here right now and go hunting for him and bring him to justice?'

Joanna settled back in her chair, rolling a silver ink pen between her elegant fingers and resting her notepad on her knee. Kate never could quite make out what she was writing but sometimes she suspected it was just the lyrics of that Madness song. *Madness... madness... they call it madness...*

'I can see how frustrating it must be for you,' said Joanna. 'Let's take a step to one side. Put yourself into the third person and just observe for a while. Help me with this... Kate Sparrow meets up with one Lucas Henry, a man she knew when she was ten and he was fifteen, and asks for his help to solve a missing persons and murder case. She knows Lucas is a talented dowser. He's found things before. So... it works. The detective and the dowser solve the case together — and then another — and then another. But this comes at no small cost. Injuries, trauma... And all the while, Kate harbours doubts and suspicions about Lucas Henry and whether he was involved in the disappearance of her sister and the murder of her sister's best friend.'

Kate nodded, rolling her eyes. 'Nicely summarised. I can see you've been paying attention.' In the six weeks since she'd last seen Lucas Henry, Kate had been attending her mandatory weekly counselling sessions religiously and this story had been unravelled, reravelled and unravelled several times over. She didn't understand why Joanna had to keep trotting her through the same stuff, though, over and over again. It was as if she was in the interrogation room back at the station... but with tissues, cushions and much nicer decor.

'So why, I wonder, didn't Kate confront Lucas sooner?' Joanna pressed on 'Why not as soon as she met him again?'

'She needed his help,' said Kate. 'Asking if he was a murderer — even politely — wouldn't have got her off to a good start. And anyway, she mostly — nearly *completely* — didn't believe he could ever have done it.'

'But she believes it now..?'

Kate had an unwelcome flash of recent memory —
Lucas Henry digging in the ground and holding up a mud-
caked bra and knickers, his face a picture of guilt and
desolation.

'Lucas took Kate to the site where her sister's underwear
was buried,' Kate said, playing along at the third person
thing. 'Kate recognised it at once. Her sister's DNA is all over
it. There was hair and blood found there, too. All belonging
to Mabel.'

'Kate, I know we've been over this before,' said Joanna.
'Your colleagues at Wiltshire Police are supporting you on
this and the search for Lucas Henry is ongoing. They're
following all the leads they have, and both Europol and
Interpol have his photo circulating. So is it possible you can
relax and let *others* do the job of finding him? Let yourself
off the hook?'

'That's exactly what I *am* doing,' Kate snapped. 'That's
why I've promised my brother — and my boss — that I *won't*
run off on some stupid wild goose chase on my own. So I
could get back to work and try to get some... *normality* back
in our lives.'

'You've gone through all the motions correctly,' said
Joanna. 'But emotionally, do you think you *are* letting go?'

There was a long pause. Kate had to admit that the
mangled plasticine body of her nemesis on Joanna's coffee
table was convincing evidence that she wasn't exactly
handling the situation well.

'No,' she said. 'I just... can't.'

'What do you think might help you detach from this?'
Joanna asked. 'Even if only temporarily.'

Kate stretched out her arms, pulled her blonde ponytail
loose and then massaged her scalp for a few seconds, eyes

closed. 'Honestly?' she said. 'I don't know. Except, maybe, an interesting new case. Something that'll distract me. Tire me out. Help me sleep.'

'Well, I hope you find one,' said Joanna. She blinked and looked a little ill-at-ease. 'At least... I'm not *wishing* a serious crime on anyone *else*, but...'

Kate had to laugh. She liked Joanna. She sometimes regretted that their relationship was purely professional, because Salisbury nick's go-to shrink would probably make a great friend. She could imagine going out for drinks with Joanna and swapping stories, gossip even, if the situation was different. Joanna was about ten years older than her, but very youthful in her demeanour, with a quirky, dry sense of humour beneath her counsellor carapace.

Kate felt her phone buzz in her pocket. It was meant to be switched off but she'd just left it on mute. She couldn't remember the last time she hadn't had it on her person, ready to alert her about somebody... found.

'I've got to go,' she told Joanna. She got up and gathered up the plasticine, mashing it into a dense ball and enjoying the feeling of her fingers pressing through it and forcing it to give.

'Remember the NLP,' said Joanna. 'At least three times a day. Go to a mirror and tell yourself — out loud — "It's OK. I don't have to do everything myself. I can let others help me.".'

Kate nodded, keen to be off now she was on her feet. She was only just resisting looking at that text.

'Say it, Kate,' said Joanna. 'Now. Before you go. There's the mirror.'

Kate sighed and turned to face Joanna's full-length mirror, sited by the door. The woman reflected in it looked tired, her blonde hair tangled by the head massage and her eyes shadowed by too little sleep. She was looking a bit scrawny too. Francis had taken to bringing her hot meals. All M&S convenience stuff, of course, but even so...

'It's OK,' she told herself. 'I don't have to do everything myself.'

She paused, wondering where the dowser was now.

'Go on,' prompted Joanna.

'I can let others help me,' Kate said, looking herself directly in the eye. Sometimes it was even convincing.

She dropped the ball of plasticine into her satchel, promised to keep up with the NLP, thanked her counsellor and left.

As soon as she was out in the Salisbury side street she pulled out her phone and found the text, which was actually not a text but notice of a voicemail waiting for her. She keyed into it fast, her heart rate picking up.

'It's me,' said DC Ben Michaels. 'There's been a body found in a field up in the Parkway Valley. A woman. Probably suicide but might not be. Chief Super wants you and me to get out there pronto. There's an interesting angle. Call me when you get this.'

Kate felt a little tingle go through her. She remembered Joanna's awkward hope that her client would get a juicy new case to work on and felt a similar stir of conflict. She didn't wish anyone dead, but she really did need a distraction. She called Michaels as she walked back to the station.

'You'll never guess who called it in, Guv,' he said, as soon as he picked up.

'Probably not,' she said. 'So tell me!'

'Your neighbour, Sally Aiken,' he said, grinning. She couldn't see him grinning but she could hear it in his voice. 'Her dog, Reggie — he found the body.'

'Oh hell, poor Sally,' said Kate, feeling a rush of concern for her neighbour. Sally was a good friend and Reggie... well, Reggie was a furry, jumpy, aggravating little sod who'd kind of saved her life once.

'I'm heading out to the car,' said Michaels. 'You nearly back?'

'Two minutes,' she said, picking up her stride.

'Good — I'll get the engine running. It gets better. I'll tell you in the car.'

He filled her in as they drove north out of the city. It was mid-morning and apparently the CSI team was already on site, tenting the area and setting up the lighting for the police photographer. The body had been found around eight-thirty. Kate had encountered some pretty grisly murders only weeks ago. She wondered if that would make this one any easier. She ought to be hardened to it all by now.

'Apparently it's one of our prettier death scenes,' said Michaels. 'No blood. No sign of a struggle. And, get this, she's laid out right in the centre of a crop circle.'

'Oh god,' said Kate, wincing. 'Croppies!'

Michaels grimaced and nodded. 'Yup.'

At least a dozen Croppies were already there by the time she and Michaels reached the site. Given the circumstances, they were a little more subdued than usual, but there was still a sedate party going on behind the police cordon. Most of them were middle-aged hippies and ought to have better things to do than haunt a crime scene in the middle of nowhere, Kate thought. But now that she saw the valley, gleaming almost neon green, she realised that for a Croppie this was hardly the middle of nowhere. With Stonehenge standing on the horizon, it had to be Ley Line Central.

'It's the energies!' she heard one woman saying in a

melodramatic tone. 'They're bound to take someone, some-time... it's inevitable. But what a wonderful way to go. I could only *hope* to transcend to the next level like that.'

DC Sharon Mulligan was already at the scene, taking notes from a weary-looking grey-haired man in a checked shirt and a waxed cotton cap, who had to be the farmer. As they approached, his morose monologue rose through the air. '...ruined. Completely ruined. That's my livelihood, that is. Trampled. It's the third one I've had in five years and it won't be the bloody last.' He suddenly glanced up to the gathering on the hill, some of whom were waving flags with alien avatars. 'And you lot can bloody fuck off!' he bellowed. 'This is my land! You're trespassing!'

He paused to allow DC Mulligan to introduce him as Bill Rogers, before rolling on: 'It's bad enough that they carved this mess into my crop — but now one of them's bloody topped herself in it! It's going to be all over the news and there's going to be a stampede of idiots coming down here to check it out. Can't you lot do something about that?'

'Mr Rogers,' said Kate, with a tight smile. 'While we feel for you and your damaged wheat, at this difficult time, we're also a *little bit concerned* about the woman lying dead in your field.'

The man gulped and shut up, taking off his cap and looking just slightly ashamed of himself.

'The upside for you is that we'll be leaving the police cordon up for some time,' Kate went on. 'So even if a stampede of idiots *does* head down here, they won't be able to reach the site.'

He nodded.

'Mr Rogers says he was up in this field until seven, yesterday evening,' said Mulligan, consulting her notebook. 'And there was nothing but wheat to be seen and no sign of any walkers in the area. The first he knew about it was when we contacted him an hour ago. His wife and son and daughter-in-law can verify that he arrived back at the farmhouse by around 7.30pm and was up and out with his tractor in the northerly end of the farm from 6.30am.'

Kate nodded. 'Did you hear anything, Mr Rogers?'

The farmer looked puzzled. 'I was a mile away,' he said, pointing to a cluster of farm buildings on a distant ridge. 'They could've been having a party down here and I wouldn't have heard it.'

'Did you hear any buzzing?' Kate pressed on. 'Either yesterday evening or early this morning? Crop circle hoaxers usually like to get drone video of their work.'

He pressed his lips together, thinking. 'I... don't think so. But, truth be told, my hearing's not so good. You could ask my boy and the missus. They might have heard something. Or Sam, my daughter-in-law.'

'We'll do that,' said Kate. She nodded at Mulligan to continue tying up her notes with Rogers and moved with Michaels towards the tented area in the centre of the crop circle. Around the small white marquee, she could make out the circles and arcs and triangles in the design. It *was* beautiful. And incredibly precise. Although she was no fan of Croppies, she could understand why some people got so excited about the crop circle phenomenon. Wiltshire was said to be the crop circle capital of the world, and it certainly had way more than its fair share of 'visitations'. Of course, they weren't from aliens. Just clever hoaxers with time on their hands. She didn't think the farmers had anything to do with it, although one or two, with farm shops and cafes, had been known to do quite nicely out of a well-sited bit of art in their field, allowing visitors to enter the circle for a fee and flogging produce, tea and cake to the crowd.

More often than not, though, the circles appeared deep into many acres of farmland and were not convenient for any day-tripper to reach.

'Bloody nut jobs,' muttered Michaels, as they paused to put elasticated plastic protectors over their shoes before entering the tent. He waved towards the excitable group on the hillside. 'They're all convinced the mothership is coming back for them.'

Kate snorted. 'Ah well... we all need a hobby.' She wondered what Lucas would make of the energy patterns in this circle. And then immediately shut that thought down, remembering how much she hated him.

Inside the tent they met with Death.

Bryan De'ath was their regular police pathologist who didn't bat an eyelid when anyone called him Death, even to his face. He'd heard every possible gag going and seemed to barely notice the smirks and guffaws any more. He had once confided to Kate that he'd wanted to be a primary school teacher but worked out that no parent was going to be keen to have little Lucy or Billy coming home with regular notes from Death in their book bags. 'Oh, but wouldn't it have been brilliant if you'd made it to head teacher?' she had chuckled. 'All those naughty kids getting sent to your study, being told "Death is waiting for you...".'

She had asked him whether he'd ever thought of changing it by deed poll... to his mother's maiden name, perhaps. 'Oh no,' he'd said, looking appalled. 'She was called Hoare!'

He glanced up at her as they entered and waved her over to the body. 'Nothing too grim this time, DI Sparrow,' he said. He blinked through round spectacles and smiled.

'Most likely suicide. Although how she managed to make a crop circle first is quite a question. No sign of string or planks or any other paraphernalia. Maybe the aliens *did* pop down and fashion this one.'

'How did she die?' asked Kate, taking in the pose, the white gown and the flowers in the hair.

'Most likely Pentobarbital,' said Death, getting to his feet and glancing down at a small metal flask lying in the flattened grass at the woman's side. 'Will know when we test it, of course, and when I open her up... but look.' He bent down and, in latex gloves, tweaked the neck of her white cotton dress to reveal a red rash across her chest. 'Rash is a common side effect for Pentobarbital overdose,' he said.

Kate sighed. The woman was in a peaceful posture, her hands folded at her waist, blue fingers interlaced. She was of average build — not fat but not thin. She had to be in her sixties, Kate would guess. Maybe she had a husband or children missing her. 'I'm guessing no ID on her,' she said, scanning the white dress for pockets and finding none. 'No note?'

'None found yet,' said Death. 'When we move her, we might find something under her.'

'Check her shoes,' said Michaels.

Kate glanced at her detective constable, surprised. She raised an eyebrow at him, and he shrugged and said: 'What? I can't think like a woman? Women put important stuff in their shoes, don't they? When they're at the beach or in the spa. So... if my mum wanted to top herself like this and she knew people would find her and wonder about her... she'd leave some ID, I reckon, or a note. But she wouldn't risk it blowing away or getting rained on. So... if she didn't have pockets... she'd put it in her shoe.'

Kate nodded, impressed. Michaels wasn't usually this

insightful. She wondered if he was experiencing a bit of personal development. He'd been a lot more serious around her in recent weeks, since Lucas Henry had escaped them all... again.

She glanced at Death, then reached into her satchel, batting aside the lump of plasticine to rummage for her latex gloves. 'Do you mind?'

'Go ahead,' he said, shrugging.

She gloved up, crouched by the woman's feet and carefully eased off one of the silver slippers. It had a soft suede sole, coated with a thin layer of mud. This was not suitable footwear for yomping through a field of unripe wheat, but perhaps the woman had been past caring. Her toes were plump and blue, and Kate felt a stab of sadness for her family, if she had any. There was no ID information in the shoe. She tried the other one.

'Well, what do you know?' said Michaels, smugly, as Kate held up a small rectangle of paper.

She stood to open it and found a handwritten note.

I go to the next level. Tell Rafe everything is in order. Be happy for me. I am released! Linda x

'That looks pretty cut and dried,' observed Michaels, peering over her shoulder.

Kate looked at the woman on the crushed wheat. The long hair, winding through the green stems, the wilting daisies and buttercups threaded through it, the floaty white gown and silver slippers. She had never met Linda before but everything about the woman suggested... flow.

So why was her handwriting so neat and orderly? Kate was no graphologist but these letters looked as if they had been scribed by a Dickensian clerk. She would have expected more loops and curls and... energy...

Oh god, I'm turning into him, spoke up a horrified voice inside her. *I'm trying to fucking DOWSE the answers!*

'Yeah,' she said. 'It *does* look cut and dried.' She was only dimly aware that she had plunged her right hand into her satchel and was violently driving her fingernails into the mangled remains of her Lucas Henry effigy.

2

3

'Shit!' Lucas Henry felt as if he'd been stabbed.

He had been. A wooden stake, come loose, had poked into his shoulder when he leaned back on his knees to stretch out his weary limbs. He stood up, reaching over to rub the area and hoping the stake hadn't actually punctured his skin.

'Tomatoes fighting back?' asked Alberto.

'Little red bastards hate me,' said Lucas, still rubbing but relieved that he wasn't bleeding. He couldn't afford to get some kind of infection. He was sure Alberto and his family would provide kindly first aid, but anything more serious would mean a trip to a clinic in Novoli... and all kinds of other complications.

'Overpower them, Larry!' said Alberto, grinning under his straw hat, and plucking more firm red fruits from the vines. 'Show them who's boss.'

It was Lucas's third week on the Molina farmstead and, not for the first time, he marvelled at how lucky he had been to call in for work here, on this six or seven acre smallholding, rather than at the megafarm just up the road. Lazlo

Palari's tomato output dwarfed Alberto Molina's by about ten to one and there was plenty of work to be had. But by now, Lucas had seen the regular busloads of dejected migrant workers travelling up there and heard stories about how things were for those staying in shacks on site. It wasn't much above slavery.

The Molina family supplied an organic sun-dried tomatoes business in Novoli and were small scale, working the land themselves alongside their seasonal workers. This time last week they'd had twenty-three men picking their crop.

Now they had only five — and one of them was the boss.

Years of post-pandemic trauma and border disputes around the restless European Union countries had made the recruitment of fruit pickers much more complex. There weren't enough to go around and now there seemed to be a constant system of poaching between farms. Last week a shiny bus had pulled up on the dusty farm track near the barn where Lucas and his fellow farm workers were staying. A man in a white shirt and a fedora hat had leapt out of it and strode straight in to hail them all as they finished their evening meal of several stone-baked pizzas, delivered from the farmhouse kitchen with bottles of local beer.

'Good news!' Fedora Guy had said. 'Make more money! We are in need of you at the *real* farm and we can pay half as much again as that miser Molina is offering. And put a proper roof over your head!'

The men had glanced at each other uneasily. Lucas caught the eye of Gino and Pepe and shook his head. 'Don't fall for it,' he said, quietly, in English. Gino and Pepe, students working their way across Europe, spoke good English. Even though he was fluent in Italian, they had recognised his accent and wanted some coaching, so they often conversed in English with the young man they knew as Larry Evans. Out here on the farm he thought this was probably OK... but if they ever went into town together he would have to insist that they all spoke Italian.

Gino and Pepe were sharp enough to spot a con, but the others — an assortment of North Africans with a desperate need to get money back home — fell for Fedora Guy's line. He told them any wages owed to them by Alberto would be collected by him, personally, at the end of the week. All they had to do was grab their belongings and come with him right now.

There was some discussion — double-checks on the wages on offer. Fedora Guy laid out the daily rate they could expect and it was, indeed, half as much again as Alberto's. 'Our working conditions are much better too,' he said. 'We have a medical team on site. And good food. Who's coming?'

Then he turned his back and walked away. 'The bus will wait ten minutes,' he said, over his shoulder.

'Shit,' said Lucas, as men began to gather their belongings, muttering amongst themselves. 'They're going.'

Gino and Pepe tried to stop them. Lucas tried too, speaking English because some of the North Africans understood it better than Italian. 'It's not what it seems!' he said. 'Don't trust him. Alberto is good to you! His family — they look after us well!'

'It is for money,' said Jamal, a tall black guy from Tunisia. 'We must make money for our families. You do not have hungry children, Larry. You do not understand.'

'But you don't know what the terms are!' Lucas insisted. 'These people... they're not good people!'

It made no difference. The men had learned that pickers were hard to come by; they imagined they could name a better price. Gino ran for the farmstead to bring Alberto back to reason with them but by the time the farmer reached the barn, the bus — and nineteen of his pickers — had vanished. Only Lucas, Gino, Pepe and Farid, a skinny, quiet boy from Algeria, remained.

Alberto had sunk onto a deserted camp bed and sighed. 'This is the third year,' he said. 'The third year that *bastard* has stolen my workers.' He closed his eyes and scratched his thinning dark hair, letting out a long sigh. 'But we will survive. Your departed friends may not. They *will* be paid half as much again for their work... but Palari will make them work twice the hours. And then he will take back half of what they earn for their bed and board.' He shook his head sorrowfully. 'And they will not find it easy to leave his employ.'

Then he had invited his four remaining pickers up to the farmstead to join him, his wife and their two daughters for dinner. 'There is room at the table for my entire workforce now!' he had laughed, with a fatalistic shrug.

The next day the weight of the crop gathering fell upon the five of them, Alberto included. His daughters, aged fifteen and twelve, were also called in to help in the fields closest to the farmhouse. Alberto promised there would be extra pay for longer hours but they all knew the harvest was at least two thirds doomed. There was no way Alberto could meet the agreed delivery of produce for the sun-dried tomato manufacturers in Novoli with a quarter of the work-force, even if they worked from dawn until dusk...

The remaining pickers toiled hard, stirred by their boss's good humour in the face of such bad luck and his refusal to be cowed by the megafarm next door. In truth, Lucas should be gone, too. He had not intended to stay this long. He needed to travel and soon. But he couldn't leave Alberto in the lurch, not now, even though every day spent in one place brought him closer to discovery and arrest.

As he worked along the vines, instinctively ferreting out the fruits at the perfect level of ripeness, he wondered again whether he should change his looks. Interpol no doubt had recent photos of him, and he still wore the same beard and unruly dark hair. Perhaps he should shave it all off... but here in Italy he could hide quite well in plain sight. Weeks of working in the sun had darkened his complexion until he looked like a local. As long as he didn't speak English in a public place or start waving Sid around, he should be OK here for a while longer.

Almost as if summoned, Sid gave a little thrum under his shirt. The old blue glass bottle stopper, dangling on a steel chain around his neck, had been pretty quiet for many days. Lucas had successfully shut down any thoughts of dowsing. He could have left his pendulum buried deep in his rucksack but couldn't bring himself to go that far. It wasn't Sid's fault that his wearer had cocked up so spectacularly that he'd been forced to flee the UK and go on the run across Europe. Also, Sid was just a bit of glass. Even the thrum was all in Lucas's head.

Even so... there was something here. Something subtly different among the patterns, ever present, in the atmosphere around him. There was metal somewhere here. Old metal. Lucas dropped a handful of tomatoes into his crate and stood up.

He closed his eyes and focused. He would have liked to release Sid and allow the pendulum to swing and direct him to the source of the energy ripple, but he put that idea firmly away. It was just about possible that some locals *had* seen a TV or newspaper report about him. They might remember the story of a suspected murderer who had led the British police to crime scenes and bodies using a glass bottle stopper to dowse the way. Which meant publicly dowsing with Sid — or any other conduit — was probably not a great idea.

'Having a little sleep now, are we, Larry?' said Alberto, from the next bank of vines.

Lucas held up one hand but kept his eyes closed. He felt a pull to his left and drifted towards the line of dense cypress bushes which marked the boundary between the Molina smallholding and the Palari megafarm. Sometimes they could hear the low muttering of workers on the other side — but not often. Men who worked for Palari were discouraged from talking. In the evenings bright light shone through between the gnarled branches and dark green leaves. Palari didn't think a little thing like nightfall should stop his pickers working. Gino said there were rumours that some had collapsed and died... and been buried in woods on the edge of the farmland. No police ever came to investigate. These were migrants; all but invisible.

Lucas dropped to his knees about a yard from the boundary. The nearest tomato vines were four or five metres behind him; here was just dirt and weeds... and... something else. He pulled a penknife from his shorts and began to work at the dry soil, digging a deep groove into it, aware of Alberto standing up a short distance away and gazing across at him.

Lucas dug down deeper, almost *smelling* the buried metal. It was old... and... if he wasn't mistaken (and he almost never was) it was gold. A moment later his fingers met with a small, cool disc. He pulled it from its shallow grave and held it up to the light, rubbing the earth away from its surface to reveal a head in profile.

'Alberto,' he called.

The older man ambled over. 'You had enough of a break

yet?' he asked, mildly. 'Or are you thinking of burrowing through the hedge and joining the others?'

'Alberto — who is Valentinian the third?' asked Lucas, holding up the coin.

Alberto paused and breathed 'Fottimi...'

Lucas didn't need Alberto to tell him this was ancient. He could sense the passing of many centuries since this coin had been buried. Well over a thousand years... maybe half as much again... He also knew this button of gold was not alone. He turned to his boss and touched his arm. 'Alberto,' he said, dropping the coin into his palm. 'There are more.'

Alberto scanned the disturbed soil, frowning. 'How do you know?'

'I... just know,' he said. He glanced at the leafy boundary, aware of Palini's wage slaves toiling not too far away on the other side.

Alberto was shaking his head. 'What... did you bury them there? Is that why you come to work for me? So you can seek your buried treasure?'

Lucas chuckled. 'If that was so, why would I be telling you? No.' He sighed, realising he was going to have to share his dowsing background with Alberto for this to make any sense at all.

'Look,' he said, pulling Sid out on his chain. 'I'm a dowser. I can find.. you know... water, with this or with twigs. Have you heard of this?' He wasn't even sure his Italian translation was correct. 'Rabdomante — sì? Cercatori d'acqua..?'

Alberto nodded slowly.

'Well... dowsers can find other things too. I sensed that there was gold here. That's how I found it. Look...' He closed Alberto's fingers around the coin. 'Go and hide it. Then I will dowse for it... show you what I mean.'

Alberto looked baffled but some kind of realisation was dawning as he eyed the pendulum. 'I *will* hide it,' he said, raising his eyebrows and tilting his head to one side. 'After you come and sit in my kitchen with my wife!'

Lucas grinned and followed Alberto back to the white-washed single-storey farmhouse, where Juliana was frying onions, garlic and peppers for a huge batch of soup in the kitchen, surrounded by pots and pans and bunches of herbs hanging from low rafters. Juliana took her catering duties seriously and made sure the workers were fuelled with the best Mediterranean food. 'Larry is here to help you for a few minutes,' said Alberto, winking at her. 'Don't let him out of your sight until I come back.'

Juliana gave her husband a wry look and waved him away before handing Lucas a chopping knife. 'You are a good boy to stay,' she said, giving him a fond, motherly glance, although she was probably no more than a decade older than him, with only a few threads of grey through her glossy dark hair.

'I know where I'm well off,' he said, slicing through some peppers and feeling a small pang of regret that she would be disappointed in him soon enough. He really wouldn't be able to linger in this idyllic place much longer.

A few minutes later Alberto came back to the kitchen and stood in the doorway with his arms folded. He smirked at Lucas. 'Go on then, Larry... dowse your way to that coin!'

'What coin?' asked Juliana, kneading some focaccia dough on a marble slab.

'You'll see soon enough, my love,' said Alberto, following Lucas out into the late afternoon heat.

Lucas glanced around and noticed Pepe, Gino and Farid were spread out among the tomato vines, hard at work and paying no attention. Good. He didn't want to put on a show for anyone but Alberto. Alberto's daughters were nearer, working the vines close to the house, wearing wide-brimmed straw hats and looking sweet in cool smock dresses and sandals. They were shy and giggly around him at mealtimes and he suspected the older one had a bit of a crush, which he was doing all he could to ignore.

He edged around the side of the house until the girls were out of sight and nothing but the lower slopes of the farm looked back at him, drifting a little in the heat haze. 'Well?' said Alberto and Lucas got Sid back out, looping the chain up over his waxed cotton bush hat and allowing the small blue pendulum to sway in the breeze. He instantly picked up the energy patterns of both the gold coin and Alberto. He could tell that the man had zig-zagged back and forth through the aisles of tomato plants and made for the drier, dustier edge of his land where the irrigation pipes ended. There he had turned east and walked along the far perimeter, which overlooked a vista of distant vineyards and olive groves, before stopping for a while and then returning to the house.

Lucas decided not to follow the exact route but to just cut to that location at the far edge. He set off through the long avenues of *solanum lycopersicum*, the heady sweet and sour fragrance of the vines percolating through the heat. Alberto followed behind without a word, trying hard not to give away his reaction as Lucas grew closer to the coin. There was an old covered well close to the hiding place but the coin wasn't there. It was a little further on, hidden among a stack of terracotta tiles left over from some recent roof repairs. Lucas paused to turn and glance at Alberto's face, which was beginning to wear that thunderstruck expression he had seen so many times before, when people realised it wasn't just a bluff... that he really *could* find lost

things. Back in the UK he'd even been paid to do it...
seeking out the watercourses around a big estate to help
with plans to build holiday homes.

Yes. Alongside painting, finding things was his talent. He
just wished those things hadn't turned out, quite so often, to
be bodies.

Lucas nodded at Alberto, with a grin, and then went to
the tiles, reaching down between two towards the back of
the pile and instantly finding the old coin. This was not a
difficult task. The purity and the history of the metal had
been singing to him from the moment he'd left Juliana's
kitchen. It was hard to explain to non-dowsers exactly what
this meant, but he understood that he had a talent for
reading energy patterns, vibrations, the perfect mathematical frequencies of nature and their myriad distinct differ-
ences. There were plenty of dowsing courses available and
many people could pick up the skill to some degree, but
only a handful were as instinctive at it as he was.

'Fottimi!'murmured Alberto, for the second time that
afternoon.

The Italian for "Fuck me!" was so much more elegant,
thought Lucas, dropping the coin back into Alberto's palm
and putting Sid and his chain back over his head and into
his shirt. 'It's pure gold,' he said to his boss, who was still
gaping at him. 'And it's very, very old. Fifth or sixth century, I
would say.'

'You are an archaeologist?' asked Alberto, in hushed
tones.

'No,' said Lucas, shaking his head and smiling. Although
nobody would be surprised to find an archaeologist picking
fruit these days; times had been tough and many professors
counted themselves lucky to be working as delivery drivers.
'I can just sense its age,' Lucas went on. 'I think there was a

big find of these near Milan some time ago, yes? And they were fifth century.'

Alberto nodded. 'The Cressoni Theatre treasure,' he breathed. 'Larry… are you saying you think we have a jar of gold coins here, too?'

'Well,' said Lucas, ambling back up the slope with the older man. 'Strictly speaking… no. I think there are a handful of coins on your side of the boundary… and a few hundred in some kind of chest… that's what I was picking up. Only… the chest is on the Palini side.'

Alberto stopped, tore off his hat and threw it into the dust, exploding: 'That bastard wins *again!*'

'Not necessarily,' said Lucas. 'Because although the chest *is* on Palini's side of the boundary, it's actually not *on* his land. It's *under* it.'

Alberto stared at him and then shrugged, not getting it.

'Well, you see, if we were to go digging on our side…' said Lucas, a slow smile spreading over his face. '…and then *keep* digging at about a forty-degree angle… for about three or four metres.'

Alberto blew out some air and picked up his hat. 'You think we can do that… we can burrow into that Palini bastard's dirt and steal the treasure from under his feet?!'

'We'll have to be very quiet,' said Lucas. 'And work in very low light… but yes. I think we can.'

Alberto whooped and leapt up into the air, punching upwards. 'Let's do it!' he said. 'As soon as it gets dark!' He paused and looked intently at Lucas. 'You're sure about this? You're not just… you know…'

Lucas shook his head. 'If I'm wrong, what have we lost?'

Alberto grinned and nodded. Then he rested his brown eyes again on his employee. 'What is your… story? What *are* you doing here on my farm?'

Lucas shrugged. 'Just, you know... working... travelling.'

'No,' said Alberto. 'You're not travelling. You're running. I can see it in you. Something made you run and hide on a little Italian farm in the middle of nowhere.'

Lucas looked at his feet, suddenly unable to speak.

'Did she break your heart?' said Alberto, softly.

'Whatever broke,' said Lucas, 'it was me that broke it.'

4

'Everybody here?' Chief Superintendent Rav Kapoor scanned the room and totted up his CID team. It wasn't a large team. Only nine officers sat around the worn desks. Kate was accompanied by DC Ben Michaels, clutching his A4 pad and pen, and sitting nearby was DC Sharon Mulligan, alongside DS Sharpe. Their new DCI should have arrived by now, but cutbacks and recruitment delays meant they were still waiting for that role to be filled and Kate was increasingly acting DCI *and* DI, even though she'd only just qualified as inspector three months ago.

An assortment of photos of the dead woman were already up on the board, along with wider shots of the crop circle and a close-up of the note found in the slipper. Marker pen alongside the images simply stated: **Linda Stewart? Suicide? Murder?**

'Kate? When you're ready,' said Kapoor.

She stepped up. 'This could be a very short case. Death is doing the post-mortem as we speak and should be able to advise us by the end of the day on whether it was, as seems likely, a suicide. We haven't yet confirmed identity, but a blue Ford Fiesta left overnight in Parkway Lane could be connected. It's registered to one Linda Stewart who lives in Burchfont and the photo ID and age seem to be a match. DS Sharpe and DC Mulligan have visited the address and found no-one home. Neighbours have nothing of note to report and at this point we still aren't certain our Jane Doe *is* Linda Stewart. The DVLA sent through Linda Stewart's licence photo — and we've also accessed her passport image — and both are about ten years old. She's not on social media, as far as we can tell, so we haven't yet picked up anything more recent. We're waiting on mobile phone info and when that comes through we might just be able to call her and find out she's alive and kicking.

'She might just have had a breakdown on the hilltop last night and got a cab home, although this seems unlikely because...' Kate held up a plastic bag with a car key and what was probably a door key hanging from the fob. 'The keys were in the car, up on the sun visor and it was unlocked. Even so, we need to put calls in to local recovery garages, too, in case any have had a request to go and pick it up. We also want any ANPR on the Fiesta that we can pick up in the previous twenty-four hours, with the main focus on between 8pm last night and 8am this morning. See if any image capture shows a lone woman at the wheel or if she had company. Or another vehicle following.'

'What about the crop circle?' asked Sharpe, scratching his grey thatch of hair with the end of his pen. 'Do we think whoever made it is connected with the deceased?'

'Those aliens are a bit hard to track down,' quipped Michaels, earning himself a dark look from Kapoor. He shrugged. 'Too much time interviewing the Croppies, sir. Sorry!'

'Michaels and I went to the farmhouse and spoke to Mrs Rogers, the farmer's wife, and his son and daughter-in-law, Christopher and Sam,' went on Kate. 'And they all confirm they were at home all evening and overnight until getting-up time at six. Although none of them were out and about in the dark, Sam Rogers did mention that she thought she heard something when she checked on the henhouse they've got in the farm garden, around 9pm. She thought she heard a buzzing sound, some way distant, which might possibly have been a drone. We do know that some crop circle makers like to get drone footage of their efforts and there would still have been just enough light to capture some at that time.'

'I can't see why they'd want to mess up their artwork by slinging a body in the middle of it,' observed Sharpe. 'I mean... these guys think they're artists, don't they?'

'They *are* artists,' said Mulligan, a little awe creeping across her Rotherham accent. 'Those things are amazing. I don't know how they do it.'

'Planks,' said Michaels, scathingly. Kate wasn't sure whether he was referring to the method or the creators. She nodded to Mulligan.

'We've taken names of the Croppies who showed up this morning,' said Mulligan. 'Asked how they heard about it. They reckon the coordinates were circulated on a Croppies Facebook page in the early hours, which we're looking into. No pictures were on social media, as far we know, before this morning and those that are getting out there now all feature our cordon and tent... nothing with the body on display. Which is something. I mean, those dog walkers might easily have put images up on Facebook before we arrived.'

'No, said Kate. 'They wouldn't do that. One of them is my

next-door neighbour, Sally. She's a decent woman. Her dog was the first on the scene. Sally has vouched for all of her group as fully paid-up human beings. They were quite upset.'

'Yeah — and I checked their phones, too,' said Michaels, with a grin. 'Nothing in their photo reels.'

'So,' said Kate, 'we press on with IDing our crop circle lady and with finding out who made that circle. The two may not be connected but that seems unlikely. How did Linda know the crop circle would be there? Was she part of the crew that made it? Was it some kind of suicide pact? There could be others. Although the Wiltshire Police drone is up and searching and nothing has shown up so far. We'll also need to check on all the ANPRs on the routes in and out to see who *else* was driving through any time from dusk onwards. We need to check on every licensed drone operator in the area, too...'

The task list rolled on, but as she doled out the duties, Kate suspected it wouldn't be very long before Death delivered a suicide verdict. That wouldn't kill their enquiries, of course, but it would let the steam out and take the manpower down a few notches. Contacting family and teasing out the sad circumstances of a suicide took fewer bodies than hunting a killer.

'Finally,' she said, picking up the marker pen and scrawling one more name. 'Who is *Rafe*? Why has she mentioned him in her note? Is this a husband? A son? brother? A lover or a friend? Or someone else? It's not a common name, so a bit of online cross-referencing with Linda Stewart could bring something up. Norriss and Craighead... please do your techie magic.'

The tech wizards nodded and got ready to attack their keyboards.

The Chief stood up and said: 'Thank you — to work, everyone.' He retreated to his office.

Kate turned to Michaels. 'Get a coffee, yeah?' she said, her eyes tracking back to Kapoor's office. 'Then we'll head to Burchfont. We've got a front door key in here.' She waved the plastic bag. 'And we've got an address. So if nobody's in...'

'OK. Shall I get us both a coffee to go... or... are you... are you going to ask again, boss?' He glanced towards Kapoor's office.

'Make mine white, one sugar... to go,' she replied, swerving the question. Her DC's growing concern was even worse than his crush. She'd thought his surreptitious checking out and occasional over-lengthy gazes were bad enough, but having the slick-haired little twat *worrying* about her was massively more annoying. All the more because she knew he had cause. She *was* obsessing. Every day. And worse, every night. For fuck's sake... she'd even been making plasticine voodoo dolls!

But could she get a grip? Apparently not.

She put her head around Kapoor's door and said 'Knock, knock..?'

Kapoor raised one greying eyebrow at her as he looked up from a pile of forms he was working through, pen in hand. 'You do realise that the point of knocking, whether verbally or with a fist, is that you stay on the *other side of the door* until someone calls you in..?'

'Sorry, sir,' she said, smiling tightly and going in anyway. 'I just wondered... if there's any news?'

Kapoor sighed and indicated the seat opposite. 'How many times do I tell you, every week, that you will be the *first* to know about any developments?'

She nodded, slumping back into the small leather chair.

'I just can't believe he can have *vanished* and *stayed vanished* for this long. It's been six weeks. He has to *be* somewhere.'

'Every patrol in the country has his photo,' said Kapoor. 'Every airport, seaport — Border Force, Interpol. We've checked with yacht charters and private plane pilots. He's either in this country, lying low, or he's managed to get abroad somehow. But wherever he is, he has no money, no passport. He is going to pop up sooner or later. He *will* make contact with you again and that's when we'll pick up his trail.'

Kate thought about the letter that had arrived in the post three days after Lucas Henry had escaped her and disappeared. She didn't need to dig out the copy she had made, kept permanently in a pocket of her satchel. She had memorised it all.

You should have waited. You should have given me the benefit of the doubt. How could you think I would kill Zoe and Mabel? How could you? What does your copper's instinct tell you, Kate? Don't you go with that any more?

She had handed the letter to Kapoor the day after it arrived at her house in the post. Forensics had been all over it and confirmed fingerprints and DNA from the man who was strenuously denying killing Kate's sister nearly seventeen years ago. She couldn't *believe* she had let him get away from her. She'd been so close to cuffing him but he'd managed to escape and run.

I am not running away. I am running to. I am determined to find out what happened in the quarry that day. Because I really WASN'T in the quarry that day. I did not kill Zoe. I didn't do anything to Mabel.

Oh no? So how come he'd led her to the site where Mabel's underwear was buried? And how come he'd been shaking and wretched with guilt as he dug them up?

I am going to find the answers and then I am coming back to show you, Kate. I am coming back to show you.

Yeah, right.

'If he would just tell us where she's buried,' she murmured, sagging into the chair and wiping a hand over her face. 'If we could just get her back... have a funeral. Get some closure at last.'

Kapoor looked slightly uncomfortable. 'Kate,' he said, 'Just a few weeks ago you would have been defending Lucas Henry. You would have been insisting that his ability to find bodies and other meaningful evidence was entirely down to his talents as a dowser. And now you've done a one hundred and eighty degree turn and decided he is a killer. Despite the cases you have worked together... despite the times when he has undoubtedly saved lives, yours included.' He steepled his fingers and watched her intently across them. 'I know you've had trauma upon trauma over the past six months but still, something else has changed. Something that's made you lose faith in him. Can I ask what that is..?'

Kate found herself staring at her hands, unable to answer. Kapoor's question was a fair one. He had been as sceptical as the next copper when Kate had first brought Lucas in to help with the Runner Grabber case, but after meeting Lucas one-to-one and witnessing first hand what he could do, her boss had been convinced.

'You weren't there,' she said, at length. 'When he took me into the woods and dug up her bra and pants with his bare hands, he was shaking with... *guilt*... I could see it all over his face. And before that he'd been telling me, as you know from the debrief notes, about a sexual relationship with Mabel that went wrong. Do you have any idea how many men I have encountered through this job who flip because of sexual issues, and murder the woman who made them feel less of a man? Everything he said... the whole "I just wanted it to stop" thing. It's absolutely textbook, isn't it?'

Kapoor didn't reply for a few seconds. He took a long breath and then said: 'Keep seeing the counsellor, Kate, and keep your faith in the rest of us. We *will* find him. He will face justice for whatever it is he has done. For now, though, please do what you said you would do. Please focus on your work and pour your energies into it.'

Kate got up, nodding.

'Oh, and when you clock off,' went on Kapoor, picking up his pen and smiling at her. 'Consider having a little fun, sometime..? See a movie. Go on a date. Remember to live.'

5

Alberto could have kept their plans secret — between himself and Lucas — and after he'd gone online and looked up the design of the face on the coin he would have had every reason to stay quiet. It was indeed an image of Caesar Valentinian III, dating back to the fifth century.

'These three figures on the back,' Alberto had called out, excitedly, from his under-stairs study area, 'they are a wedding group! Oh my! Oh dear god in heaven! If there really *are* more...'

He had called everyone together, taken them to the shady pergola outside the farmhouse for a lunch of focaccia bread, roasted vegetables and spiced chicken, and told them what Lucas had told him. Lucas did not want Alberto to mention how he had found the coin, but there was no way to explain how he knew the whereabouts of the rest of the trove unless he confessed to his dowsing talent... and he couldn't convincingly explain why he didn't want to do that.

So they had all sat around the huge old oak table —

Pepe, Gino, Farid and Alberto's wife and daughters, too —
and made a plan.

'This will be good for us all,' said Alberto. 'If we find
these coins, I will give each of you a five per cent share of
whatever money comes from them.' The pickers looked at
each other, a mixture of emotions drifting out from them
which Lucas was easily able to discern and understand.
Mostly they were bemused. In essence, they had seen one
tiny gold coin and heard that Larry, their fellow picker, was
some kind of magical treasure finder who believed there
was a pot of gold at the end of an underground rainbow...
which landed beneath a neighbour's property.

'You have been loyal and hardworking,' Alberto went on,
warmly. 'I regard you all as family now and I would like to
reward you if I can. So... tonight we will dig. Larry, here, has
a plan.'

All eyes turned to him and Lucas grinned uneasily. *Shit.
Way to go to keep a low profile, Dowser Boy!*

'OK,' he said. 'I know this all seems a bit like a fairy tale
and I might be wrong... but I don't think we have anything
to lose by trying, and personally, running an underground
heist into that bastard Palari's farm and stealing some rare
coins out from under him... that's something I can get on
board with. How about you?'

They started grinning at each other, excited. Tomato
picking was hard, hot and monotonous. This was something
much more interesting... and could be done in the cool of
night.

'First,' said Lucas. 'We're going to dig down there.' He
pointed south to the lower boundary of the farm, not far
from the covered well and the pile of terracotta tiles. The
others looked baffled. It was the opposite end to the
boundary with Palari's farm. 'We are going to dig a deep

hole and leave it open, with some bright lights around it,' Lucas went on. 'We may even shout to each other about the excitement of our discovery. Then we will come back to the boundary with Palari's farm and we will work in silence and very low light. We will be digging deep, at a forty-degree angle. This will take us beneath the boundary and two or three metres under the Palari land. That is where we will find some kind of chest and the main deposit of coins. But it's *crucial* that nobody hears us or sees any evidence of what we are doing.'

They stared at him, slowly nodding as understanding and growing excitement dawned in them. He could sense that they were increasingly buying into his plan.

'Once we have extracted all the coins we will fill the hole back in and then transport our find down to the other pit. We'll put it in place and take some photos and video, proving exactly where we found it. Understand?'

Everyone nodded and Gino asked: 'Is this for real? You really think it's there?'

Lucas pressed his fingers into the old warm wood of the table and sighed. 'I have had quite a high level of success at dowsing in the past. I am pretty sure there is... a lot of gold.'

'And... you're trusting us... with this information,' Gino went on, glancing from Lucas to his boss.

Alberto nodded. 'I hope you will make some good money,' he said. 'I am never able to pay you as much as I would like. This place...' he waved around them. '...it's our home and we love it. We can only just afford to stay here because of our tomatoes, but this year...' He shook his head. '...it may be our last. Palari is trying to squeeze us out. He wants to crush me and buy my land for a pittance. And he probably will.'

His wife reached over and squeezed his hand. 'No,' she said. 'Never.'

'My family has been here for two centuries,' said Alberto, squeezing Juliana's hand in return. 'It would break my heart to leave. My daughters deserve to inherit this land.' His daughters smiled at him. 'But we cannot withstand someone like Palari without money of our own. If Larry is correct... if these coins can be found on my land... it could change everything. So, yes, Gino, and Pepe and Farid, I am trusting you because I see that you are good people. And I will, I promise, give each of you five per cent of whatever money these coins sell for. It may be only hundreds... but it could be thousands.'

'It could even be *millions*,' breathed Sofia, his older daughter, who had been surfing websites about rare coins for the past hour.

'Ssshhh, don't jinx it!' whispered her mother.

'And even if it is nothing,' conceded Alberto, 'And Larry here has just gone mad from too much sun, that's fine. We will have tried.'

'We're in,' said Gino, grinning at Lucas. 'What have we got to lose? Let's tunnel from one end of Palari's slave camp to the other!'

'But first,' said Alberto. 'We have more tomatoes to pick!'

'Only one other thing,' added Lucas, tentatively. Everyone looked at him. 'This thing I do... my dowsing. I don't want anyone else to know about it. Can I ask you all to keep it to yourselves?'

They glanced at each other and then back at him, nodding.

'We've all got something to hide,' said Pepe, with a wink.

Lucas didn't think one of them would guess what *he* was hiding.

The plan kicked off at twilight. Everyone but Juliana headed down to the far end of the farm, carrying shovels and buckets and lantern torches. The scent of the vines and the wildflowers along the borders of the land was intense as the day cooled into night, and moths and crane flies spun around the lights set down on the soil. It was pretty hard-baked, here in the peak of the summer heat, but it didn't take long to break the surface and start to dig. They went down around a metre and a half, turning up some bits of old clay tile, stones and many affronted worms. It was unlikely anyone was close enough to hear them, but they made plenty of noises — excited noises — as they worked.

Then, as the evening wore into night, they left the lights where they were and made their way silently back up to the Palari boundary, Alberto sending his daughters inside to go to bed at this point. Everyone fell silent as Lucas led them back to the spot where he'd dug out the first coin, shining just one low torch beam across the ground to guide them. He stood over the small pit he'd dug and got Sid out to give him a more precise reading of what was down there... and where.

Chinks of bright white light fell through the gaps in the cypress hedging, and the distant mumble of pickers could be heard. The Palari farm night shift toiled on just a few metres away from them, unaware of what lay beneath their feet as they occasionally wandered close to the perimeter with their crates of produce.

Lucas knelt down and dug his trowel into the earth he'd already loosened. It made a deafeningly loud crunching noise as it hit buried pebbles. He sat back on his heels and shook his head. 'No,' he said. 'This is too loud; we're too close to them. I think... we need to come back later. When do those poor pickers get to bed?'

Alberto considered. 'The lights are usually out by midnight,' he said. 'They give them about six hours off to sleep.'

'So... I think we should get some sleep, too,' said Lucas. 'And come back here at around two, when we can be sure they've all gone.'

Alberto nodded. 'You are right. We cannot risk this. It is too important. Come... let's sleep. Well, you can *try* to sleep! I don't think I will close my eyes!'

Ten minutes later Lucas was back in the barn and settling onto his camp bed, Sid still nestling under his shirt. They all stayed dressed, ready to get back to their subterranean heist in about three hours. 'Larry,' called Gino, softly, his camp bed just a few steps away. 'Are you sure you're not pulling a big fat prank on all of us?'

Lucas snorted. 'Yeah. There's nothing down there at all. I just want to see how good you all look smeared in sweat and mud.'

'You know you want me, Larry!' replied Gino, in a loud stage whisper. 'You're so hot for me!'

They all sniggered — even Farid — and Lucas lay on his back, forearms across his eyes, grinning. He began to drift, tired from another long, hot day at the vines and then the added effort of excavating the fake treasure site. He could see his hands in the soil, digging and digging... and then coming back up, mud and leaf litter dropping away from what he'd found. Scraps of soil-encrusted material, hints of the original pink in a crease... He jolted out of sleep, cursing inside his head. He could really do without this nightmare right now.

But as he drifted again, it only got worse. Now he was digging into a pile of rocks, uncovering the fixed dead stare of one of his best friends beneath. Zoe was entombed, murdered... but always seemed to be still alive in his dreams. 'Why did you do it, Lucas?' she asked. 'Why did you show her? What did you expect her to think?'

'What were you doing with my bra and pants, anyway?' asked Mabel. She sat a little way above them on a cheese-wedge shaped overhang of the quarry, wearing a white dress, her blonde hair floating on the breeze. 'You should have left them where they were. That was a shrine to me, that place. Well... a shrine to my knickers, anyway.' She laughed — threw back her head and cackled, the way she always used to whenever she'd embarrassed him.

'She's going to come for you,' said Zoe, but Lucas didn't know who she meant. Kate Sparrow? He knew she would be searching for him. He knew she would never give up; never let him go. But then Kate morphed into her big sister and it seemed that Mabel was the one who would never let him go.

'You've never let me go,' he muttered. 'Not for nearly seventeen years. Why can't you just stop haunting me?'

'You know why,' said Mabel, running her finger along his lower lip. 'You know why.'

And then it was Kate again, standing so close to him on the edge of that wood where her sister's clothing still lay buried. Standing so close he could breathe in the air she exhaled. Standing so close he knew they were just a millisecond from touching lips and the compulsion to reach out and pull her into him was almost overwhelming. 'I'm coming for you,' said Kate, running her finger along his lower lip. And then she threw him on the ground, flipped him onto his chest and straddled him, screaming and weeping while she grappled his wrists into her police issue handcuffs and read him his rights.

Fuck. Lucas rolled over and rubbed his face. *WHY had he*

taken her there? Why could he not have just sat down in a cafe with her, made his confession, and then explained that he'd recently been picking up energy patterns that were drawing him to the woods below Pepperbox Hill? Why on earth had he thought it was a good idea to lure her along to the beauty spot to meet with him, start wittering about all the humiliating things Mabel had done to him... and then dig up Mabel's underwear?

If he had just got the sequence of events in the right order, he might not be here now. He might be working *with* Kate to find the answers to the Quarry Girls case, rather than fleeing across the continent to try to do it on his own.

It was no small miracle he'd escaped. Her police colleagues had been very close on his tail, and it was only a series of lucky breaks that had seen him safely away from the UK. He had no passport, no money, nothing but the clothes he stood up in and some bank cards in his wallet which he didn't dare use, as they would immediately signal his whereabouts. No matter how much good he had done, assisting Wiltshire Police over the last six months, he was now once again the prime suspect for the murder of the Quarry Girls.

As he'd stumbled through the woods his mind was feverishly working out how he could get out of the country. That was when he'd realised, in a moment of clarity amid the surging panic, that Mariam was in Poole Harbour. That very week. She had gone to stay with friends aboard a yacht. He didn't know the name of the friends or the yacht, and he couldn't phone or text his friend and mentor to ask, but he could get to the harbour and dowse.

Killing his mobile, detaching the battery and sim card, he scattered the parts into bogs as he ran through the thick undergrowth. The only way they could track him was by drone, helicopter, CCTV or witness sightings... and he thought he knew how to avoid those. Drones and helicopters gave off very distinct patterns and when he was running on adrenaline he was very attuned to the threats around him. There was nothing in the air yet; no heat-seeking tech to flush him out. Not yet. He could do this. He could make it to Poole.

Sid informed him that a vehicle moving slowly along the farm track he was pounding along was a possible way out. Lucas scrambled inside undergrowth on the roadside just as a tractor rounded the bend, lugging a trailer of hay bales. Further along this path he could sense warm, simple life forms. The feathery kind. Two pheasants were bumbling at the edge of the road. As the tractor drew closer, Lucas waited for his moment, and then, while the vehicle was still a few seconds from passing him, he clapped his hands hard, hoping the sharp shot-like vibrations would cut across the approaching rumble of the tractor engine.

It did. The pheasants both reacted by bouncing into the path of the oncoming vehicle and then circling in a confused amble, clearly unable to decide whether the massive machine bearing down on them was more of an issue than a random clap. The driver slowed down to walking pace, drawing level and then passing Lucas, and he heard a weary shout of 'Get outta the way, you stupid birds!'

It was all the time he needed to sneak onto the trailer. He climbed easily over its low back end and discovered a spare bit of tarp which he pulled over his head. The journey that followed was bumpy and uncomfortable and seemed to last for ever, but it got him far enough away from the searching police to stand a chance. He did hear a drone overhead and sensed a chopper coming from the north-east.

He hoped the heat of the big tractor engine and the barrier of the hay would confuse any thermal-imaging gear.

He slid, unseen, off his ride when deeper into farmland and began to make his way south along streams and through copses, hugging any area with trees to hide his passing. He took off his jacket, turned it inside out to show blue lining, and tied it around his waist. From a pocket he pulled a khaki biker's snood and put it on his head like a bandana. Whenever he was forced to walk in open land, he adopted a loping, easygoing gait, hoping to pass for a local out on a walk. He didn't dare to move like a fugitive.

Finally, he picked up the A338 and managed to hitch a lift with a Polish truck driver heading directly to Poole Harbour. As soon as the truck pulled in and the driver waved him up, he spoke to the man in French, reasoning that if he could come across as a non-native, his haulier friend might not connect him with any news reports of a murderous English bastard who'd killed a couple of teenage girls a decade and a half ago.

It worked. He reached the harbour and then all he had to do was find Mariam, explain how catastrophically wrong everything had just gone, and see if she would help a wanted man to get out of the port.

Once again, Sid came to his aid. Before even reaching the marina, Lucas found Mariam in a local bakery. She was alone, picking up fresh bread to take back to her friends on their boat. The baker was trying to chat her up when Lucas spotted her through the wide glass window display. She was a good looking fifty-something with Egyptian colouring and stylish streaks of grey in her glossy dark hair, so this wasn't uncommon. Lucas felt his heart thump with gratitude at the sight of her. As soon as she stepped out onto the sun-warmed pavement he moved up alongside her and said: 'Hi.'

She glanced at him, did a double-take, and then said: 'Oooooh, Lucas. It's all over the radio. I just heard it in the Co-op ten minutes ago. You are in some *serious* shit now.'

'Yup,' he said, keeping his head down. 'Um... any chance you could help me vanish again?'

She sighed, handed him her canvas bag, filled with bread and wine, and paused long enough at a kiosk to buy him a peaked cap with I ♥ POOLE on it. 'Look like a tourist,' she said, handing it to him. He whipped off the bandana and gratefully put on the cap.

What he would have done without Mariam, he had no idea. His former university lecturer had saved his skin a number of times over the past year — first by giving him exhibition space and prompting him to paint a collection which was later to sell out, then by shielding him from the police as he scrambled through her attic, escaping an earlier Lucas Henry manhunt. More recently she'd got him dowsing work at a stately home, the payment for which had kept him going until now.

Mariam swiftly made the decision to introduce him to her friends, a couple in their sixties who owned a large yacht and were, by her description, 'stupidly rich but somehow not stupid'. Jeff and Sonia Markham had been fascinated by the fugitive brought below deck to meet them and trusted Mariam when she assured them both he was not a murderer. The trio had masterminded his escape — the older couple positively revelling in the adventure.

They contacted another couple, Henri and Genevieve, friends who lived on a private island just off the French coast. These friends had their own waterfront and anchorage. They were also stupidly wealthy *and* up for a bit of adventure. The plan was to sail out to meet them halfway across the channel, and transfer Lucas to the other yacht and thence back to the French couple's island retreat.

Lucas had been astounded that Mariam could convince her friends to do this — even more that *they* could convince their other friends who had never even met him.

'What you have to understand, dear boy,' said Jeff. 'Is that having everything you need, and pursuing a non-stop holiday in your retirement years, can get boring as shit.'

'What if you're caught?' Lucas had said. 'Harbouring a fugitive? Smuggling him abroad without passport or papers or..?'

But by then Sonia had already called her friends and arrived to tell them that it was all arranged.

It shouldn't have worked. They should have been caught. Lucas's luck had to run out. But... it hadn't. And the plan worked perfectly — although leaping from one yacht to another in the middle of the Channel had proved less straightforward. It was too lively a swell to nimbly step between the decks and too dangerous to attempt a winch, so in the end he had leapt into the water in a life jacket and grabbed the life ring on a rope in the water, flung overboard by his French rescuers. He arrived on board soaked, frozen and knackered. All he had left behind was the handwritten note to Kate, which Mariam had promised to post back in England — from a remote box in the middle of nowhere, out of sight of CCTV or passers-by, a few days later. He had even put the letter into a plastic bag with instructions to be sure she didn't leave any incriminating prints on it.

'I will leave no trace,' she had told him, squeezing his hand. 'Lucas... be careful. And... don't come back until you have your proof, OK?'

'The police will come and talk to you,' he had warned her.

'Well, good luck to them,' she had said, with a wink. 'I know *nothing*.'

He spent two days with Henri and Genevieve while they helped hatch plans to get him onto the French mainland and away to wherever he needed to go. They took a motor launch trip and dropped him onto the beach at Saint-Cast-Le-Guildo, giving him five hundred euros in cash and a rucksack with some of Henri's spare clothes. When he promised to pay the money back they waved him away as if it was a handful of coins. 'We've never had such excitement,' Genevieve had told him. 'It's excellent value!'

Entertainment. Yes. He could believe that was a big motivator. Of course, any one of them could have a crisis of conscience and give him up, but he doubted they would. They didn't need reward money, they didn't seek notoriety and they certainly wouldn't want to spend their leisure time helping the police.

He had been incredibly lucky to find such people, and so far that luck had held. Hitching rides all the way to Italy, he hadn't chosen a dud. Every single stranger had been kind. Right up to Alberto and his small family. Lucas turned over in bed, drifting in and out of sleep. He was going to have to leave this place. Not just because of his dowsing revelation and the way this might expose him if anyone ever talked, but because his senses told him more forcefully every day, that he was close. That the answer to who committed the Quarry Girls crimes was almost within reach.

His map of Europe was folded in his rucksack and every time he found a private place and suspended Sid above it, the pendulum pulled towards the last leg of his journey. He hadn't been certain until the last few days, but he was sure now. The person who had ended Zoe and Mabel was across one more body of water — just a ferry trip away; he was convinced of it. But if he left it much longer, they wouldn't be. As soon as the treasure had been dug up tonight, he would have to go.

With only an hour to go before the moonlit dig, he at last slept, and dreamed of green circles.

6

There were days when being sexy was so fucking boring.

CHRISTINA ELIADES LAY on her bed, her toes high in the air, and considered the merits of stripping the peach nail varnish off and replacing it with red to go with the cocktail dress she would be wearing later.

THE POUNDING OF THE PLUMP, sweaty man between her thighs had been going on for a couple of minutes but if she knew anything about Stav it was that he didn't go for long. This was a blessing for which she was regularly thankful. Sex with Stav didn't really take much effort, beyond the perpetual pretence, whenever he looked at her, that she was in transports of ecstasy. In truth, she probably didn't need to try that hard. He always took his glasses off before clambering on and he was incredibly short-sighted, so the odds were that even if she were weeping and mouthing the Lord's Prayer, he probably wouldn't notice.

HE WOULD NOTICE, though, if she forgot to shave her legs or put on lipstick or keep her toenails varnished and chip-free. She wasn't just a great lay; she was also a trophy wife. How she looked in public reflected on Stav. He gave her a healthy allowance to keep the shine on her appearance and expected to see the results whenever he *did* have his glasses on.

'OOOH... OOOH... NEARLY...' he grunted, almost bang on three minutes.

'OH BABY,' she sighed, doing her bit. 'Oh yeah.' The red nail varnish. She couldn't wear the peach with a scarlet dress; it would clash horribly. Even if the men didn't notice, all those bitches they were married to would. God... she would be glad when all this was over. She reckoned she could make it through another couple of weeks.

SHE HADN'T DECIDED how best to do it but glancing at the spectacular marine aquarium at the end of the kingsize bed, while Stav collapsed, panting, on top of her, she got some inspiration.

DROWNING WOULD BE GOOD.

7

The village of Burchfont was right out of Midsomer Murders. Kate felt as if she were a guest actor as she and Michaels got out of the car by the parish church.

DS Sharpe and DC Mulligan's visit earlier in the day had already told them Linda Stewart's home appeared to be empty and there was no car parked out front. The vehicle registered to this name and address was currently in the evidence pound, so that was no surprise, but seeing the parking area still empty indicated nobody else was likely to be living or staying at the address.

Linda Stewart's home was a small mid-terrace cottage with actual honeysuckle around the door. The front garden was neatly kept, with pots of blue hydrangeas under the bay window. There were no nets or blinds to be seen behind the glass, but a series of crystals on fine cord hung there, scattering the mid-afternoon sunlight in rainbow diamonds. There was no way to get to the back of the house from this side, and, at this early stage, it might later be hard to justify breaking in if their dead New Ager turned out to be someone else. So it was fortunate they had the key.

KATE KNOCKED FIRST, loudly. They waited for thirty seconds before she slid the key in. It turned easily and the blue painted door swung inward. The house smelled of pot pourri or perhaps incense. It was small but pretty, with stripped and varnished floorboards along the hallway and pendant light shades made of shells hanging above. The front room had an original cast-iron fireplace filled with fir cones, and shelves of books from floor to ceiling on either side of the chimney breast. There was an elderly Chesterfield sofa in wine-coloured leather with heavy and dented cushions in its corners, an old trunk for a coffee table, set upon a faded Persian rug, woven many years past in shades of maroon and bottle blue. The entire window sill was cluttered with crystals — quartz, amethyst... something yellow... citrine? There was no television or any kind of screen in the room and, as they worked their way through to the dining room and small galley kitchen, Kate got the distinct impression that they wouldn't find any tech at all. The pictures on the walls were ethereal... images of the planets, rendered in a vividly oversaturated style and charts of the lunar cycle, astrological signs... some Leonardo da Vinci sketches and what looked like some homemade watercolours of local scenery. There were some old family photos on the walls, too, but none of them resembled the woman in the crop circle.

. . .

TO KATE'S MIND, the crystals and the otherworldly contents of the book case — *Mysteries of Wiltshire, Ghosts and Spirits, The Crystal Bible* — were building a picture very much in keeping with the woman who lay dead in a crop circle that morning. By the time they'd toured the two bedrooms and bathroom, finding not so much as a transistor radio, Kate was convinced the inhabitant of this cottage had no truck with the advances of the 21st century. On a telephone table in the hallway — straight out of the seventies — was a single landline phone with a circular dial. This appeared to be the only concession to communication, beyond pen and paper.

'THIS PLACE IS A BLOODY TIME CAPSULE!' marvelled Michaels. 'My nan had a telephone table like that!'

'WE NEED TO SEE HER HANDWRITING,' said Kate, going back to a bureau she had seen in an alcove in the dining room. The bureau gave up its treasure almost at once. There were notebooks filled with drawings and poems, and the handwriting was, as she had suspected, free-flowing — loops and curls in abundance. Not at all like the script she'd seen on the so-called suicide note — although the poems looked to have been written in fountain pen ink. In the bureau she also found three A5 fliers — all the same — with **THE CHURCH OF THE ENLIGHTENED ENERGY** emblazoned across them in glowing turquoise print, above a picture of a man with long golden hair and a Christ-like beard, holding out his open palms in a circle of light. It read:

. . .

CIRCLES OF LIFE
  A talk by the CEE leader.
  Join us on St Michael and Mavis Hall.
  SU 1503 7335 11am, 24/07
  Have your mind opened to the truth.

SHE HEARD MICHAELS, back in the hallway, lifting the receiver of the old-style phone. Then she heard the dial click and whirr. She pocketed one of the fliers and leant around the door, looking at him quizzically.

HIS DIALLING FINGER was safely covered by a latex glove and he lifted the receiver from the table with the same hand when he was done. In his other hand he held his mobile, thumb at the ready to make a note. 'Just dialling 69,' he explained. 'See who called her last.'

SHE NODDED. 'GOOD THINKING.'

'GOT ONE!' He thumbed the number into the note facility on his mobile as he held the clunky old receiver an inch from his ear. 'It's a Salisbury code,' he added, hanging up and wrinkling his nose. 'Wasn't sure that would even work on this antique. Why would you keep something like this? The exchange barely supports them any more and they're useless with a digital menu. Anyway — I can call this number if you like...'

. . .

'STORE IT,' she said. 'We can wait a little longer before we start rattling relatives or friends. Just want to be completely sure our deceased *is* Linda Stewart. Remember the Cranston case?'

MICHAELS NODDED AND GRIMACED. A couple of years back an enthusiastic Salisbury DC had rung the relatives of a young man who'd been pulled out of the River Avon, after the tech guys had dried out the phone found in the deceased's pocket and got into the contacts. It later turned out the mobile had been stolen from its perfectly fit and well owner, who just happened to closely match the description of the cadaver in the mortuary. Daniel Cranston's distraught parents had come in to ID their drowned son and were just staring, horrified, into the puffy dead face of a stranger when their *actual* son phoned up to ask if he could borrow his dad's car.

FAR FROM BEING grateful that they had been spared such a tragedy, Mr and Mrs Cranston took legal action for the shock and trauma — and won a substantial payout.

KATE TOOK one of the notebooks and bagged it before dropping it into her satchel. 'OK,' she said. 'Not sure what more we can learn here at the moment. Let's go walkabout, shall we?'

· · ·

THEY LET THEMSELVES OUT QUIETLY, unnoticed by any neighbours, and made their way towards a small parade of local shops, around the corner from Linda Stewart's address.

'I SUPPOSE there are worse ways to go,' mused Michaels as they strolled along the quiet street of pretty cottages facing a small green and a pond. 'Drink something that just knocks you out gently and float away to the great beyond in the middle of a crop circle. If you believe in all that earth energies crap, it's probably about as good as it gets.'

'YOU'RE ASSUMING she *chose* to die,' pointed out Kate. 'We don't know that yet.'

'SHE LOOKED PRETTY PEACEFUL,' said Michaels, shrugging. 'No sign of a struggle.'

'THAT WE COULD *SEE*,' said Kate. 'Death will tell us about that later. I mean... if you're drugged up to the eyeballs it's kind of hard to struggle.'

'YEAH,' said Michaels, dropping his head and shoving his hands into his pockets. 'Fair point.'

SHE FELT, rather than saw him reddening up. It took a lot to make Michaels blush but she reckoned he'd just remembered that she had, only a few months ago, been drugged and helpless herself, at the hands of a serial killer. The recollection that she'd been stark naked throughout was probably what was warming up her DC's cheeks.

'IT'S ENTIRELY possible it *was* a nice, gentle suicide,' she said, distracting him from his hot collar. 'I'm not assuming it's foul play... but not counting it out, either. It was ritualistic and where there's ritual there's often a dead-eyed, stone-hearted psychopath within spitting distance.'

THE POST OFFICE and general store was the obvious place to go, although Michaels was already eyeing up the chip shop next to it. 'Go on,' she said. 'It's been at least an hour since you last ate. Just... ask about Linda Stewart while you're waiting for your pea fritter.'

HE GRINNED. 'WANT SOME CHIPS?'

'I MIGHT NICK A FEW OF YOURS,' she said. He rolled his eyes. 'I'm only saving you from yourself,' she added. 'It's a kindness.'

THE POST OFFICE was quiet but two older ladies were chatting by the till, one on either side of it. There was a rather surly looking man behind the counter, staring into a Royal Mail computer, but Kate made straight for the ladies. 'Hi,'

she said. 'Can you help me out with something? I'm trying
to locate a Linda Stewart..?'

THE CUSTOMER LOOKED blank but the woman at the till said:
'Oh, Linda... yes... she lives just down the road. You can't
miss the house... it's like a crystal grotto! I hope you're not
planning to take that to her door,' she added, eyeing the
mobile in Kate's hand.

'WOULD THAT BE A PROBLEM?' asked Kate.

THE WOMAN, in late middle age, greying and of sceptical
expression, snorted. 'Oh yes, Linda's not one for tech. She
believes all the... what does she call it? Electromagnetic
smog or something... it's poisoning us all. She won't go
anywhere near it. Doesn't have a mobile, doesn't believe in
the internet! Thinks it's all a massive conspiracy to enslave
us all.'

KATE GLANCED down at her mobile with a wry smile. 'She
might have a point. So... have you seen Linda today, er,
Karen?' she asked, eyeing the name badge on the woman's
blue tabard. She's not at home. I just called in there.'

'SHE'S PROBABLY off out with those New Age weirdos,' said
Karen. She put her hand over her mouth in an affectation of
embarrassment. 'I shouldn't say it, I know. But she does
seem to attract the nutters. They came over to the green and

did this dancing, chanting thing back last month. Next thing you know they were all stretched out on the ground, burying their faces in the grass, *soaking up the earth's vibrations*. Scared the ducks right off the pond, it did. People complained. Bloody weirdos. We get 'em *all* round here.'

'OH COME ON, KAREN,' said a mild voice behind them. 'That's a bit harsh.' Kate turned to see a man had arrived in the shop. In black with a white dog collar, it wasn't difficult to work out what his job was, but Karen helped out on that too.

'REVEREND BENNET, how nice to see you,' said Karen, suddenly colouring up. Kate couldn't be sure whether it was because she was embarrassed to be overheard bitching by the local vicar, or for other reasons. The vicar was uncommonly good-looking. His hair was wavy, light brown and sculpted back across his head as if it had been chiselled by a talented Greek sculptor. His eyes were a warm brown and his mouth was pressed into a smile, as if he were trying not to laugh.

OH MY, Kate thought. *I bet he gets a lot of cassock-chasers.* 'So, you're happy to welcome the New Agers in?' she asked.

HE SHRUGGED. 'They're harmless. We get a lot of tourists, seeking out ley lines and stone circles and ancient monuments. They're good for business, aren't they, Karen?'

·   ·   ·

KAREN SNIFFED and tidied a rack of postcards featuring Avebury Ring, Stonehenge and other tourist spots in the county. 'I suppose so,' she said.

'NOT SO GOOD for *your* business, though, is it?' Kate asked him. 'Not many New Agers beating a path to the church door on Sunday, I'm guessing.'

'NOT UNLESS I tell them about the ley line intersection under the crypt,' said Rev Bennet, with a grin.

KATE GRINNED BACK, and then discreetly flashed her badge. 'Any chance I could pick your brain about something, Reverend? Outside..?'

HE FOLLOWED her out to the street, where Michaels was sitting nearby on a weathered wooden bench, hoovering up chips. Her DC gave a greasy salute and started to get to his feet but she waved him away. 'Get your lunch down you, Ben,' she said. Then she turned back to the vicar. 'Do you know Linda Stewart?' she asked. 'Lives down in Cyclamen Lane..?'

'YES, I KNOW LINDA,' he said. 'She's been a great supporter of our little church for many years.' His eyes narrowed. 'What's this about? Is there a problem?'

.   .   .

'No,' said Kate. 'It's routine stuff — just hoped to find her at home today but she's not in. Um... you say she's a church supporter? Only... I was getting the impression she was one of the lawn-hugging New Agers...'

He dipped his head and looked a little strained. 'Linda is... shall we say... open-hearted. A bit impressionable. Artistic and creative. She gets excited by all kinds of things... and people. Her attendance at church... fluctuates. But she knows she is always welcome back. Whenever she chooses to return. And she always designs our Midnight Mass order of service, every Christmas. She's very talented.'

'OK... so, when did you last see her, Reverend?' Kate asked, as Michaels screwed up the chip wrapping and shoved it in a nearby bin.

'Please — call me Jason,' said Bennet. He rubbed his chin, thoughtfully. 'I'm not sure... a week ago maybe? In passing. Just along this road I think. We exchanged a few words as she went into the Post Office. Can't really remember what... lovely day... that kind of thing.' He shrugged. 'Sorry if that's not very helpful. I'm getting a little worried now. Is she missing?'

'You've been a great help, Jason' said Kate. 'Thanks.'

. . .

SHE REJOINED MICHAELS. 'So... no chips left for me?' she asked, arching an eyebrow.

HE GRINNED and handed her an unopened paper package. 'Better,' he said. 'Battered sausage...'

8

All was darkness on the far side of the cypress hedging when the five-man team returned to the original spot where Lucas had found the coin. It appeared the overworked pickers at Palari's had finally been granted some rest.

'Let's go!' breathed Alberto, his eyes glittering in the moonlight.

'Wait,' said Lucas, holding up one hand. The men looked at him, random angles of their faces highlighted by the single lantern that Alberto held low between them. Lucas got Sid out and closed his eyes, focusing hard and asking whether there was anyone else they needed to worry about.

The answer was... maybe... but not *yet*.

'I think Palari has patrols,' said Lucas, at length. 'Maybe with dogs.'

'He does,' said Pepe, nodding. 'I saw them at his gate one time. He has two guard dogs — Alsations — nasty brutes. Another way of keeping the workers too scared to run away in the night.'

'OK, that fits with what I'm picking up,' said Lucas. 'But we're OK for now. I reckon the dog patrol will reach this boundary in twenty or thirty minutes.'

Alberto shook his head. 'How can you *possibly* know this?'

Lucas grinned. 'I'm not a clairvoyant. I can just about detect their energy patterns moving north and we're on the southern perimeter. From the speed they're moving, I can guess it'll be twenty or thirty minutes before they get down to us. So... let's get going.'

Only two could comfortably dig together at a time, so the others were stationed along the boundary, ready to give a quiet signal if they heard any patrols approaching or saw light on the other side of the hedge. Alberto and Lucas started the dig, with forks at first, to loosen the earth, and then with spades to lift it. Three times in the first five minutes, Lucas halted Alberto and sifted through the clods of earth with his fingers to find another coin and hand it to the farmer. Each time, Alberto chuckled quietly with delight and wonder, tucking the coin away into a leather zip-up money bag, strapped to his waist.

After twenty minutes they were both sweating and tired, but too wired to really notice. The others periodically edged closer to see how the treasure hunt was going, before returning to their posts. 'I think there are three more coins on this side,' Lucas said, quietly. 'Then we have to go down at an angle and work our way under the roots of this.' He gave the sturdy hedging a shake.

After they'd found the next three he urged Alberto to rest while he and Pepe continued to dig. They were knee deep in the earth when Farid gave a low, warning hiss. 'Patrol!' he said.

'Everyone — move back!' Lucas muttered. The dogs

were sure to scent five sweaty, overexcited men just beyond the boundary. They downed tools quietly and retreated at speed to the first bank of tomato vines, where they folded themselves in among the leaves and fruit and stood perfectly still. Above the thudding of his heart, Lucas could hear the patrol approaching, the dogs panting and the men speaking to one another in low voices. They took their time, ambling past the dig point, but three minutes later Lucas sensed the dogs were far enough away for them to continue.

The next stage was tough and unrewarding. Getting deep enough to pass under the roots of the cypress hedging took a lot of work. This was high summer and the earth was hard-baked to some depth. Gino ran off and came back with a connected hose and they softened the unyielding soil into mud, which helped with digging but made the load on their spades much weightier. Eventually though, after an hour of labour — sharing the patrol and the digging duties — they had the makings of a serious tunnel.

It was necessary to pause and hide a second time as the human-canine patrol approached and passed again on the far side. They all took a well-earned drink of cool water and then returned to the hole. 'I think it's going to have to be me down there, from now on,' said Lucas. 'I will be able to find the coins much more quickly. I will scoop them out and pass them through to *you*, Farid. You're the skinniest so you should have room to manoeuvre if you come down into the tunnel behind me. Is that OK?'

Farid nodded, his young face wreathed with excitement. Lucas could sense that every man here was having a moment of absolute regression. This was the ultimate boys' adventure, acted out by them all, no doubt, in some wood or park when they were under ten. Only, back then the treasure was imaginary and here it was real.

Digging sideways underground was the worst part of this adventure. It got amazingly hot in almost no time and Lucas was dripping and slippery with sweat as he used a small gardening trowel and fork to grind through the stony earth, periodically softening it with the water gun on the end of the hose which had been fed through to reach him. But now the pickings were getting easier. He found coin after coin, collecting them in a small plastic tumbler which he handed to Farid whenever it was close to full. Farid would pass it further along to the men on the upside, who would send another empty vessel back in return.

Keeping silent in the midst of such extreme excitement was a bit like reaching a long drawn-out climax, Lucas reflected, with the partner of your dreams, whilst hiding under a bed containing your lover's lightly sleeping parents. Everyone wanted to whoop with delight and leap around and punch the air — he could feel wave upon wave of intense thrill emitting from his fellow diggers. All he could do was grin and draw immense satisfaction from stealing gold from beneath the very feet of Alberto's enemy. He just wished he could do something that would improve the lives of the men captive in the rows and rows of huts half a kilometre away from here. Their collective wretchedness was strong enough to pool down into the very earth and leave a dull bass hum of misery in Lucas's dowsing mind. He did his best to ignore it, but it was making his flesh crawl. It seemed somewhat obscene for them all to be revelling in their heist while hundreds of human beings were being brought so low, so close by.

Hitting the motherlode distracted him from these thoughts. His fingers caught a line of something metal, which was not gold, but iron. The edge of the box. It was wooden too, but the wood was rotten and simply fell to pieces when he pressed his thumb against it. The collapse of the ancient casket produced a glittering torrent of coins and it was all he could do not to cry out in wonder at it. Then he felt, rather than heard, the others fall silent. Farid froze behind him. 'Ssshhhh…' he urged.

Lucas turned himself to stone, his cupped hands brim full of coins, as the patrol passed overhead. He caught his breath as a shower of earth rained down over his neck and shoulders and realised that they were stepping literally over the top of him. He had not asked Alberto to provide any props for the tunnel because the earth above was only a metre or so thick and bound up with root networks. On this side, though, he realised, it was different. Away from the boundary hedge he could sense there was less than half a metre of earth over him, and it was not stable.

It might have been fine if at that point he hadn't caught the quickening of excitement from a canine source. The dogs… the dogs could *smell* him. Maybe Farid too. The men up top would have retreated to the tomato vines again, but the young Algerian was still crouched silently behind him.

'What is it?' he heard one of the patrolmen say, muffled by the earth and grass that separated them. 'Stop pissing around, Caesar!'

Fleetingly, Lucas bit his lip in amusement. He wondered if the other dog was called Valentinian. But the amusement was spent a second later as more earth rained down on him and the distinct sound of dogs digging permeated through the earth. *Shit! SHIT SHIT SHIT!* He should have thought of this. He should have stopped and dowsed for those dogs every few minutes instead of getting caught up in his childish desire for gold. He wanted to drive Farid backwards — to get him away and safe, because this could end very badly. If these dogs got through to him he was going to **a.**

have his ears bitten off and **b.** be in no position to explain what the hell he was doing down there without giving away the escapade the neighbouring farmer had set his workers to. Quite apart from anything else, there was a *lot* of gold on show. Maybe he could bribe the guards... but he didn't much fancy his chances.

'What are they after?' said the other patrolman, his query just audible over the fervent scratching of claws. 'What the hell is buried down there?'

Lucas cringed. He shoved Farid with his foot and hissed: 'Get back out! You need to get away.' He thought the dogs might be too obsessed with *his* scent to notice Farid's when the boy emerged out of the hole on Alberto's side of the boundary. But if *he* went, too... it was going to pull those dogs right towards the boundary and invite curious torches through the leaves... maybe even a stepladder and one of those arc lights they loved to use. Farid, though, was stock still and would not leave him.

More earth fell through, dislodging further coins and causing a small, chinking avalanche which sounded incredibly loud to Lucas's ears. How the men above weren't already completely acquainted with what was happening beneath their feet he couldn't guess. From where he was crouching, it seemed screamingly obvious.

And then... the dogs suddenly stopped digging and hared away to the east, causing their handlers to shout out in annoyance as they were yanked along on the end of the leads. 'What the fuck has got into you?!' bellowed one of them as his footfalls faded away.

'OK,' breathed Lucas. He had no idea how he'd got so lucky but he knew there wasn't much time to cash in on that luck. 'We have to finish this *fast!*'

And they did. The unsettling of the ground from above

helped dislodge the wooden casket further until its side collapsed completely, showering Lucas in gold as if he was the jackpot winner on a cheesy TV gameshow. He and Farid worked in a frenzy, collecting the coins in the plastic tumblers and sending them back with speed, until literally no coin was left. At least none that Lucas could sense... and that meant *none.*

At last, he and his helper crawled back outside, but the work wasn't done. 'We have to fill it in again,' he whispered. 'If it collapses... they'll find out someone was there. Can't risk it...'

But he and Farid were urged to rest while the others filled in the tunnel, pushing the earth in hard to pack out the area once taken up by a treasure beyond reckoning. Beyond Lucas's reckoning, anyway. He lay on the ground, absolutely exhausted, until the job was done and then, with only a few minutes left before those dogs returned, the party, soaked in perspiration and mud, staggered back to the farmhouse holding a sack of coins between them.

'I... I thought I was done for,' gasped Lucas, as soon as they were far enough from the boundary to speak. 'Those dogs were about a minute away from digging down to the top of my head. What happened? Why did they run away?'

Alberto and Pepe grinned at each other. 'Well,' said Alberto, 'I'm sorry to tell you that none of us will be having the joint of roast lamb my darling wife intended to cook to perfection for us tomorrow. Pepe here stole it from my kitchen, ran away down the boundary and threw it over the top.'

Lucas laughed and shook his head. 'Genius,' he said.

'No,' said Alberto. '*You* are the genius, Larry.'

Back in Alberto's farmhouse his wife met them, eyes

wide with excitement and disbelief as they dragged the sack inside and showed her what lay within.

'We must clean them all!' she said, holding a coin up to the light and beaming.

'Not all,' said Lucas. 'Keep a few back to put into the other hole at the other end. You can take some photos in the morning — it needs to look like you found them there.'

Alberto nodded his head, understanding. 'They will send men to inspect, once we've told of our find. I will have to report it officially, of course. The government might take a share of this... but most of it will come to us,' he told his wife. 'As the owners of this land.'

'There's going to be a lot of press interest,' said Lucas, letting out a long sigh. 'So... can we all agree that nothing is said to anyone until the photos have been staged tomorrow? Then...' He knew his time was up. He would have to leave now. He could not be here to meet the media. He could picture the cheery line up of farmer and pickers with their treasure, on the front page of the local paper and on websites all over the world. There was no way he could feature in that line up.

Everyone was agreeing that nobody would speak of this until the scene was fully set. Alberto reiterated that his faithful pickers would be well rewarded. As Juliana ladled out hot Mediterranean pepper soup and passed around plates of focaccia he took Alberto to one side. 'There is something else I have to do,' he said. 'Before the sun comes up. Will you come with me?'

Alberto looked surprised. 'Now? But you must take some soup and then you must rest before the morning, Lucas.'

'After the soup, but before we go back to bed,' said Lucas. 'I need you to walk the perimeter with me once more... further east... towards the woods."

'You think there are more coins?' Alberto looked thunderstruck.

'No,' said Lucas. 'I don't think there are any more to be found. But... I don't just find coins or water. I have a knack for finding other things too.'

'Like what?' Alberto asked.

'Like bodies,' sighed Lucas.

9

Sally caught Kate as she arrived home at the end of the day. 'Any news?' she asked, leaping out of her front door like a trapdoor spider as her neighbour got out of the car.

Kate smiled, locking up the Honda. She would never normally share work information with Sally, and Sally wouldn't ask. Well, not more than *once* anyway. She met Sally at the wall which ran between their front gardens and sat down on it, resting her back against the brick of their terrace. 'Most likely it *is* suicide,' she said, with a yawn. 'But it's all still open for debate right now. We're pretty sure we know who she is. We still need to get hold of the relatives, though — get a formal ID.'

She glanced at Sally. Big, blousy and warm, her neighbour was a decade older and quite maternal towards Kate and Francis; had been ever since their mum died a few years ago. Sally was one of the reasons Kate and Francis had made the decision not to sell the family home but instead to convert it to a flat for each of them — Francis upstairs and Kate down. 'So — are *you* OK?' Kate asked. 'Sorry I didn't have time to talk to you much this morning — lots to deal with. A bit of a shock for you, though.'

Sally shook her head, glancing back along her hallway, where Kate could make out sounds of company inside. 'I'm fine,' she said. 'It *was* bit of a shock but no worse than seeing my old dad dead in the nursing home. In fact, quite a bit nicer, as these things go. I mean, she looked really peaceful, didn't she?'

'She did,' agreed Kate.

'Some of my dog-walking friends were pretty freaked out, though,' said Sally, glancing back into the house again. 'A few of them are here now — stopped in for a cup of tea and a chat, you know. Waiting to see what shows up on *South Today*.'

'I'm sure they didn't expect your country walk to end like that,' Kate said. 'Did many of them see the body up close?'

'No — only a couple of us — me and Nicola. We told the others to stay away and they did. They had to look after all the dogs, keep them on their leads. It was funny, actually. Once we realised what it was in the crop circle and once I'd taken Reggie back for Dee to hang on to, all the dogs just stood there with their humans, quite still and silent — even Reggie. It was like they *knew...*'

'They probably did,' agreed Kate. 'They could smell it, quite apart from anything else.'

'Come in and say hello,' said Sally, taking hold of Kate's arm. 'I've got cake!'

'I shouldn't really,' said Kate. 'I won't be able to tell them anything, you know. Not that they don't already know.'

'It's my *carrot cake*,' Sally went on, with a wink.

Sally's carrot cake was legendary. Kate laughed, wavered, and gave in, clambering over the wall and following her neighbour into the house. Four of the friends were sitting in the conservatory, which had its doors open onto Sally's neat back garden. The only dog with them was Reggie, who was lying on his back, having his belly scratched by a woman with short wavy hair.

'Kate,' said Sally, 'this is Vicky, Nicola, Mark and Dee. Everyone — this is Kate, my neighbour... or DI Sparrow, I should say, who we met this morning.'

'Please — just Kate right now,' said Kate, raising her hands as she found a spare wicker seat. 'I'm off duty.' Before anyone could ask her for news she grabbed a large slice of carrot cake and bit into it. 'Sally, this is bloody amazing,' she mumbled through a mouthful.

'Kate was saying it probably was a suicide,' Sally said to the others. 'And we're not allowed to ask a load of questions because she's off duty and she probably mustn't tell us anything anyway. The family haven't been informed... and it's an ongoing case, you see?' Sally was clearly enjoying sharing her procedural insight.

'Well,' said the one Kate remembered as Vicky. 'We won't ask about that, then... but... are you the Kate Sparrow who was caught up in the Runner Grabber case? And then the Gaffer Tape Killings?'

Everyone stared at her, agog, and she realised she was going to have to bolt her cake and run. But then Sally sat down and gave her friends a reproving look. 'She's had a long day,' she said. 'Leave her alone.'

Kate finished the cake, getting ready to make her excuses, but was saved by her mobile phone going off. She smiled apologetically at Sally. 'I've got to get this.' Sally waved her out into the garden and she stepped outside, grateful to escape the scrutiny of the tea party.

'It's me,' said Michaels. 'We've found a phone number for Linda Stewart's son. It was a bit long-winded because she'd gone back to using her maiden name after she got divorced a few years ago. Her son's called Marcus Dundrill. Lives in Salisbury with his wife Diane. Looks like he was the last one to phone her on that landline too.'

'OK — so have you put in a call?' asked Kate.

'Erm no... not yet,' said Michaels. 'It's a bit weird. This Marcus Dundrill... he's already been interviewed by Sharon Mulligan. It appears he was one of the dog walkers who found the body.'

Kate paused, blinking, and then glanced back into the conservatory at Sally's guests, checking off the names she'd been given. Vicky... Nicola... and Mark... and Dee... *what the hell?* She moved further down the garden, well out of hearing of the group in the house. 'Are you telling me that he was on the scene when his mother's body was found and didn't think to mention it to anyone this morning?'

'Looks that way,' said Michaels. 'Just wanted to run it past you before I called him. See what you thought.'

Kate considered. 'Have you got a mobile number for him,' she said.

'I have,' said Michaels.

'OK,' she said. 'Give it two minutes and then call him.'

'Right... OK,' said Michaels. 'Erm... any particular reason for the wait?'

'I'm in my neighbour's garden,' she explained. 'She lured me in for cake and some of the dog walkers are here now. I think Marcus Dundrill and his wife may be among them. I'd just like to see their reaction when you call.'

'OK,' said Michaels. 'Well... I'll get right on it. In two minutes...'

Kate took a deep breath, put her phone away and headed back into the conservatory. 'I should be going,' she told Sally. Then she crouched down to where Reggie still lay on the floor, paws up, ready for love, and scratched his rib-cage area. 'Not before I've said hello to *you*, though, Reggie!' she said.

'Sally told us Reggie saved your life,' said Vicky. 'Is that true or is she just winding us up?'

Kate grinned, still petting her furry saviour. 'Well, I think he nearly ended it several times when I used to take him out running with me, but yeah, he did redeem himself eventually. He got in between me and a serial killer at precisely the right moment.'

'Told you!' Sally said, with much pride.

Before they could prise further details from her — details which she was pretty sure Sally had fully briefed them on some time ago — a mobile phone went off. Mark fished out his device, frowning at the unfamiliar number on it. Kate glanced up, keen to catch his reaction as he picked up the call, but Mark got up, saying: 'Sorry... better answer this,' and went into the garden.

'Oops — think I may have left my phone out there,' improvised Kate and followed him.

'Hello... er, yes... um, who?' Mark was saying. She pretended to find her phone on Sally's garden swing, while keeping her ears carefully pricked and surreptitiously watching his body language.

'Yes... yes I am,' went on Mark, scratching his dark hair and looking worried. 'Yes... she is. What's all this about?'

She could see his shoulders stiffen and the side angle of his face suggested genuine puzzlement and then concern. It was hard to gauge much more. If Marcus Dundrill *had* spotted his mother's body in that crop circle, from a distance, and chosen to hide his recognition, she was having a hard time working out why. Nothing in his demeanour suggested guilt. But that didn't mean he *wasn't* guilty. She would need to be looking him directly in the eye to get a feel for that.

Mark put the phone back in his pocket, looking dazed. 'Dee!' he called, and his wife, a dark- haired and energetic thirty-something, like her husband, arrived on the lawn.

'What's up?' she asked.

'That was... the police.' Mark turned to take Kate into his field of vision. 'Your colleagues at Salisbury Station,' he explained. 'They want to know when I last saw my mother. Apparently she's... gone missing.'

'Oh,' said Kate. 'I'm sorry. Have they asked you to go in?'

He nodded. 'Don't know *why*,' he said. 'I mean, she's a free agent. She doesn't have to check in with *me* every day. She's probably just gone off somewhere with her wifty-wafty mates.'

Dee looked concerned. 'So... who reported her missing?'

'Nobody — but they found her car abandoned,' he said. 'With the keys still in it. And they can't raise her at the cottage.'

'We'd better get there and find out what's going on,' said Dee, squeezing his arm. 'Come on.'

As the couple left, amid anxious expressions of sympathy and best wishes, Kate couldn't honestly say their reaction was in any way suspicious. It was pretty much what she'd expected, apart from that comment about the wifty-wafty friends, perhaps, which was telling... Michaels had obviously thought it kinder to get them into the station before dropping the bomb of the mother's apparent suicide. She suspected he wanted to see their faces for himself. She was mildly aggravated by this but didn't really blame him. He was working late and so probably deserved any revelations that were coming when he broke the news. She should trust him by now — if there was something guilty in Mark or Dee's reactions, he would pick it up.

She cornered Sally in her kitchen while her other two guests chatted on in the conservatory. 'Do you know anything about Mark's mum?'

'Oh, *her,*' said Sally. 'He and Dee are always telling us about her mad escapades. She's a bit eccentric. Very New Age and into all kinds of conspiracy theories. I think she's taken up with some kind of cult... at least that what Mark says.'

Kate dug into her satchel, remembering, for the first time that day, the leaflet she'd picked up from Linda Stewart's bureau. She glanced at it and said: 'This so called cult... is it called the Church of the Enlightened Energy?'

'Yes,' said Sally, her eyes wide. 'Have you heard of it? Oh my god, is it *really* a cult? Has she been kidnapped?'

'Sally... have you ever met Mark's mum? Or seen a picture of her?' Kate asked, putting the leaflet away again.

Sally shook her head. 'Don't think so. I mean... they just talk about her sometimes. We all talk about the people in our lives — the little dramas — you know, while we're out on our morning walks. It's therapy!'

'So... you wouldn't know her if you met her?' Kate persisted.

Sally shrugged. 'Not from Eve. Unless she was wearing a badge saying "Mark's Mum". Why do you ask? What's going on?'

Kate wanted to prepare her for what her little dog-walking group was going to have to deal with shortly, but until there had been a positive ID on that body, she couldn't. At this stage it wasn't even certain that any foul play was involved. Death had confirmed that the deceased had indeed taken Pentobarbital, a poison commonly used for suicide by those who could get it (it was a favourite of depressed vets). Kate had shared her thoughts on the handwriting with the team that afternoon, after she and Michaels had got back to CID, and the graphologist was going to take a look, but other than her own misgivings there was so far very little to go on.

'I don't really know,' said Kate. She yawned again. 'Quite a day for all of us, yes? Look...' She checked her watch. 'It's nearly time for *South Today*. I'll leave you to watch it. Although don't expect much. We've not released any statements yet.'

She headed next door, letting herself in with some relief, her thoughts tangled and tired. She paused by the pinboard in the small hallway she and her brother shared. Ahead of her was his door at the foot of the stairs and to the left, her own door. They didn't lock them. After the traumas of the last few months, it had become habit for each of them to check on the other. She wondered if that would change once one of them got their next boyfriend or girlfriend.

Kate wondered what kind of boyfriend... or maybe husband... her big sister would have been with by now. She turned to focus on the photos of Mabel on the pinboard. There were assorted family shots on the board and she and Francis had long ago agreed to leave them there. It wasn't like this hallway was a shrine to the dead... more of a reminder that they *had* been alive. Alive and happy. Well, Mabel, anyway... here in her sunhat and off-the-shoulder top, poking her tongue out at the camera. Mum's photos were definitely happy before her daughter went missing, presumed dead. After that, Mum was never truly happy again, although she put on a good show for her surviving children.

'Live your life,' she used to say. 'Be happy. In remembrance of Mabel, live it all to the fullest!'

Kate stared at Mabel, committing her face to memory once again. It troubled her sometimes that picturing Mabel without the aid of a photo was getting harder as time went by. She traced her fingertip down the side of her late sister's face. 'Where are you, Mabel?' she whispered. 'I so want to find you and bring you home to rest.'

She didn't add: 'And bring the bastard who killed you to justice.' That thought never left her head these days, so it seemed superfluous to mention it.

Inside her flat, at a desk which had a view down the long garden to where it met the meandering reaches of a River Avon tributary, she flipped open her laptop and looked up the Church of the Enlightened Energy online. She got a few hits but no website. Whoever they were, they weren't working hard on their social media profile. There were some fleeting mentions of them on Facebook, from people who appeared to be followers of assorted fringe and New Age interests. One name came up repeatedly in the discussions, immediately grabbing her attention — Rafe Campion. *Rafe.* The very name in the dead woman's note. It appeared he was the leader of the Church of Enlightened Energy. Kate searched his name more broadly and aside from a long-deceased genealogy reference, a handful of pages appeared to relate to one person, currently alive in the South of England.

This Rafe Campion was thirty-eight, a Winchester College alumni and a former city stockbroker. An online article in *Pagans Today* magazine told his story.

'I was an empty man,' says Campion. 'I made my living buying and selling worthless notions of what is of value in

this world. I was materialistic and shallow and in pursuit of nothing more than my own pleasure.'

Kate glanced at the photo — noting it was indeed the golden-haired guru featured on the leaflet. Rafe Campion wouldn't have struggled much in his pursuit of pleasure. He was good-looking and clearly charismatic.

'One day I was visiting my parents' home in Wiltshire,' Campion continues. 'When I heard about a crop circle in a neighbouring farmer's field. I went to see it and, for some reason I couldn't really fathom, felt an incredibly strong compulsion to lie down in the centre of it.'

Kate almost *heard* her detective radar go ping. This was *very* interesting.

'So I lay down in the centre,' Campion explains, his face filled with disbelief even now, five years later. 'And I felt the most extraordinary sense of happiness and energy and... *enlightenment*. I realised straight away that something otherworldly was happening to me. I understood at once that whatever had created this — and countless other crop circles all over the world, for centuries — had a message. For me and for all mankind. *We are not alone...*'

Kate sighed. Wiltshire was full of crop circle and ley line devotees. She didn't generally have a problem with them — most were sweet enough when she encountered them. They meant well. And who was to say they weren't *right* about aliens popping in every so often to leave pretty patterns in a cornfield? Kate was sure she would be very much on board if it weren't for the *complete lack of evidence*. The idea that massively intelligent beings from other worlds were dropping little notes to humanity was an entertaining one, but she couldn't help wondering why, if they had mastered intergalactic travel, they couldn't manage to write their messages in even one Earth language. Or, perhaps, drop in for a selfie with a croppie fan..?

The Church of the Enlightened Energy, it turned out, was what Rafe Campion had founded shortly after his crop circle enlightenment. There was no shortage of followers ready to get involved, despite the fact he had so little online presence. One of the tenets of his new religion was that modern-day tech was damaging to the body and soul — and definitely to the chakras — and to be used only when absolutely necessary. Kate had to hand it to him — to get any kind of following these days, without tarting yourself about on every social media platform going, was impressive.

So... she took out the leaflet and read the details. The time and date — 11am, 24/07 — that was tomorrow. SU 1503 7335 was clearly a set of map coordinates. She entered the letters and digits into Google maps and sure enough, there it was — almost on the intersection of the old St Michael and Mavis Hall ley lines. Some farmer's barn, perhaps. It looked like it from the satellite view.

Well, now she had a place to be tomorrow morning. There was a knock at the door and she found Sally standing there, shock and distress upon her face. 'The others have gone,' she said, 'And I'm so glad, because Dee's just called to tell me... that woman Reggie found..? I can't believe it... she was Mark's *mum!*'

10

Dawn wasn't far away as Lucas and Alberto walked the eastern end of the boundary with Palari's farming empire.

Lucas had fashioned a Y diviner from some fine metal pegs found in his boss's shed. 'I can use Sid,' he explained, 'but if I'm walking any distance it's easier to use rods or twigs or a Y diviner. I have to stop and take fresh readings quite a lot with a pendulum but this will stay fairly steady as we walk. He let the metal rods rest lightly in his fingers, holding his arms outstretched a little from his chest, where Sid nestled, thrumming away with energy in support of the newly deployed diviner.

'You really think you can find bodies on Palari's land?' asked Alberto. 'I mean... you hear things, don't you? There has been talk... but nobody knows for sure. Those men who disappeared; they probably just escaped and moved on.'

Lucas glanced at him and shook his head, sadly. 'Maybe some did but others didn't, I'm sure of it. I started picking up some vibrations while I was down in the earth. There are bodies, trust me.'

'But even if there are,' Alberto went on. 'They're on Palari's land. We can't go over there and start digging, can we? Not unless you think one of them is close by and we can go under the boundary again.' He shuddered at the thought.

'No, I wouldn't do that,' said Lucas. 'But... I'd get a dog.'

'A dog?'

'Yep... a spaniel, probably. They're the best. Your girls would love it.'

'What *are* you talking about?' Alberto raised his hands and dropped them, tired and exasperated.

'Here,' said Lucas, stopping abruptly as the Y rod flipped up. He pointed into the thicket of trees and shrubs on the boundary. 'Maybe three or four steps into his side. About a metre down. Not deep.'

Alberto gaped. 'A body? *Really?*'

'Really,' said Lucas, a sense of great sadness enveloping him. 'And at least two more further along this line. They were buried at the edge, well away from any machinery, well away from the cultivation area. At least we know their remains aren't feeding the tomatoes.'

'But how can you *know?*' hissed Alberto.

Voices rose on the other side — the patrol was back at this end of the perimeter. The two men who had stood over his head not two hours ago were still on duty, although they seemed to have left the dogs behind now. Lucas and Alberto stayed still and silent until the men had passed.

'*They* know,' he said. 'This is their last pass on shift. They're doing this section without the dogs and I know why - alsations aren't as good at sniffing out bodies as a spaniel, but they'd still notice and maybe start digging.'

Alberto nodded slowly. 'So... you want me to get a spaniel to sniff out bodies?'

'Just here,' said Lucas, 'the boundary is thin. Foxes come

through — see?' He knelt down and shone the torch at the gap. 'A spaniel could get through. It could get through and start to dig. And then it would probably find something... interesting. It would be your civic duty to report it. The police would be called in. There would be an excavation.'

'I can't just call them and tell them anyway?' said Alberto.

Lucas shrugged. 'You could — but without evidence they might not go in and dig up a corner of his land. You need that spaniel.' He clapped the man on the shoulder. 'Think about it. There's no hurry — those dead men aren't going anywhere — but Palari shouldn't get away with what he's done... what he's still doing. He deserves what's coming to him.'

They walked back to the house in silence and Lucas wondered whether to tell Alberto he was leaving. On the one hand it would be safer if he slipped away quietly before dawn... which left him only a couple of hours now. But on the other, if he did, Alberto might still feel compelled to include him in the narrative of how they'd all found the treasure. He was a big-hearted guy and he'd want Lucas to get the credit he deserved.

No. Lucas knew he was going to have to confess.

As they reached the farmhouse he leant against an old post of the pergola and inhaled deeply, cherishing the scent of the night, here in warm southern Italy. 'I'm going to miss this,' he said.

Alberto shook his head. 'There is much more to be done! Plenty more work! And then, when we know its value — your share of the gold coins money.'

'Alberto, I can't stay,' Lucas said. 'I can't be here when the papers show up to take photos and ask how to spell our names.'

The Italian shook his head slowly. 'You *are* running from something,' he said, emitting a long sigh.

'No,' said Lucas, 'I'm running *to* something. There's something... some*one*... I have to find. I've been following my dowsing instincts, tracking them across Europe. I'm close now. I can sense it — and Sid, when I get the map out and check — confirms it. I'm nearly there. But if you mean, are the police after me, well, yes... they are. The British police and maybe Interpol, too. They think I did something bad, but they're wrong. I need to find the truth and clear my name before I can go home.'

Alberto rubbed his face, looking sad. 'If you must go, you must go, Larry,' he said. 'If that's actually your name.'

Lucas smiled and didn't enlighten him.

'You must have your wages,' said Alberto. 'And a bonus, which you have surely earned. How will I contact you when I have your treasure money? Do you have a mobile phone number?'

'No,' said Lucas. 'I can't risk that. But... I'll keep an eye on the press reports and when it looks like you're rolling in money, I'll get in touch for my share. Will you keep it safe for me?'

'Of course,' said Alberto. 'Go and pack your things. I will get your wages.'

Half an hour later, while Pepe, Gino and Farid still slumbered deeply, Lucas crept from the barn with a full rucksack and a heavy heart. He had found friendship and almost some level of peace at Alberto's little farm. But the discovery of the coins had only hastened something he was already sensing. It was time to go. The night before last he had pulled out his map book, turning to the pages that spanned Italy and neighbouring countries around the Mediterranean. He had suspended Sid above the map, steepled between his interlaced fingers, and asked where he must go next. *East,* he was told. And not just to the coast but well beyond it. Across the Adriatic. He wasn't sure whether Greece or Albania was his next destination... Sid seemed to prevaricate between the two.

Then he saw the island that lay in the path of both countries... Corfu. 'Is it Corfu?' he had asked, and Sid had spun wildly in his agreement. If Lucas hadn't found those coins the very next day, he would already have departed. He couldn't wait any longer.

Alberto gave him a month's wages in cash, even though he was only owed for the past two weeks. He also gave him a heavy packet of food, from Juliana — bread, meat, tomatoes, sweet spiced pastries and bottled water. 'Can I drive you somewhere?' Alberto asked. 'To the station? To the port?'

Lucas shook his head. 'It's better that you don't know. If anyone ever asks, you won't have to lie. If you could just not mention the dowsing..? When the journalists come..? And ask the other guys to not mention it, either..? I'd be really grateful. Just set the scene at the other dig site, like we said. Say you found a coin under your boot and then started digging together for the rest. I was never there... I'd already left, more fool me.'

Alberto folded him into a tight hug. 'We will meet again, Larry!' he said. 'And when we do, I will be a rich man... and you will be richer, too.'

Lucas left the farm and walked down the winding lane just as dawn began to paint the eastern sky. The port of Brindisi was his next destination.

He thought he might make it by lunchtime if he kept moving.

11

'All life is a circle. All of existence... is a circle. Everything you do in this world is *part* of a circle.'

Rafe Campion stood on a wooden platform while two hundred or more of his followers sat on fold-out chairs in a barn. There was a significant lack of mud, straw and tractors in it but there was a well-maintained wooden floor underfoot and artful lighting in the rafters overhead.

'I'd go further,' Campion went on, fixing them all with a beatific smile and lifting his hands in that Christ-like pose Kate had first seen on the leaflet. In fact, in his white collarless shirt, with a low spotlight shining just behind his head for the full halo effect, he might have been auditioning for *Godspell*. 'Everything you do is part of a circle that takes in the *universe...*'

There was a mumble of agreement from the audience.

'Not exactly evidence-based is it?' muttered DC Michaels, in the chair next to Kate. She didn't reply. They already stuck out like two sore thumbs, even sitting at the back, and she didn't want to add furtive whispering to their rap sheet.

The people in this room wore a lot of tie-dye. The audience's average age was above forty but there were a few people here in their twenties. They collectively smelled like sandalwood and the nose-piercing count was moderate to high. In truth, Kate would rather mix with a crowd like this than a chapter of bikers or a mob of football fans, but in her blue needlecord jacket, black jeans and townie boots, she knew she *screamed* establishment.

'In our everyday lives we are both travelling on our own circle and intersecting with the life circles of every other being we meet,' Campion explained. 'If you look at a crop circle, it is representing this very essence of who we are and how we exist on this plane.' He waved a hand and there was a clunking and a gentle humming noise behind them. An image suddenly flicked up on a screen to his left, depicting a crop circle of great precision and beauty. 'Observe the circles within circles — the intersections,' Campion continued. 'Of course, not every crop circle is the same and some have different patterns.'

Kate glanced back, amused to see that the image was being shone onto a screen via the mote-speckled shaft from an old-style slide projector. A man with a white beard, in a loose-weave green tunic, was attending to it with great concentration and palpable pride. She remembered what Sally had told her — that this church eschewed social media and mobile phones and other such 21st century trappings. Karen, in the shop in Burchfont, had also mentioned that Linda Stewart avoided the electromagnetic smog of such gadgets. Clearly the slide projector wasn't considered too dangerous, then.

'I believe *these* carry other messages,' Campion said, as another crop circle image was shone onto the screen, this one with a design of triangles and stars. 'And I believe it is our task, within The Church of the Enlightened Energy, to decipher these messages and reveal them to the world. Those of us who are chosen... those of us who can sense the power of these imprints from another dimension... it is our destiny to read the meaning and take it out into a world which will... what? Embrace it? Thank us for it? Rise to it? No. No... for many years the world has laughed at it, in much the same way people laughed when it was proposed our planet was a sphere and not a plate. The way people laughed when it was first suggested that surgeons should wash their hands between operations.'

The audience collectively nodded and murmured its agreement.

'It may be that full enlightenment does not reach this planet... or even this country... in your lifetime or mine,' said Campion, scanning the faces before him with a sad smile. 'But remember... life is a circle. We all come back around again, perhaps here on Earth, and what we endeavour to do in this life may mean our message is widely accepted as fact and wisdom by the time we return. Imagine that! Imagine being born into a world where the human race finally understands its true place in the universe. Where we are connected and at one with the Otherworlds and the Otherworldly Beings. Just... *imagine...*'

At this point some heavenly music was piped through the PA system and the slide projector wizard went into a well-oiled segue between a series of crop circle images and fantastical cosmos graphics. Campion stepped aside, allowing all eyes to shift from his well-moisturised counte-nance to the screen for several minutes.

It was an organised, slick affair, albeit low-tech, Kate thought. Campion was a master at channelling the hopes and dreams of his audience, lifting their otherworldly aspirations with music and well-rehearsed rhetoric. He was eloquent and charismatic, she had to admit. And just the right side of hard-sell... so far.

The music ended and a woman with long black hair and implausibly violet eyes stepped up to ask the audience if they had questions for Campion. Hands went up enthusiastically, but there were few questions. Mostly it was personal testimony. Everyone had a story about how a crop circle had affected their lives, which Campion encouraged them to share, nodding sagely.

Eventually, sensing his increasing frustration, Kate let Michaels out of his trap. 'Go on, then,' she said, with a nudge. His hand shot up.

'At the back,' said Campion, his eyes drawn immediately to the unwavering arm Michaels was holding aloft.

Michaels stood up. 'Mr Campion,' he began.

'It's just Rafe,' interrupted Campion. 'We don't do titles here.'

'Rafe, then,' went on Michaels. 'Have you heard about the crop circle that arrived near Stonehenge this week? It was discovered yesterday morning.'

Campion nodded. 'I have,' he said. 'It was on the local news last night, I believe. I don't have a television but heard about it on BBC Radio Wessex this morning. Josh Carnegy, the breakfast presenter, has asked me to speak about it on tomorrow's show.'

'So... you heard about the dead woman..?' Michaels said.

Campion nodded again. 'I did hear. It's a very unusual occurrence. Very rare and, if I may say, rather wonderful.'

'Wonderful?' Michaels echoed. Every head in the audience was swivelling between the two men, and Kate could see many expressions of benign amusement. Clearly this young man *did not understand*.

'For those of us who believe,' said Campion. 'Leaving this world — when our time has come — and ascending to the next plane from the centre of a crop circle... that would be a privilege and a blessing beyond reckoning.'

Michaels nodded slowly, his face tight with scepticism, and sat down as Campion went to another raised hand. 'Let's get him to talk without the audience, shall we?' suggested Kate.

They had to wait for the signing queue to die down first, as Campion autographed a glossy hardback for at least half of the people present. It was called *LIFE CIRCLES: A Decoding Of Messages From Otherworld.* Predictably, a spectacular crop circle was on the front cover. Just as predictably, thought Kate, a spectacular portrait of Campion was on the back, along with a sycophantic blurb about its contents and its author.

She picked up a copy and purposefully waited at the end of the queue, Michaels loitering nearby and looking at his phone until the purple-eyed lady asked him to switch it off. 'You're polluting your body, mind and soul with electromagnetic smog,' Kate heard her say. 'The mobile phone network is strangling our planet as surely as fishing nets strangle our turtles.'

Campion sent off his last fan with a warm handshake and a promise to see them soon at another meeting. Then he turned to Kate and gave her a wry smile and a tilt of his golden head. 'I do hope this is covered by police expenses,' he said, nodding towards the book in her hands.

'Oops. We've been made, Michaels,' Kate said as her DC approached. 'No flies on Mr Campion here.'

'Well, I hope you enjoyed the talk, even if it was just in the line of duty,' said Campion. 'Perhaps you learned something..?'

'We learn something every day,' said Kate. 'I'm Detective Inspector Kate Sparrow from Wiltshire Police, and this is Detective Constable Ben Michaels. Mr Campion, do you know a woman called Linda Stewart?'

Campion sat back in his chair and stretched his arms out before clasping his hands behind his head and eyeing the rafters thoughtfully. 'I did know Linda, yes. And it's Rafe... please.'

'Why the past tense, Rafe?' She narrowed her gaze at him.

He took a breath and brought his elbows back to the table, leaning across and fixing her with a piercing stare. 'Because I believe you're about to tell me she is the woman whose body you found yesterday morning.'

'What makes you think that?' asked Michaels.

Campion didn't glance at the DC but stayed focused on Kate as he replied: 'I heard that the body of a mature woman was found in a crop circle. I noted that Linda wasn't here today. And as you have just asked me if I know her, I reached the conclusion that Linda has indeed gone to the next level... in the most extraordinary and marvellous way. Although I will miss her in this life circle, I rejoice for her. I really do.'

'Can you tell us where you were on Tuesday evening?' asked Kate, cutting to it before Campion could dribble any more verbal syrup over her. 'And overnight into Wednesday morning?'

'I was at home,' said Campion. 'With my wives.'

'Your *wives*?' she checked. 'As in more than one wife..?'

'I have three wives,' he said with a serene smile. 'Although we are not married in a way that organised religion would recognise.'

'Except your *own* organised religion, of course,' said Kate.

He laughed and shook his head. 'I am not running a religion. This is not a cult. It's a gathering of enlightened people who share the same outlook and the same life goal.'

'So, your wives, they can all confirm you were at home?' asked Kate, although the question was fairly pointless. Of course they would. And their testimony would be largely worthless. A man like Campion would have an alibi in every corner.

'What car do you drive?' asked Michaels, on a more practical channel. ANPR might be able to track any journeys. 'Or do cars mess up your chakras too much?'

Campion gave him a tight smile. 'I would very much like to live without a car, but out in rural Wiltshire the bus service isn't too reliable, and I must reach my followers. I drive a vintage Jaguar, inherited from my father.'

'That doesn't sound very eco-friendly,' said Michaels.

'It's not, which is why I drive it only when necessary,' said Campion. 'I applaud the spirit of the move to electric cars, but the batteries in them make me ill. I run my Jaguar on bio-fuel made from rapeseed oil.' He got to his feet as Purple Eyes started stacking his remaining books. 'Now... if you would like that signed, I'd be very happy to oblige.' He held out his hand and Kate passed the book over, noting the huge R and C in the man's autograph and the wildly looping script flowing from his fountain pen. The message with it read: ***Wishing you a rising life circle, Kate! Rafe***

'May I just check your address, sir?' asked Michaels, his baleful glare daring the man to insist on first names again. Campion only nodded and rattled it off — the house name and the village, a few miles west of their location. A road name and number wasn't necessary when you were resident in the local manor house.

'Thank you for your help,' said Kate. 'We'll be in touch.'

'I very much hope so, Kate,' he said, smiling at her warmly and fixing her with his intense gaze. 'Feel free to call me on my landline, any time... day or night. I'll get back to you.'

'He's after Wife Number Four,' muttered Michaels, as they left the barn. 'Sleazy bastard.'

'You're telling me you wouldn't fancy three wives?' she said, smirking.

'Jesus — even one would be bloody terrifying,' grunted Michaels as they reached the Honda. 'Probably the death of me.'

12

Even if she said it herself, she looked hot. She'd seen her reflection in the glass of the chapel door and couldn't help but admire the way the silk Chanel dress clung to her slim frame. The seamed stockings and high-heeled Jimmy Choos set off her long, shapely legs. The black outfit worked well with her red hair, styled in its restrained glossy pleat. She could have been a model. Had turned down an offer from a French agency once, in fact.

The widow's veil on her hat — not considered old-fashioned around these parts — wasn't hiding any tears, but it was doing a good job of disguising the relief and excitement of her new status.

Christina Eliades sniffed loudly as she approached the open grave, hitched in an emotional breath, and scattered a handful of earth onto her late husband's coffin. A flash of memory flared through her mind... a similar movement... her hand scattering water in her husband's face. He had always rather liked that kind of thing in their big, circular sunken bath. She would splash his face and he would grab her around the waist and bury his face in her soapy tits.

He liked it less in the sea, while he was struggling to get back on board the *Contessa*, their luxury motor yacht. 'Let me on!' he'd gasped, purple in the face, staring in disbelief at the boarding ladder she had pulled up out of his reach. 'Get me up!'

But she'd already got him up too many times to count. It was like getting him up was the point of her, really, and she was bored now. It was time to move on. She had leaned over the stern, holding onto the chrome rail with one hand and reaching down towards him with her other. And as he had swum harder towards her, his T-shirt and chinos weighing him down, she had simply scooped up a handful of seawater and splashed his face.

Something in her expression finally brought home to him the situation he was in. Four or five miles out to sea, no other vessel in sight, with a wife who, despite being as pretty as a picture and having the smoothest of legs and the shiniest of toenails, wanted him dead.

His mouth dropped open and his eyes widened in horror. 'You... you *bitch*...' he spluttered, still doggy-paddling hopelessly. 'I gave you *everything!*'

'You didn't,' she replied, with one last, teasing splash. 'You didn't give me one single orgasm. I had to fake all of those.'

'Please,' he cried. 'Please... throw the ring...'

But she just got up and padded barefoot across the deck, heading for the skipper's seat. A minute later she had started the *Contessa* up, and the engine noise as she pulled anchor and piloted the vessel away drowned out the sounds of... well... drowning. If the fat bastard had wanted to get back on board *that* badly he should have spent more time in the gym, building his upper body strength.

She didn't head straight back to harbour but a couple of

nautical miles east, before dropping anchor again and
having a glass of champagne. Then, half an hour later, by
which time she was sure her husband would by now be
floating face-down, slightly below the surface of the Aegean
Sea, she put in a Mayday call, distraught almost to the point
of incoherency. After that, while she waited for the coastguard to show up, she retreated to the circular bed in the
master cabin, loaded some fresh batteries into an expensive
toy and had a little personal time.

It was almost absurdly easy. She'd killed before, for
lesser reasons, when it had been much more strenuous to
pull off, but this... this had been a walk in the park. After a
day and a half of weeping and gnashing for the benefit of
the emergency services and his family, she was rewarded
when Stavros Eliades' body conveniently washed up on a
beach near Skiathos.

And now here they were, all saying goodbye, and she
was getting all the attention, sympathy, and admiration for
how well she was holding up, broken-hearted as she was.
Her performance for the past eighteen months had been so
convincing. Around all the other trophy wives she had been
the very model of adoration for Stav. While they bitched
and whined about *their* husbands, despite the lavish
lifestyles such spouses bestowed upon them, she had been
resolutely loyal to Stav, constantly parroting his opinions,
sharing his business successes, and even bigging up his
sexual prowess. Not for her the pool guy trysts or the tennis
pro affairs — she was squeaky clean. She had even
converted to Catholicism to please Lucretia, his sinewy old
bag of a mother.

As the days passed, she knew there would be suspicion.
Hot young wife out on a yacht when rich old husband
vanishes into the sea. But literally nobody could pin this on

her. No cameras anywhere. No drugging. No bruises on his body. Just enough alcohol inside him to lessen his chances of getting back on board that yacht after he'd slipped and fallen over the rail while his wife was sleeping off half a bottle of champagne. It had been their anniversary. It was so... so cruel.

A week after the funeral she left Athens to take up residence in her favourite of the Eliades villas, many miles away from Lucretia, who was still keening and wailing every single bloody morning and had set up a literal shrine to Stavros in the hallway of the family home. Fine. The grieving mother could have the big Athens house all to herself for now. The grieving widow was in need of some fun.

Arriving in Mirtio, she hired local staff and had the villa's pool deep-cleaned and the house brought up to her standards. It had a breathtaking view across the Ionian Sea from the terracotta tiled terrace, with a balcony overlooking its own private beach, complete with cave, and a private mooring for the *Contessa*, which she'd had sailed out to her a few days after she'd arrived. People might think it was morbid to keep the vessel from which her husband had fallen to his death, but she wasn't concerned about their opinions.

The young Italian who had delivered the boat caught her attention. He was dark, handsome and fit — a perfect salve for her starved libido after a year and half of flabby, greying Stavros. They had noisy, animal sex in the villa for a day and a night before he headed back to another country at dawn, both parties satisfied.

Yes. She really had it all now.

Except... a sense of *purpose*. Her attention span was frighteningly short; she would need a project. But what? She spent the morning naked, in the centre of the kingsize bed, wrapped in sheets which still smelled of her Italian one-nighter, watching non-stop TV news.

Which was when, on Sky News, she happened upon a report of a newly discovered crop circle in Wiltshire, England.

She sat up straight and then shoved the sheets aside and stepped closer to the massive wall-mounted HD screen as it showed first a drone's eye view, hovering above the green circle with the small white tent at its centre, and then cut to a view of the police cordon and officers standing in the wheat field.

A smile spread across her face. *Well.* Wasn't life just one big circle..?

13

'I'm not convinced this is a good use of our resources.'

Chief Superintendent Rav Kapoor sat back in his seat, his fingers gently drumming the top of his battle-scarred oak desk.

Kate and Michaels glanced at each other and back at the boss. 'Really?' said Kate.

Kapoor shook his head, lips pursed, and then added: 'It looks like a suicide. The son has told us that his mother was fit and well and, as far as he knew, quite happy — but the path report tells us she had stage three ovarian cancer. Medical notes tell us she refused treatment for it six months ago. She appears to have made a decision to take matters into her own hands.'

'Stage three,' said Kate, 'isn't a terminal prognosis.'

'Perhaps not,' said Kapoor. 'But DC Mulligan spoke to her consultant, who said Linda Stewart was against the radiotherapy process and thought it would be more damaging than helpful.'

'So...where did she get the Pentobarbital?' asked Michaels.

Kapoor raised his hands. 'These things are all too readily available, if you're determined enough.'

'But what if she was... coerced?' said Kate. 'Because you need to see this Church of the Enlightened Energies guy in action. He all but put it out there during the talk he gave this morning... ascension to the "next level" from the centre of a crop circle is the ultimate cool to these people. And when we asked Rafe Campion about Linda Stewart, he responded that her death was *rather wonderful* — and that's verbatim.'

Kapoor narrowed his eyes. 'Did you say Rafe Campion?'

'I did,' Kate said. 'Do you know him?'

'There can't be many Rafe Campions,' Kapoor mused, leaning forward onto his elbows and steepling his fingers. 'I believe there was a Rafe Campion at my eldest son's school.'

'Your son went to Winchester College?' Kate asked, trying to hide her surprise. The fees for a school like that were astronomical, even for a man of Kapoor's rank.

'He did,' Kapoor said, giving her a wry smile and raised eyebrow. 'He gained a scholarship. He is now a practising surgeon at Southampton's neurological unit.'

'You must be very proud,' said Kate, dropping her eyes.

'There was a Rafe Campion who was head boy while Sami was there,' Kapoor went on. 'Destined for great things, he was. Always up on the stage, making speeches and shaking hands with the headmaster and visiting VIPs. I always thought he was an oily little chancer, myself.'

'I think I'd go along with that,' said Kate.

'Oily *and* sleazy,' added Michaels, who was clearly unleashing his inner puritan today.

'But would you put it past him to set up a death cult?' Kate asked.

'Actually,' said Kapoor, 'I wouldn't. Even so... it's thin. A one-off like this, even if our victim was a member of his so-called church and even if he *was* advocating some kind of heavenly ascension from the middle of a crop circle... it's quite a leap to say he was actively encouraging anyone to kill themselves.'

'Section 2 of the Suicide Act 1961,' said Kate, glancing at her notebook. '...*encouraging or assisting suicide.* It's indictable. I mean, nobody knows if she was assisted but I'd say there's a good chance she was encouraged.'

'What does he have to gain from this?' asked Kapoor. 'Have we checked on her finances... her will... any bequests?'

'We don't know,' said Michaels, consulting his own notes. 'But the son thinks she recently visited her solicitor.'

Kapoor sat up straight. 'I see. So... how do we establish that Campion both encouraged *and* assisted. Does he have access to the poison she took? Did he create the crop circle or commission someone else to do it? How did he persuade her to go and lie down in it and take her life? And can we establish that he was *aware* of the monetary gain if he did this? What is the financial status of his organisation?'

'It's a foundation,' said Kate. 'DC Mulligan has done some digging and apparently Campion is applying for charitable status for it, for the tax break, I'm guessing. His followers make regular donations for ongoing research into crop circle energy fields.' She waved the hardback. 'You can get the BACS details right out of his book! There's a quarterly magazine — recycled paper only — which subscribers get, along with discounted tickets to his various workshops and retreats — none of which are cheap.'

'And Campion's account? Is it looking healthy?'

'I'm just about to get on to the Financial Investigation Unit and find out,' said Michaels. 'That's if you still think this is a good use of our resources.'

Kapoor shot him a glance, gauging the sarcasm level, then appeared to find it tolerable. 'Fine,' he said. 'I'll leave the both of you on this. The rest of the team have a backlog of other work that's just as pressing... but you two can shake this tree until the end of the week and then we'll take another look at what's dropped out of it.'

'Thank you, sir,' they chorused.

As they went to go, Kapoor called Kate back. 'Sir?' she said, as soon as the door was shut behind Michaels. As ever, a spike of adrenaline went through her. What had he discovered?

'I thought you might like to take a look at this,' said Kapoor, spinning his laptop around to her. A grainy image, clearly a CCTV capture, lay before her. A man with dark hair and a beard, walking along a street in bright sunshine, a rucksack on his back and what looked like an Aussie style wide-brimmed hat on his head. Kate sucked in her breath and peered at it more closely.

'Could it be him?' asked Kapoor. 'It was picked up two days ago, in the port of Brindisi on the south-east coast of Italy. Passport control hasn't flagged anything, but as Lucas Henry fled the country without one, he's most likely picked up a fake passport somewhere in Europe. That's if it's him, of course. It's very hard to be sure. Lots of dark-haired men with beards in Italy.'

Kate stooped lower to the screen and stared at the picture. It wasn't, in all honesty, possible to be sure. But... there was something about the sense of movement in it... something about... *No*. She couldn't be sure, and she knew she had to restrain herself from leaping to conclusions because she so badly *wanted* to find Lucas Henry on camera somewhere.

'Honestly?' she said, standing up again. 'It could be

him... but it could be someone else, too. It's just not clear enough.'

Kapoor nodded, approvingly. 'That's what I thought you'd say. I've asked for more CCTV around the port and on the ferries around that time period, just in case we pick up a better capture. I'll keep you informed.'

'Can you send me that image?' she asked. 'Just... in case.'

'No problem,' said Kapoor. 'And I'll let you know if there's anything else.'

'Thank you, sir.'

'We will get him,' he said. 'Trust me... he's going to slip up sooner or later. We'll get him and we'll get justice for your sister.'

14

———

Kirsty Pope was neat, dark and attractive; a woman in her early forties, already a senior partner at Wellwright, Lambrook and Pope. She walked across the reception area of the small solicitors' practice, clutching a folder which Kate dearly hoped held the last will and testament of Linda Stewart.

As she reached Kate, Pope paused and a flicker of recognition crossed her face. 'Have we met before?'

Kate smiled and nodded. 'Yes — you looked after my mother's estate when she passed away a few years ago. Emily Sparrow..?'

A series of connections crossed the lawyer's face, like a fast-moving weather front. 'Ah,' she said. 'Yes, I remember now.'

'But, obviously, I'm not here about my mother,' Kate went on.

'Of course. You want to discuss Linda Stewart,' said Pope, turning and waving Kate along a short corridor towards a client reception room. 'Ah... it's not just that we've

met before.' She glanced back, narrowing her eyes curi-
ously. 'I've seen you on TV quite a lot in recent months.
Detective Kate Sparrow... you've had quite the time of it,
haven't you?'

Kate didn't answer until they were inside the carpeted
room, the door shut behind them. 'Yes. I have. Now... about
Linda Stewart...'

'I'm sure you know,' said Pope, sitting down and placing
the folder on a glass-topped table. 'That it would be highly
unprofessional of me to disclose any details of Linda Stewart's estate to you without consulting the executor. It's not
even gone to probate yet... and I'm guessing you've not
brought a warrant to compel disclosure.' She raised one
eyebrow, fully aware that the timescale meant there was no
way this was a possibility.

Kate smiled sadly. She had been hoping this small firm
would be more helpful than bureaucratic, especially as Pope
had agreed to see her so quickly.

'Oh, stop looking so worried,' said the solicitor, with a
laugh. 'You're in luck. *I* am the executor of the will and — as
long as you can promise me your *absolute* discretion — I am
willing to waive privilege and talk to you. Not least because I
liked Linda... we were friends. I think she would have
wanted me to help.'

'You knew her socially?' asked Kate, sliding thankfully
into the seat opposite.

'Yes — we met now and again. She used to be in the
same choir as me. Nice lady. I was sad to hear of her passing.' She pulled a number of documents from the folder. 'So
what do you want to know?'

'Um —when she last updated her will would be a good
start,' said Kate.

'That's easy. It was June... the twenty-sixth. A month ago,' said Pope.

'Really?' Kate nodded slowly. 'Did she change anything meaningful... like who the beneficiaries are?'

'She did,' said Pope. 'Her cottage and all its contents — that goes to her only son, Marcus Dundrill. That's always been the case. The rest of her estate is savings and some bonds. These are worth, at most recent estimates, sixty-four thousand and three hundred pounds. That, minus legal fees, all goes to... the Church of the Enlightened Energy.'

Kate let out a dry chuckle. 'Did it strike you as odd,' she said, 'that Linda suddenly upped and changed her will? I mean — that's a lot of money to bequeath to any kind of church.'

Pope considered, pursing her lips. 'It didn't strike me as *that* odd, because we'd had conversations like this before. She'd chopped and changed a fair bit in recent years... with an assortment of beneficiaries coming and going. But she told me she felt this organisation was like her true family. She believed in everything it represented. She wanted to donate towards what she saw as important work.'

'Did you try to talk her out of it?'

Pope smiled. 'That's not really my job — although I did ask her to think about it and come back to me when she'd had time to reflect. I asked her to tell her son, too, although I don't think she did.' She sighed. 'It's not much fun, having to deal with disappointed relatives. Bereaved people aren't at their best when there's money at stake.'

'And she was of sound mind?'

'Linda? Oh yes. Definitely. Eccentric, certainly, but I've known her fifteen years and she was always just the same. No issues with her mental capacity.'

'Any sense she was being pressured?'

'No. Linda was a woman who very much knew her own mind. Even if she changed it quite a lot.' Pope shrugged and smiled. 'People are allowed to change their minds.'

'So, the other beneficiary... Rafe Campion. Is he aware of what's coming his way?'

Pope shrugged. 'He might be. I don't know. Linda didn't say whether he'd been made aware and we haven't been in touch yet, since we've only just learned of Linda's death. And to be clear, the money has been left to the foundation, not to Campion himself. Although it would be hard to judge the difference, as he's the sole director and has nobody else to answer to, financially, other than HMRC.'

'I see,' said Kate. She got to her feet. 'Thank you — you've been very helpful.'

'A pleasure,' said Pope, sliding the paperwork back into the folder and standing too. 'And it's nice to meet you finally. I hope the last chunk of your mum's estate was enough for your big trip. Gap year, was it?'

Kate blinked. 'Um... no. My brother and I just used the life insurance pay out to convert the family house into two flats. We didn't go off on any big trips. What makes you..?'

'Oh, I'm obviously confusing you with another client! So sorry,' said Pope. Her head was down as she turned to open the door, her dark fringe obscuring her face. Kate could see the side of her cheek, though, and it was definitely colouring up.

She was about to probe further when her phone went off. DC Michaels spoke fast. 'Another crop circle,' he said. 'Near Avebury.'

'Oh god,' Kate said, intuiting what was coming next.

'Yep... another body.'

———

THE MAN in the white shirt and pink jeans couldn't have been older than fifty. He might have been forty. Once all animation had fled a face in the wake of death, it was often hard to judge.

The crop circle was smaller than the first and in another green wheat field further west, with a distant view of Avebury Ring — a detail that wasn't lost on Kate. It was quite a sheltered spot, which might explain why there had been no earlier discovery, because the circle, if not the body, surely had to have arrived in the hours of darkness. Nobody ever made crop circles in the daylight — unless they were being filmed for a documentary on faking the phenomenon.

'Looks very similar, doesn't it?' Kate said to Death, as he knelt beside the corpse, under the flapping roof of the forensics tent.

'It does indeed,' he said, checking for anything lodged inside the blue-lipped mouth. 'We might have a copycat suicide here.'

'We might,' said Kate. 'But there have been no details of Linda Stewart's death in the media, and this is strong on detail, wouldn't you say?'

Death nodded. 'Yes, at first glance, I couldn't disagree.'

The man's long brown hair was spread around him and wilting buttercups and daisies were threaded through it. His dull grey eyes stared upward, like Linda's had, and his mouth hung open in much the same way. The small empty bottle at his side was glass, not metal.

'We checking the shoes again, then?' asked Michaels, stooping down, already gloved up. Death nodded his assent and Michaels worked the man's pale brown loafers off skinny, unsocked feet. There was no sign of a note.

'He has jeans on,' Kate pointed out. 'With pockets.'

Michaels carefully felt inside the man's pockets and withdrew another note on cream paper. 'Here we go,' he said, glancing at it and showing it to Kate. The careful ink script on it read:

I am transcending with joy. Tell Rafe I hope to see him on the next level. Callum

'Rafe's getting a lot of shout-outs in the great beyond, isn't he?' said Michaels. 'Time to bring him in?'

'Not just yet,' said Kate. 'Let's wait to hear back on cause of death. Find out who this is — and whether he's been to see his solicitor recently.'

'It's a neat way of fundraising, isn't it?' said Michaels as they left the tent and headed for the outer cordon where a handful of locals were beginning to gather, including, by the way they were bouncing up and down, a fair few croppies. 'Just convince a bunch of idiots that they need to go up to the next level, and pay in advance on this one.'

'Hmmm,' said Kate.

'Make them a nice crop circle,' Michaels went on. 'Tell them it's the alien mothership calling them home... offer them the magic transporter juice...'

'It would take some doing,' Kate mused. 'Have we found any gear yet? Planks? Rope? Stepladders?'

'Nope. All tidied away. But I reckon there's going to be plenty of willing hands from that bunch of tie-dye tree-huggers. It's serial killing by power of suggestion, isn't it?'

'Or serial suicide,' said Kate. 'If that's a thing. It may be that this guy knew Linda. Might even have had a bond with her — heard about the detail of what happened from one of the dog walkers, maybe. Decided to go the same way. Either way, I don't think two in a row qualifies as serial. We'd need at least one more.'

'Careful what you wish for,' said Michaels.

15

The two figures at the front gate could only be police. Christina tensed as she viewed them on the feed from the state-of-the-art security cameras, and then told herself to relax. The murder of Stavros was completely unprovable. She had learned a lot over the past few years, about the importance of self-cleaning long cons. This one had been perfect.

Maybe it was something else... door-to-door enquiries about a local incident. Although there weren't many doors to knock around here — the super-rich tended to keep some distance from their neighbours. So...what? What could it be..? She was tempted to lie low and not answer, but her Ferrari was on the front drive, clearly visible between the gilded wrought iron of the gates, indicating she was at home. No. Whatever it was, it was better to know than guess.

'Hello?' she called, affecting just the right balance between courtesy and concern.

'Mrs Eliades?' asked the woman, leaning in towards the telecom, her features bulging through the fisheye lens set into it.

'Yes,' said Christina. 'Can I help you?'

They identified themselves as detectives Adamos and Gazis from the Athens police. Ah. So not local. They had come to talk about Stavros, no doubt. She took a deep breath. She could handle this. In the full-length mirror on the marble wall of the entrance hall she saw a composed, sad widow, elegant in a grey dress, wearing not a scrap of make-up, red hair combed but unstyled. A widow in a state of becalmed mourning after the stormy desolation of the past couple of weeks. She pressed the button to release the gates and they drove in.

They were all polite smiles and professionalism, and accepted her offer of cold drinks on the terrace in the late morning sun. 'Amazing view,' said the female detective — Gazis — middle-aged, with a face like a sun-dried raisin, leaning over the wooden balustrade and watching the waves rolling into the crescent-shaped cove forty metres below.

'It is,' said Christina. 'I'm very lucky.'

'You certainly are,' said Adamos — around the same age as Gazis but better preserved.

Christina dropped her eyes to her hands, folded in her lap, and twisted her wedding ring. They seemed to remember that she was a recent widow, and coughed, as if they'd embarrassed themselves.

'Why are you here?' she asked. 'Is it something to do with Stavros... with his business..?'

'Yes... we're here about your husband's death,' said Gazis. 'We wanted to check something with you... a small... anomaly.'

'Oh?' Christina raised her eyebrows. 'What's that?'

'We wanted to check the timings of what happened on the day he died,' the detective went on, consulting a sheaf of paper in her folder. 'From what you told our colleagues in

Athens, you made a Mayday call to the coastguard at just after midday, is that right?'

Christina nodded, her face crumpling as the traumatic memory of finding her husband missing played through her mind on a slightly creaky projector. 'That's right,' she said.

'And you said you'd noticed he was missing just a couple of minutes before the call, but that you hadn't actually seen him for some hours, yes?' the woman went on, tracing a stubby finger down her notes.

'Yes, that's right,' said Christina. 'It's all there in my statement. I was asleep.'

'Were you aware that there are cameras fitted on board the *Contessa*?' asked the man.

Christina blinked. There were no cameras. She had checked. This must be a ploy. They were watching her closely for a guilty reaction. They weren't going to get one. 'I wasn't aware of that... no...' She drew in a quick breath and leant across the table towards them. 'Do you mean you found some film? You saw what happened? Did you see what happened to my Stavros?' She found tears springing obediently to her eyes. 'Oh god... you can tell me what happened! Is that it?'

They exchanged glances and then the woman said. 'No. I'm afraid there is no film of your husband falling overboard... nothing to prove exactly how that happened.' She paused, allowing her eyes to rest upon the widow for a few seconds.

'So... what film *is* there?' asked Christina, fear just beginning to prickle deep inside her.

'Ahem...' The woman glanced at her notes again while her partner leant his elbows on the table and seemed to be biting back a smirk. 'Perhaps your husband didn't make you aware of this, but it seems he was in the habit of filming, erm, in the bedroom.'

Christina's jaw dropped.

'There's a camera fitted into the ceiling above the bed,' the woman went on. 'And we discovered, when his mother allowed us to access his laptop back in Athens, that he had quite a collection of private films stored on it... dating back some years.' She coughed. 'It would seem you feature in the more recent series.'

Christina felt a thud of rage. That pervy old bastard. Jeezuz — she wished she could drown the fucker all over again.

'But we're not interested in any of his previous recordings,' the detective went on. 'We're only really interested in what we found on his laptop two weeks ago. It seems his films would be automatically backed up to the cloud from a connection on the *Contessa*, and he would download them later on his laptop.

Christina gulped.

'So... it seems the video recording was going on throughout the day when your husband died. There is a recording of you... in the master bedroom, on the bed. You're not asleep though. You appear to be experiencing... some personal pleasure... with a sex toy.'

Christina felt heat rising through her, along with an intense rage. Close behind the rage was the dawning realisation of what they were getting to. The time code on the video would clearly show her getting her celebratory rocks off *after* she had put in her Mayday call. In her statement she had said she'd spent the whole time between that call and the arrival of the coastguard endlessly searching the sea for a sign of her lost husband, shouting herself hoarse. By the time a boat had shown up on the horizon she had brought those well-trained tears out in abundance and had indeed, screamed herself hoarse for several minutes as it approached, all the better to play the part.

But now they had proof that she had done no such thing until she'd sighted the coastguard. And it was going to be a hard sell, convincing anyone that a swift session with a fully charged vibrator was just a coping mechanism. It wasn't like she'd been sobbing her way to orgasm.

Shit. Fucking Stavros! What a total arse-wipe of a bastard!

They were waiting for a response, so Christina gave them one. She went rigid. She dropped her glass, which smashed spectacularly on the tiles, and began to make weird clicking noises, her eyes rolling up into her head.

They stopped smirking at each other and stared at her, taken aback.

'What the hell?' said the man. 'What's she doing?'

'I think she's having a seizure,' said the woman, getting to her feet, alarmed.

Christina went limp and allowed her eyes to pull back into focus, dribble running down her chin. 'Me... me... med..medicine,' she burbled. 'In... the... kitchen... by... sink...'

She started the twitching and juddering again while the male detective ran to the kitchen. As soon as he was out of sight she slumped sideways in her chair, face slack and eyes glassy. The woman approached her, looking freaked out.

Three, two... Christina counted as she got ready... *ONE.*

She sprang as if she'd been flipped from a trap and cannoned into the woman with all the velocity she could summon, sending her crashing backwards against the balcony with barely more than a gasp. The old wood cracked and gave, and the detective vanished with a small shriek. She might have got out a full-throated scream if she'd had time but her head struck a rocky outcrop as she plummeted past, meaning she was almost certainly unconscious two or three seconds before she hit the beach. She now lay far below, spread out like a starfish. Perfectly still.

Christina would have liked to study her work for a while, but there wasn't time. The male detective was already on his way back, yelling that he couldn't find any meds in the kitchen. She pressed herself against the villa wall, in the shadow of a large potted fig, and watched as he came out onto the terrace, paused and murmured, 'Whaaaat?' before approaching the broken balcony to stare down at his dead colleague in horror.

He turned his head just in time to see her coming for him. But not in time to save himself as she swept up a wrought iron patio chair and swung it against his backside, toppling him face-first into oblivion. He *did* get a full scream out, toppling head-over-feet-over-head until his acrobatics were brought to a sudden stop a short distance from his partner.

Caught in the momentum, Christina very nearly followed him, only just saving herself by grabbing a bit of the balcony that was still steady enough to hold her. She dropped to her belly and wriggled forward to stare at the scene below. Adamos had fallen more awkwardly and made a broken, unnatural shape on the sand, like a human swastika.

'So... now what?' she breathed. It was a very good thing she had sent the staff home. And that there was nobody down there on her private beach. Scanning the sea she couldn't see any boats, either. Or any sign of walkers in the surrounding cliffs. 'Right,' she said, getting up. 'Work to do.'

She walked the two hundred and thirty steps down to the beach, carrying large hessian sacks from the gardener's shed. On the way she'd toyed with the idea of dragging the bodies down to the water and letting the tide take them, but it was too risky. There wasn't really much tide around these parts and the bodies might wash around in the surf for days. She could weigh them down but that would entail dragging them onto the motor yacht's rib and dropping them overboard further out to sea, roped to rocks, probably in the night. It might have been worth it if she didn't know that their journey to her villa would have been on some police duty log back in Athens and their mobile phones easily tracked right here. There wasn't time.

No. She needed to tidy up quickly and go. There was no question she could stay here now and continue her beautifully set up new life.

Years of gym sessions had made her a lot stronger than she looked, which she was glad of as she dragged the bodies on the sack, one by one, across the sand towards the cave. First she'd ransacked their pockets for ID, wallets and phones, putting these in a neat pile on the bottom step. Getting the dead weight to the cave got a little easier as she reached the shallows that fed into the rocky chamber, sloshing and gurgling back and forth. The salt water gave helpful buoyancy. She floated them in, one by one, and guided their limp, broken bodies to the back of the cave where the water eddied and swirled before partly exiting via a submerged tunnel which connected to another part of the beach. Further in, the tunnel wasn't wide enough to swim through and only a very skinny kid would dare to try, before discovering it was a dead end for anything bigger than a fish. It would be easy to get jammed and drown.

But it was perfect for sliding a body into. She posted the woman in first, a scarlet river of blood trailing through the water from the shattered skull. She had to pull the floating limbs in tight to the body and pack the dead woman, like a wayward Barbie into a presentation box.

Then she went back for Adamos. On her return to the cave, she found the woman's lower legs had floated out again, and so drove her colleague's head and shoulders in hard, wedging him like a cork to keep the first body contained.

She found some rocks — movable under the water — to pack in, along with the sacking, around Adamos's feet, pinning them tightly in place and hopefully buying some more time. She had no doubt the bodies would be found, but not any sooner than she could help.

She emerged from the cave and returned to the landing sites where a lot of blood and other matter was spilled across lumps of rock that rose out of the drifts of sand. A dozen gulls flew, squawking, away from it as she approached. She spent ten minutes dragging rocks and shingle over the evidence. The rising tide would clean it all away in a matter of hours, but it paid to be thorough.

She was exhausted but also exhilarated. She'd done it again. She counted through her kills and realised she'd just reached seven. *Lucky seven.* Each one a memory to be stored, retrieved, and re-examined at a later date. Her early kills were clumsy and amateur, but she had a fondness for them, all the same. There had been a passion and energy about her debut in the quarry which couldn't be topped, all this time later. Watching the life go out of young Zoe Taylor's eyes... there hadn't been much time to fully take it in while it was happening, but she would never forget it. You never forgot your first. The ending of sweet, well-behaved Mabel, not long after, was also a tremendous rite of passage. Around that time she was just grasping the visceral delight of planning for the future and had left some fun evidence behind to mess with minds — and to keep herself safe. None of it had ever led back to her.

Not that it was *easy* back then. No. The trauma of it all had shaken her to the core. She wouldn't ever kill lightly, even now. She wasn't going to be one of those serial killers who got caught up in a pattern, feeding their desire in ever-decreasing circles of time, like a crack addict whose hits get less and less effective. She was much more Mr Ripley than Dr Shipman.

It was definitely a game. Chess, probably. She understood that she had to be sparing with herself, if her pleasures were to last a lifetime. And there was exquisite satisfaction in playing the *long* game.

This, though, was not a long-game situation. She needed to act fast. She stripped naked and bundled the bloodied dress and her underwear together, seeking a burial spot. There were plenty of options among the stones and she concealed the material quickly, deep in a rock pool, pinned under a boulder among some surprised crabs and shrimps. Again, she knew it would probably be found at some point, but by then she would be long gone.

She ran up the two hundred and thirty steps, adrenaline driving her upward and onward, and arrived on the terrace where the cool drinks still stood on the patio table, the folder of police paperwork still resting beside them. The tipped-over chair, the smashed glass and the broken balcony were the only clues to the kind of day she was having. Back in the house, she took a brisk, hot shower, and dressed in her least eye-catching running gear — navy blue long-sleeved T and matching calf-length tights. The detectives' vehicle couldn't be seen from the road, but an overhead search — a drone or a helicopter — would spot it easily enough. There would probably be cameras along the

route to her villa, too, which would have logged the one-way
journey. She needed to do something about this.

She brushed and tied back her hair, tucking the ponytail
up into a navy blue baseball cap. She put on some fresh
latex gloves from the cleaner's supply cupboard and paused
in the utility room to thoroughly scrub the car key, the
mobile phones, warrant cards and wallets, using an alcohol-
based spray cleaner, and put them all into a paper bag. Still
gloved, she collected the files from the patio table, too and
took the whole lot with her to the Fiat.

It took her ten minutes to drive the Fiat back down the
winding road towards the nearest town, during which time
one of the mobiles rang six times in the paper bag before
lapsing into silence. Leaving them switched on was part of
the plan. A couple of other cars passed her and no doubt the
vehicle was picked up by a traffic camera or two en route.
The sun visors were down on both sides to block as much of
the view through the windscreen as possible and she kept
the brim of her cap well down, obscuring her face. She
drove to a remote beauty spot and pulled up in its car park,
under some trees, tucking the Fiat well away from any eye in
the sky.

Scanning for witnesses, she saw none and got out, grabbing the paper bag before locking the vehicle. She didn't
pause to look back but simply jogged away through a track
in the woods and back to the coastal path which led to her
villa. She did not meet any other runners or even dog walkers... it was too hot for most of them to be out at this time
of day.

She was back at the villa within half an hour of leaving
it, having dropped the Fiat key and the contents of the paper
bag off the cliff path, five minutes from the beauty spot car
park. She'd chosen a dip in the path where a runner would

disappear from casual view of anyone nearby, and tossed the evidence far out into the air as she ran. The sea was battering the rocks below and the personal effects would be scattered, smashed, and sunk in no time. No boat was anywhere nearby. No possible witnesses. The folder of files on Christina Eliades she'd left on the back seat.

Now she paused in the house, taking long, slow breaths and thinking through her plan. Anyone following the detectives' mobile phone signals would conclude that they had visited her home, stayed for about an hour, and then driven away to a spot further down the coast. The local cells would confirm the progression of the mobiles along the cliff path and then the point at which they blinked off the network. It would look a lot like the detectives had fallen — or jumped — off the cliff.

Of course she knew this was only going to buy her a little time. There was no doubt that the police would come to the villa to question her and, on finding no response, most likely break in and search. When they eventually found the bodies... and her buried clothing spattered in police blood... there wouldn't be much doubt about what had happened. Forensics would be able to work out how the detectives had died and who had mostly likely pushed them — and why. It was all over for Christina Eliades. Which meant it was just beginning for... hmmm... Brigitte had a nice ring to it. Brigitte Anderssen. It was one of three passports she hadn't yet used.

It took half an hour to gather up everything she would need. She thanked her lucky stars that she had spied on Stavros and memorised the code to the safe at the villa. He had left fifty thousand euros in it, along with some of the diamond and emerald jewellery he occasionally liked her to wear, which was worth at least the same again, although she would need to get it to a very reliable fence to realise around half that.

She regretfully left the car and all her designer clothes. She didn't have time to dye her hair just yet, but tucked it up into a wide-brimmed cotton sun hat. She'd go blonde later. She put on walking boots, shorts and a T-shirt and shoved the money, the jewellery — including her wedding and engagement rings — and other necessities into a deep zip-up inner pocket of a rucksack. Her phone she left, switched on, beside her bed. There was nothing incriminating on it. She knew better than that. Although she guessed it was all going to be academic once they got into that cave in a few days' time... maybe sooner. Perhaps the Athens police were a bit quicker off the mark than the Corfu plods.

She was about to leave by the front door when she was struck by one final thing she could do. She left her gear in the hall and retraced her steps back through the house — stopping to pick up her phone after all, and a set of keys, along with her Christina Eliades passport. She went through the garden and back down the steps to the beach, taking the route to the small jetty instead of down to the rocks and sand. The tide was already coming in and the *Contessa* was floating prettily on its aquamarine inlet. Pulling the keys from her shorts she got aboard and. started the motor yacht up, setting its direction and autopilot. The boat gently motored off, straining at the ropes tying it to the jetty. Christina put her passport on a shelf by the skipper's seat and walked back along the vibrating deck, jumped off and untied the mooring rope, quickly slinging it back on board. The vessel set out at once on its straight course out into the Ionian Sea. With luck it would go unnoticed as it ploughed its lonely way across the water. She hoped it would miss any big ships and get as far away as possible before striking any trouble. Although in some ways it would be good if it did strike something... if it could sink itself before it was tracked and a police boat or the coastguard came alongside... well, that could only help, couldn't it?

Widow vanishes in luxury motor yacht mystery just weeks after husband drowns... Yes. She could see the headlines now. And whether or not the police believed she had drowned or escaped, they would still be concluding that she had left the island in a panic.

It was late afternoon when she climbed over the wall of the villa's road-facing grounds, leaving the electric gate closed and her Ferrari on the drive, and walked away up the quiet single-track lane. She experienced a regretful pang that she'd not had longer to enjoy the villa's little luxuries. But she also felt a thrill at the adventure ahead. She was now a mature student from Sweden, studying Greek, on her way home because she'd broken up with her Greek boyfriend a week ago and her money was running out. At least, that was what the first person to give her a lift to the port was going to hear.

Just a few hours later, she was dyeing in the poky bathroom of a budget hotel, stripping the red from her hair and replacing it with a golden blonde. After hitching a ride to Ano Korakiana, she had purchased some Garnier colourant from a market stall in the village.

Then she lay on the bed and slept for several hours, being chased by dreams. This was unusual. She didn't normally dream at all but on occasion a nightmare might shock her from sleep. As she drifted awake in the mid-evening, aware of tourists celebrating noisily in the taverna across the street, she realised she had been back in the quarry.

She supposed it wasn't surprising — not with what had

happened earlier that day, and with her recent sighting of
Kate Sparrow on the BBC news. Her biggest regret about
shoving those detectives over the cliff was that she now
didn't have time to investigate Kate Sparrow's latest adventures at leisure, the way she liked to every so often. Not
everyone would know she was Mabel's little sister, since
she'd changed her surname from Johanssen to Sparrow, but
Christina — now also renamed Brigitte — had easily
worked it out and followed the young detective's career with
interest. Over the past year it had got so very entertaining.
Her escapades with Lucas Henry were gripping stuff. The
pair had become quite the cause célèbre in Wiltshire,
solving all those murders together. A detective and a dowser.
The newspapers had loved that!

She supposed she should be worried. The whole Quarry
Girls story had returned to public consciousness a few
weeks ago, when Henry was named as prime suspect —
again — for the murder of Zoe Taylor and the abduction
and probable murder of Mabel Johanssen. Although it
would be useful for Lucas Henry to be caught, charged and
convicted for these crimes, part of her, perversely, didn't
want that. It was too dull an end to the story. Too
predictable. Of course, she wasn't going to put her *own*
hands up, but even so... she liked the way the mystery had
hung around for nearly seventeen years. All the while her
crimes remained unsolved, she could tinker around the
edges, occasionally messing with the minds of those
involved. The occasional call, silent and brooding... a whispered message... a clue to a clue to a clue.

She had never had the urge to do this with anyone
involved in her other murders, but the Quarry Girls case
was different. It was much more personal and, of course, her
first outing.

It was time to go out for some food, but before then she had a little more work to do on her new look. She put her new blonde hair into plaits and then foraged in her back-pack for a little plastic container. Inside were contact lenses, floating in solution, which she slid across her silver-blue eyes, converting them to dark brown. She also found an expensive eyebrow ink pen — the kind that would only wash off with soap and a very hot flannel — and, checking Brigitte Anderssen's authentically doctored passport photo for guidance, applied three large moles to her face: two on one cheek and the other on the side of her nose. Nothing ugly about them — no bumpy melanoma effect — just a smooth brown freckle in each position. Just noticeable enough.

One thing she had learned in her years of creating new identities was that adding a notable physical marker to her appearance was valuable. It was a way for a tired border guard to double check your passport and connect the dots and only remember the dots — literally, on Brigitte's features. She had once used a massive port-wine birthmark on her cheek and chin, which had smoothed her passage remarkably through border control. Not only was it totally unlike the smooth, unblemished face of her last incarna-tion, it was also —universally — rude to stare.

She left the hotel and went to get dinner in a nearby taverna, chatting to the barman in broken Greek, with a smattering of muttered Swedish between her phrases. Her talent for languages — and accents — was another gift in this long and unusual career of hers. Now that she was Brigitte it was fun to bring Swedish back into play again. With Stavros she had been Australian-Greek; something he had never questioned, along with her story that she was alone in the world after her parents had died in a fire in

Queensland the year before. Only Stav's mother had seemed suspicious, but not enough to prevent the wedding, especially after her daughter-in-law's conversion to Catholicism.

The Greek barman was hot and she could really do with some sex right now — she was always so charged up for it after she'd killed — but she knew it would be unwise. She planned to buy a ticket and walk onto the ferry back to Italy in the morning, leaving as little trace of Christina Eliades as possible. She was pretty sure her new face and hair would be good enough to settle her into her latest identity, but this was a small island and she was a great lay. Hot barman would remember her, maybe see a photo of Christina on TV in the coming days, and make a connection. Especially if things got steamy enough for one of her moles to smudge.

So she ate her meal and drank her drink and returned to the hotel for a dull night alone. Only it wouldn't be dull, not really. Because she had a whole new life to plan.

16

Another field, another crop circle, another body. Kate definitely *hadn't* wished for another early morning call like this.

The third was a woman — Asian in appearance, middle-aged, in a white dress with buttercups in her dark hair. She had rolled onto her side and reached one arm out across the flattened wheat as if trying to move away from the centre and the small metal flask lying close by. Maybe she had changed her mind about "ascending", thought Kate. Too late, obviously. She felt a wave of weary sadness. This was looking undeniably like a death cult situation.

Another note was found, tucked into the instep of one of the woman's golden strappy sandals. It read: *I ascend, with love and joy. I will see you all on the next level. Justine xx*

'Heaven's Gate,' Kate murmured, as she and Michaels retreated from the forensics tent at the edge of the field. At this rate they were going to run out of tents, FIs and police pathologists and would have to start calling them in from neighbouring counties. Kapoor had deployed all the Wiltshire-based teams now and this was fast escalating into a major incident.

'What's that?' asked Michaels.

'A death cult, in California, back in the 1970s. The leader of it convinced about forty people to kill themselves, promising they were just leaving their earthly bodies behind and ascending to a higher realm. They washed down the poison — and I think it was Pentobarbital — with apple sauce and vodka.'

'Jeezuz,' muttered Michaels. 'People will believe any old bollocks, won't they?'

'Sad, lonely or damaged people,' said Kate, 'looking for something to believe in… to make sense of their suffering. They get groomed. They get seduced. They usually get taken for everything they have along the way.'

'Are we bringing Rafe Campion in?' Michaels asked, literally rubbing his hands.

'Yup,' said Kate. 'But not before we've IDed the deceased, established whether they're his followers and had a word with their solicitors and life insurers.'

'Would be a bit careless, though, wouldn't it?' said Michaels. 'Putting your followers up to topping themselves after they'd changed their wills or set up life insurance you'd benefit from. I mean… people are going to check.'

'True,' said Kate. 'But that would depend on how rational you are. Campion seems to be buying into his own legend. We really need to speak to more of his followers — get some statements about the way they've been recruited and what they've been asked to do. Or strongly influenced to do.'

'Not going to be easy,' said Michaels, shaking his head. 'No social media presence — no website — not even a phone number.'

'It's all part of the mythology,' said Kate. 'You score a much higher mystery count if you're not too readily accessible. Think how many films stars have lost their kudos on Twitter.'

'Why not just go in and get Campion now? We know where he lives,' said Michaels.

'We will... soon...' said Kate. 'I just think we should build a bit more of a case. We're going to need everyone on board with this and Kapoor's not going to deny us a full team — not now. This is going to be massive in the media by the end of today.' She glanced up as a helicopter rose on the horizon. 'Here they are now,' she sighed, recognising the white and red livery of the regional ITV station.

'And the road crew,' said Michaels, nodding back towards the verge which screened them from the B-road. The top of a satellite truck could clearly be seen coasting along beyond the hedgerow.

Kate's phone buzzed and she picked up the call right away. 'Sir?'

'Is it as bad as I'm hearing?' asked Kapoor.

'I'm afraid so,' said Kate. 'We've got a third one.'

'Right — team briefing in an hour. Get back to base as soon as you can.'

They left the area well-guarded by uniforms and headed back past a knot of rubberneckers and journalists.

'DI Sparrow — are we looking at another serial killer case?' called out one young woman, waving a microphone in her direction. 'Are you going to call in a dowser?'

Kate glared at the woman, biting back a curt response.

'Keep walking. Don't rise to it,' advised Michaels, through gritted teeth.

'Are you still looking for Lucas Henry?' the same woman called. 'Did he kill your sister?'

Michaels steered her into the driver seat of the Honda. 'Come on — don't get distracted. You know they just want to get a rage-y photo of you for the next edition.'

As they pulled away she shook her head. 'Is that what's going to happen every time? Every case I have... *Hey, Kate... what happened to your pendulum-waving sidekick? Can you solve a case without him? Oh... and what's the latest on whether he murdered your sister?* Shit. Shit, fuck and bollocks.' She thumped her fist on the steering wheel.

'Don't even think about it,' said Michaels. 'We solved plenty of cases before Lucas Henry showed up and we'll go on to solve plenty more now he's gone. We're good at what we do. No short cuts, no gimmicks — just proper policing.'

Kate nodded as she drove carefully through the incoming media and gawping sightseers. She knew he was right. But in her head some traitorous voice whispered: *'Yeah... but a shortcut is just what you need here, isn't it? Because three suspicious crop circle deaths in one week might just be the start of it.'*

'You're right,' she said.

He nodded and added: 'I can't wait to get that smarmy bastard Campion in for questioning.'

A blue Ford Focus was trying to get past in the opposite direction, but it had hit a bottleneck. This skinny B-road was never intended for serious two-way traffic. Kate resisted the urge to slap on the blues and twos and took a long breath as the car tried to pull tight to the verge, close enough for her to pass, driving its wing mirror deep into the hedgerow. Then it stopped and a window wound down. 'Hang on,' called a voice. 'I'll back up if I can.'

Kate glanced across and saw a familiar face. 'Reverend Bennet? Jason..?'

'Oh — yes — hello again,' he said, a smile breaking out as recognition dawned. 'What have I got caught up in here?'

'Possible crime scene, I'm afraid,' said Kate. 'Can't really tell you any more, but...' she glanced up at the media chopper circling overhead. '...you'll get plenty of juice on tonight's news.'

'Oh my,' said the Rev. 'That's very unfortunate. I'm sorry to hear it. Looks like I chose the wrong shortcut back to Burchfont.' He glanced back and noted there was space further back up the lane. 'Look — I'll back up to a decent passing point and let you get past. Then I might try to turn around myself.'

'Thanks,' said Kate. 'Appreciate it.'

He spotted the ambulance up ahead as he shifted into reverse. 'Look, if it turns out to be anyone local and you think I can help...' He gave her another warm smile. 'Do let me know. Really wish I could have done more to help poor Linda...' His smile turned regretful.

'Thank you,' said Kate.

'You know where to find me, DI Sparrow. Anytime!'

'You got a thing for church leaders?' Michaels asked, with a wry grin, as Bennet's car reversed back up the hill and swerved into a passing point.

'Don't be ridiculous,' she said, driving on with a courteous wave.

He snorted. 'Well, they seem to have a thing for *you*...'

17

'Justine Patak, fifty-eight, from Westcott, and Callum Fanshaw, forty-two, from Shedhampton,' said Kate, indicating the photographs of the latest crop circle dead up on the board. 'Both died from Pentobarbital poisoning, both found in crop circles. And both... according to their solicitors... have left money to the Church of the Enlightened Energy.'

'So when are we bringing this anointed Rafe Campion in?' asked DS Sharpe.

'He's in and being processed now,' said Kate. She checked her watch. 'We should be interviewing him by teatime. Between now and then we need to crack on with the victimologies. We need to know exactly who Justine and Callum were, who their friends were, who their enemies were, if they had any. Social media trawling please, mobile phone logs, anything at all. It won't be easy because they will have sworn off a lot of this stuff if they were true believers. But perhaps only recently, so look for mentions of them on Facebook and other platforms... you might find an unlisted page somewhere.

'We also need to be making contact with Campion's followers. We need to understand what that group dynamic is — how much they know about what's occurred this week. Some of them are probably going to be getting scared by all of this — especially since Linda's been IDed in the media — and they might be able to tell us something we need to know. Next — who's making the crop circles? Can we check out any known hoaxers? It's unlikely anyone we have on file is involved, because they've tended to be drunk students or academics with a debunking bee in their bonnet. Either way, where are they now? Where have they been this week? And do they know where other hoaxers are who might be able to help us?

'Croppies — you can find plenty of those on social media. We need to get them to help, too. If they're getting advanced intel of where and when circles are emerging, there has to be a way to chase that back to its source.'

'What about family?' asked Sharpe, flicking his pen against his paper folder like a bored student. 'Anyone being brought in to ID the bodies?'

'Yes — we have a daughter, coming down from London,' said Kate, with a sigh. 'It's pretty academic because Justine, like Linda, parked nearby and left her driver's licence in her car. The photo looks like her and the signature on it matches the signature on her farewell note. We haven't found a vehicle for Callum but he was wearing an emergency ID bracelet for diabetes and we've traced him through medical records. No family in this country, but a neighbour is coming in to ID him formally.'

She stopped and exhaled, thinking of the sad ripple effect these deaths were bound to have on families far and wide. Then she pressed on. 'In the meantime, we need checks across ANPR and mobile phone cells for the past 18 hours to see who was travelling in and around these locations.' She pointed to the map where three small circles were marked.

'Guv... what about that lot?' asked DC Sharon Mulligan, glancing out of the CID window and grimacing. Representatives of local — and national — media were loitering on the front steps, awaiting news. Their colleagues were also staking out all three crop circle locations but being kept well away from the cordons, although there was little that could be done to prevent the media choppers from getting their aerial views. These were already decorating news channels around the world.

Kate wasn't surprised. Crop circles alone were enough to get global coverage — people never seemed to tire of them — but crop circles with *bodies*; that was just journalistic catnip.

'I will be making a press statement at five o'clock,' said Chief Superintendent Kapoor. 'A media liaison officer is working with us. And I should stress at this point, that this is not a murder enquiry. At present there is no firm evidence of foul play. These *are* suspicious deaths, however.'

'Are we talking death cult?' asked Sharpe.

'The next Heaven's Gate,' said Michaels, who had obviously remembered his conversation with Kate. 'Could be our Rafe Campion's planning to wipe out the lot of them, crop circle by crop circle.'

'Let me make this *very* clear,' said Kapoor, sharply. '*Nobody* says anything about a death cult beyond this room. We've already got a significant press problem to handle here — we do *not* need to fan the flames any further.'

'It's not, anyway,' said a boyish figure in a brown tweed jacket, who was resting on a table at the back of the room. Kate glanced across in surprise — she had not seen him arrive. Their occasional criminal psychology expert was back in CID, clutching his usual folder and smiling his usual benign smile. Conrad Temple nodded at her, raising one eyebrow, and then scanned the rest of them as he went on: 'Cults like Heaven's Gate have historically been very secretive — much of the brainwashing went on behind closed doors and the suicides weren't planned to be public — well, not until it was too late.

'If Rafe Campion wanted to wipe out his followers he'd be planning a big, under-the-radar event to get them all in one hit before the authorities could wade in and stop him. This is different. The crop circles, the white clothing, the flowers in their hair... it's big on ritual and public statement.'

'So are you saying you don't think Campion's so-called church is behind this?' asked Michaels. 'Because if so, you should have been at the meeting of the faithful that Kate and I went to. Think you might change your mind, Yankee Boy.'

Temple grinned at Michaels as if he'd just said something very clever and endearing. 'You're right to be suspicious,' he said.

'Well, thanks,' said Michaels, nodding heavily. 'You make a humble detective constable very happy.'

'I'm not saying Campion isn't involved,' Temple went on. 'I'm just saying I don't think a mass suicide event is on the cards. If that was the plan he's blown it. No element of surprise now.'

Kate moved on to assigning the tasks, keeping an eye on the clock. Her interview with Campion was ten minutes away. She was desperate to watch his face while she laid out some choice titbits of the last forty-eight hours' policing in front of him.

'Nice to see you looking so well.' The warm Bostonian

accent was close behind her as she gathered her file of notes and images to take to the interview room.

She turned and smiled at him. 'Well, it's been at least six weeks since anyone tried to kill me. That always puts a spring in my step.'

'I heard about the holiday camp,' Temple said, tilting his head and fixing his brown eyes on her. 'Tough break.'

'Next time I'm thinking of a relaxing getaway to the Gaza Strip — or maybe Syria,' she said.

Someone tapped her shoulder and she turned to see Michaels, already revving up. 'Campion's ready for interview,' he said. 'If you don't mind, professor,' he added, with a side-eye at Temple.

'Let's go,' said Kate.

'Coffee and a catch up some time?' said Temple, as if Michaels wasn't standing right there, seething at him.

'Sure,' she said. 'That'd be nice.' It *would* be nice, too. She'd been hoping he might ask.

'Tosser,' uttered Michaels as they headed out of CID.

'He speaks very highly of *you*,' she couldn't stop herself saying, with a grin.

Campion was very relaxed, or giving a good impression of it, when they arrived in the interview room. She wondered if he'd smoked a joint before arriving at the station, but her highly-tuned olfactory system did not detect any evidence.

'Thank you for coming in,' she said, sitting opposite him.

'I'm very happy to help the police,' he said, 'in whatever way I can.'

'Do you know why we've asked you to come in and talk to us today?' asked Kate, as soon as the tape had been set rolling and the introductions made.

'I'm guessing it's the crop circles and the bodies therein,' said Campion. 'It's all over the news.'

'I thought you didn't do news,' said Kate. 'No tech. No live media feeds.'

'I have a wind-up radio at home,' he said, giving her a lazy smile. 'I listen to that when I need to connect with the outer world. There's another radio in the car. I caught up with the news as I was driving in. I'm not able to run things without *some* contact with the modern world, I'm afraid.'

'Are you aware that the three people who have died in a crop circle this week are all members of your Church of the Enlightened Energy?' she asked.

He blinked. 'I wasn't aware of that. I knew about Linda, of course, since you enlightened me yourself, but I had no idea there were two more. May I ask who?'

'Justine Patak and Callum Fanshaw.'

He blinked again and shook his head. 'Well... that's... unexpected,' he said, with a sigh. 'I will miss them both.'

'You won't miss their money, though, will you?' said Michaels. 'That's going to cushion the blow.'

He glanced from Michaels to Kate. 'Money? I'm sorry... I don't understand.'

She raised her eyebrows. 'Don't you?'

He looked uneasy for the first time. 'Look... people make donations to the church, it's part of how we run things. Our research needs resources and true believers are very willing to help with that. Linda and Justine and Callum — they all made contributions, but they were under no duress to do so. We welcome everyone regardless of their financial status.'

'So — the money left to you in Linda's will — did you know about that?' asked Kate.

He bit his lips together and breathed slowly through his nostrils before responding. 'It seems to me that I should probably be talking to a lawyer before I discuss this any further.'

'Mr Campion, just two days ago we watched you spell out to your followers that ascending to the *next level of consciousness*, as you put it, was a highly desirable goal,' said Kate. 'And that to do it from a crop circle was about as good as it gets. Did it not occur to you that some of your audience were vulnerable and suggestible? That they might take you at your word?'

'I was *not* encouraging anyone to kill themselves!' Campion protested, sitting up straight and shaking off any of the Zen he'd brought in with him.

'I might argue with that,' said Kate. 'And, in case you're wondering, inciting suicide *is* an indictable offence, punishable by law.'

She nodded at Michaels, who slid some photographs of the small flasks and bottles found beside the bodies from his folder. 'Do you recognise these?' he asked.

'DC Michaels is showing Mr Campion some images of three vessels, each found at the scene of the crop circle deaths this week,' Kate said, for the tape.

Campion stood up without glancing at the photos. 'Am I under arrest?' he said.

'No,' said Kate, leaning back in her chair and watching him closely. 'You're helping us with our enquiries, which I believe you said you were very happy to do.'

'Right, well I'm going,' he said. 'And if you want to interview me again, it'll be with my solicitor present.'

Kate stood up, too. 'That's your right, of course, if you feel you need a solicitor,' she said. 'So... *do* you think you need a solicitor?'

'I'm not guilty of anything, if that's what you're trying to get me to say,' he snapped, raking one hand through his immaculate golden hair. 'You know your problem?' He turned and narrowed his eyes at her.

'Enlighten me,' she said, almost straight-faced.

'You're just the same as every other so-called authority figure. You live by the rules of empirical evidence — a narrow world view that you protect at all costs, because you're too terrified to look beyond the feeble constructs of western society. Too scared to imagine there is anything in or off this world other than what your blunt five senses tell you. You bury your spirit and your creative inner mind and ignore anything which does not fit your safe daily narrative. You are boxed in and wilfully blind.'

'Is *that* it?' she said. 'I thought it was just a wheat allergy.'

She reached across to the recorder. 'Interview terminated at seventeen-thirty-seven.' She switched off. 'Please show Mr Campion out, DC Michaels. We'll speak again, Rafe.'

18

L ucas wandered the ferry, restless, even though it was nearly midnight.

Yesterday he had reached Brindisi too late to catch the lunchtime *or* the late ferry to Corfu. It was high season and one ferry was getting repairs, so the crossing was booked out until the next evening. He had no choice but to keep a low profile in the port for another night and a day, stopping at a budget hotel and passing the time with a book and the TV with its intermittent signal. He bought tickets for the sailing shortly after nine the next evening and now, finally, he was on his way.

There had been the usual prickle of apprehension as he entered the ticket hall, pulling out his passport, created and artfully aged by a useful contact in the South of France last month. Lawrence Tonioli — half English, half Italian — was thirty-two and travelling Europe to research a travelogue book he hoped to get published one day. Friends called him Larry.

He had been tempted to put 'artist' in the occupation section but couldn't risk it. He had bought pencils, paints, brushes and a watercolour pad in a French art supplies store during his first week on the run, needing the comfort of the tools of his trade, and aware that he might also need the street artist income. As a wannabe author, the supplies in his rucksack would still make sense. Lawrence Tonioli hoped to illustrate his travels, obviously. Lucas knew that living up to a fake legend for himself would be harder if it was too far removed from his own instincts and talents.

The well-padded recliner seats on board the ferry were amply comfortable for some decent kip and, once he'd boarded without incident, he'd been able to drift off to some degree. An uneasy night in the cheap hotel, followed by a day spent wandering the port before he could board the ship, had tired him a lot. But then he'd woken up with a raging thirst and a need for hot carbs. Lasagne and a Coke revived him as he sat in the café with a handful of other wakeful passengers, enjoying some middle-of-the-night sustenance. There was only a gentle swell and he found the motion of the vessel soothing as he settled into a corner with his hot pasta dish and his bottle of fizz. A TV suspended on the wall nearby was showing twenty-four-hour news and he wondered if the discovery of ancient coins in Southern Italy would have made it into the media yet. He hoped Alberto was managing it all as they had discussed... that there would be no questions raised over where the treasure was found. He guessed the red tape of Italian bureaucracy would mean there would be no money coming for a while, but his anonymous online research in a library during his wanderings around the port had reassured him that the last lucky finder of such a momentous stash had managed to recoup a lot of its value after the state had bagged its share.

He wondered next how long it would be before Alberto

bought that spaniel. He very much hoped the dog would have an excellent nose and as good an instinct for uncovering bodies as Sid. He instinctively patted his T-shirt and then remembered he'd taken Sid off and balled him up in a sock, buried deep in the rucksack. He was pretty sure Interpol would have posted alerts for anyone wearing a blue glass bottle stopper on a chain. In a country filled with dark haired, lightly-bearded young men, it was one of the few distinctive features they could call on. As he continued to travel unrecognised, it was easy to get complacent, but he knew he mustn't. Back in England there were people who firmly believed he had killed two teenagers. A search for the killer of young girls was never likely to be given up.

Not by him, anyway. If he was right he was getting closer to the person who had ended Zoe and Mabel. Once he'd found that person he might have some hope of returning to his old life, picking up the threads... maybe even of going back to his bungalow in the wilds of Wiltshire and completing the new series of paintings he had barely started. Perversely, now that he was many hundreds of miles away from his canvases, he was getting plenty of inspiration.

The rolling news had moved to curious events around the world and he suddenly found his dreams of a new direction for his next collection interrupted by the familiar sight of a wheat field in England... with a *crop circle* in it. Lucas sat up straight — peering hard at the screen and tracking the Italian subtitles running along the foot of it, trying to translate them at speed. Although he spoke the language easily enough, he'd never spent much time reading it.

Something surged inside him as he read: **Morte nel cerchio nel grano vicino a Stonehenge nel Wiltshire.** What was going on in his home county? The news report zoned in on people jostling at a police cordon — a white tent erected in the centre of the circle, the ancient stones misty on the far horizon.

And then there was Kate. He nearly choked on his Coke and put the bottle down with a shaking hand. Kate was among the knot of people inside the cordon, near the tent, talking animatedly to what looked like a local farmer. The familiarity and yet the *strangeness* of seeing her took his breath away. It also made him feel faintly foolish. He realised that, despite his every waking — and sometimes sleeping — conviction that she was doggedly in pursuit of him, this clearly wasn't the case. Here was Kate... his nemesis and his obsession... simply getting on with her job as a detective, as if nothing had happened.

His rational brain told him that *of course* she was getting on with her job. Kapoor, her chief superintendent, whom he'd met and, actually, quite liked, was never going to let her investigate the Quarry Girls case — and the prime suspect now on the run from it — when one of the victims was her sister. He wondered how she was coping with that; being made to be patient and allow others to do the detective work for her. If he knew Kate — and he *did* know Kate — she would be bouncing off the walls. That plasticine habit of hers was probably going into overdrive. Mostly with effigies of himself, he suspected.

The news moved on but her face, the angle of her body, the jacket he'd seen her wear before and the drift of her blonde ponytail across her cheek as she stood in the Wiltshire breeze... all of this was instantly burnt into his memory. It was both a shock and a relief to see her on screen. The last time he'd seen her she had been wrestling him to the ground, her features drenched with hatred and anger. It still stung him to the core to think of it. Now he'd had a refresh. It was easier. Kate... just being Kate.

Don't underestimate her, his inner self spoke up. *Whatever it looks like, she'll never give up.* And nor should she. In her position, *he* wouldn't. And in truth he was not at all far from being in her position. She had lost a sister — *he* had lost two friends, his reputation, his freedom in his own country. His assets, such as they were, had most likely been frozen. He couldn't be completely sure of this, of course, because he had been nowhere near a bank or a cashpoint with his card. He'd only dealt in cash and he'd not carried a phone since he scattered pieces of his mobile during his escape. He hoped someone was keeping an eye on the bungalow and his Triumph Bonneville motorbike, no doubt languishing in some police evidence pound since he'd abandoned it in that countryside car park. He wanted his home and his bike back one day.

The temptation to unearth Sid and check his map was strong, but there were people around and maybe CCTV cameras, although he had covertly checked for lenses when he settled into his seat — as he instinctively did wherever he went these days — and he was pretty sure he wasn't featuring on any video feeds.

There were two hours of sailing time left and dawn was only just lighting the sky, but he knew he wouldn't be able to sleep again. He got up, picked up his rucksack and, keeping his head low and the brim of his hat between his eyeline and any camera, headed for the upper deck.

Outside it was surprisingly cool for late summer, the sea breeze steady in his face as he clung to the guard rail. He could see a misty shape on the horizon which must be Corfu. He didn't need Sid. His instincts were up and singing to him like a philharmonic choir. This was the place. *This* was where the killer was. He had no doubt. He *was* going to track his quarry down. But whether he could bring them to justice... that was another question altogether.

He passed an hour on the deck and then managed to get a little doze in, back inside, before the ferry docked at six. He felt as vulnerable as ever as he queued with the foot passengers to get off, keeping his head down and his attention focused on a magazine he'd found on board, pretending he could read Greek. In some ways he'd do better to get a smart phone of some kind, because it didn't look odd on a CCTV camera if someone was constantly head down, staring into a device. This passed for normal behaviour here in the 21st century.

But his instinct told him that even a pay-as-you-go phone might trip him up. The temptation to call Kate was too strong. Just a text... a little line saying: **It wasn't me. Don't go around thinking it was me. I will prove it. Just give me time.**

It would be madness, but sometimes, in the early hours of the morning when he'd lain awake in the camp bed at the farm, he had convinced himself that Kate would believe him if he made a call or a text. That she would apologise for ever doubting him. That she *knew* him the way he felt he knew her.

And by the cold light of day, he had shaken his head and congratulated himself for never buying a phone. It would be his downfall. Of course, he could always get one with no SIM card and just play games on it in the next passport control queue. Anyway, he and his passport received only a cursory glance as he passed through.

He found a cafe and got some feta cheese, olives, focaccia bread and coffee. He was burning to get Sid out and dowse his newly-purchased map of Corfu but that was not invisible behaviour. He would need to find a secluded place to do that — and soon. He was picking up patterns of elevated energy... movement. The answer to his simple question — *What happened to Zoe and Mabel?* — was close at hand; he could sense it in every cell of his body. But with this certainty also came a lot of emotional fog and he would need Sid and a map, and a good few minutes in the dowsing state before he could be clear on where to go next.

He continued his breakfast, half-listening to an excitable local presenter broadcasting through the old portable radio blaring from the kitchen area behind the serving counter. His wanderings of the continent over the past decade had given him enough of a grounding in Greek to understand there had been a double murder... of two Greek detectives. Their bodies had been found in a cave on the west coast and a recently widowed heiress was also missing, possibly at sea, and wanted urgently for questioning. Kate would have been all over that, he thought, his skin prickling.

He took a deep breath, got up and paid, and then headed along the street, seeking a good spot to calm his mind. To his right was the road to the old harbour, the island's old Venetian fortress hanging on the hill above it, surrounded by trees. It was early yet, and the fortress probably wouldn't be open to tourists for another couple of hours. It seemed like a good place to settle in the shade and seek out the quiet mind that would usher the dowsing state in and help him locate his target. 'Time to come out, Sid,' he muttered, opening his rucksack and reaching far down into it, where his pendulum lay stifled in the balled-up sock.

North. That was where he needed to go. Sid was pretty definite about it, swinging in a confident arc from his port location to a route that suggested the main inland road. Lucas sat back against the trunk of the tree he was sheltering under, stared up at the Venetian fortress and tried to make a plan.

He could maybe catch a bus part of the way, but he felt concerned that doing so would take him too far east. Walking would give him ample opportunity to stop along the way and recalibrate. Because he was now getting a very strong instinct that his target was on the move too. Towards *him*. Almost as if the target *knew* he was here. Maybe he should just stay put and wait.

But no. This place was too busy. It would be very easy to lose yourself in the crowd, which would help in some respects, if he was tailing someone — but also hinder if that someone realised they were being tailed and chose to slip into a knot of tourists and vanish. Out in the more provincial parts of the island he might be in with a better chance of locating the target on approach and finding a place to lie in wait.

And then what? Citizen's arrest? Take them down and march them to the local police station, demanding phone calls to the UK? He shook his head, impatient with his own fantasy.

No. The best option would be to follow and see where they were holing up these days. Once he had proof of an address he could dig out his digital camera and get some shots to send back to Kate, along with the address and any other details he could find out. He was going to need to turn detective in the more conventional sense. A dowser's hunch was hardly enough to prompt a call to Interpol; he would need to find out much more.

He realised there was another hole in his walking plan. If he did encounter the target, only to find they were driving, he'd catch only a glimpse of them at best and then they'd be gone. He might not even get the chance to note their registration number. So... He could see the sign and the hut from here. He smiled to himself. It had been a long time. He got up and crossed the car park and the road to Corfu Vespa Hire, grinning and humming *'On the road again...'* in the style of Donkey from *Shrek*.

———

BRIGITTE ANDERSSEN, formerly known as Christina Eliades, hauled her rucksack higher on her back and set out south along the farm track. There were perfectly good roads with perfectly good drivers to hitch a lift from, but she was getting a tightening in her belly which was warning her against this. She calculated it was forty-four hours since detectives Adamos and Gazis had taken the quick route down to her private beach. The police would by now be crawling all over the villa, having eventually traced their lost colleagues back there, where they had no doubt spotted the broken balustrades above a killer drop and deduced that this was a FUCKING BIG CLUE.

The police had indeed thought to check out the cave and so quickly found the bodies. Brigitte knew her manoeuvre with the car and chucking the mobiles and ID over the cliff had won her a little more time, and sending the *Contessa* out to sea was a stroke of genius, but Christina Eliades was now wanted for murder, if not of her husband, then definitely of the two detectives. It had been all over the news on the TV in her hotel room, which she had booked for a second night while she took time to plan her next move.

Although she didn't do guilt or regret, she cursed her post-homicidal horniness. If she had just held off a bit longer with her little post-murder celebration, she'd have been in the clear for ever. Of all the things that might have tripped her up over the years, she'd never have guessed a few solo masturbatory minutes would be her undoing...

So... Brigitte Anderssen should get to the port and get off this island pretty sharpish, before there was extra scrutiny of any young woman travelling alone. Her DNA wasn't on any database as far as she knew... but she could be wrong. She hadn't known how to be careful seventeen years ago and for all she knew there was evidence tucked away in a plastic bag held by Wiltshire Police. A swab by a suspicious border patrolman might end her freedom.

Of course, she *could* lie low on the island for a bit longer and wait until the fuss had died down before boarding that ferry or even catching a flight. That might be a better plan. She could get a job in a hotel for a few weeks, cleaning rooms, waitressing — really lay the Swedish accent on thick. Ipsos was a good option — a seaside village with plenty of gap-year students and travellers working the bars. When she'd set out this morning, she'd instinctively begun to walk towards the east-coast resort. But... should she really just head south and brazen it out on a ferry now? Or even catch a flight? Her disguise was good and her fake passport excellent.

She shook her head impatiently. It was unlike her to be indecisive. Normally she made a plan and saw it through. Why was she vacillating? What was going on here?

Up ahead was a footpath across the valley, further inland, which might be a shortcut. She instinctively veered onto it, knowing it would be less frequented by tourists than the coastal path. This route was probably used by Corfu natives, trekking from village to village across farmland and olive groves.

It got less picturesque as she walked on, cutting across a weedy area of neglected pasture with a hill of tyres and discarded farm machinery piled up against a wire-fenced border. The heat of the day was building and she could almost hear the ping and twang of old metal expanding under the sun. She could hear buzzing, too, and initially thought it might be flies. Was she about to stumble on a body..?

Her antennae twitched. She had never seen a dead body, other than those she had made herself. She'd never observed the aftermath, once a corpse started to degrade — she was much more about the moment of departure; the unique expression in the eyes of a person grasping the shock of their imminent demise — and of the person dealing it.

But there was no disturbed cloud of flies, rising off the putrid, bloated face of a dead farmer. Just a large metal trap-door set into the ground — probably an underground silo for animal feed or maybe diesel. Judging by the dirt and weeds growing in its hinges, it hadn't, like the machinery around it, been used in years. Idly curious, she grabbed the warm metal ring on one of its half-moon shaped doors and pulled. The trapdoor rose up more easily than she had expected, revealing a pit cut into the earth about two metres deep, lined with corrugated iron. Four rungs led down into it but there was no sign of any feed here now; just compacted earth and spider webs.

The buzzing continued, though, and now she realised what it was... one of those little mopeds that tourists loved to ride around the island, sounding like an angry wasp in a tin can. Instinctively, she slid into the shadow of a mature cypress tree, close to the wire fence perimeter, as the Vespa and rider approached. She needed to avoid being seen if at all possible.

But instead of passing by, the rider came to a halt at the

side of the road. Weeds grew high and woody against the wire fence, so she didn't have a clear view of why they had stopped. To consult a map, probably, and work out why they were on this track alongside unlovely dilapidated farmland rather than on the coastal road with its gorgeous views.

There was no sound from the Vespa rider. It was unnervingly quiet. She stood very, very still, her skin prickling a warning of danger. Another vehicle was approaching... slow and lumbering... a tractor. Under the cover of its noise she slipped the rucksack off her back, shoved it into a hollow between the roots, and climbed the tree. She needed to move quite fast if she was to get high enough into the branches before the tractor passed and she might be heard. She managed it. Another tribute to her many hours spent doing pull-ups and squats in the gym. She balanced on her haunches on a steady bough, one arm hooked around the trunk, the soles of her white trainers gripping the bark securely.

From this angle she could see the rider. His Vespa was on its stand and he was holding a map in one hand. So, she'd guessed right. He was just seeking a better route. Only the goosebumps were still travelling her skin like a Mexican wave because there was something about the figure below her that was familiar.

He took off his helmet but turned away from her sight-line as he did so, revealing only long, unkempt dark hair and one plane of a bearded face. She narrowed her eyes, staring down and waiting for him to turn around, her heartbeat speeding up almost painfully. He didn't turn, though. Instead he picked up the rucksack he must have shrugged off earlier, and started rummaging through it, pulling out what looked like a balled-up sock. From this he extracted a glinting steely chain, with something dangling on it.

Her heart crashed so hard she thought it might be audible to the man beside the bike. Her breath was funnelling in and out of her open mouth as if she'd just been dunked in icy water. The man was now slowly turning towards her, holding a blue pendulum on a steel chain, eyes closed. It was, without doubt, *Lucas fucking Henry.*

———

LUCAS FELT A SENSE OF UNREALITY. Sid was pulling him along, like a bloodhound on a lead, eager to make him travel... just a short distance. There was nothing to be seen here but some run-to-seed meadow and the rusting remains of some long-abandoned farm machinery. Nobody in view for miles. But Sid definitely wanted him to be right here.

Maybe this was an intercept point — this might be the track his target was travelling along, shortly to reach him. That made sense. He glanced back, a surge of adrenaline rocking him, as a tractor laboured up the track towards him, but he quickly dismissed it. Wrong direction. Wrong patterns.

No. This was the place he needed to be. He glanced towards a cypress tree, just the other side of the weed-choked wire fence and decided this was where he needed to go next. If only to wait in its shade and view the approach of the next vehicle coming from the north. This was the road the target was travelling, and they were close. Very close.

He should be able to spot the car at a distance, use his small binoculars to track it and note its registration before it reached him — and then be on his moped, helmeted up, and ready to follow as it passed. He manoeuvred the Vespa around to face the other direction, so it would look less suspicious when he pulled out and began his discreet tailing, as if he had been travelling south in the first place. He grabbed his binoculars and then scrambled, awkwardly, across the wire fence, which sagged and wobbled under his weight.

His heart was racing as he strode to the tree. Any time now he might be looking right into the eyes of a killer.

At the foot of it he found another rucksack. In less than half a second the pulsing, jagged patterns that had led him to this spot twisted into a sharp spike of certain knowledge. He glanced up, jaw dropping, and looked right into the eyes of a killer.

19

'SHIT — NO!'

Kate shot up in bed, tangled in the sheets, sweating and panting. She stared around, taking in the grey light of dawn and the familiar shapes, shadows and planes of her room, reminding herself where she was. At home. In bed. She went through a more detailed mental checklist as she unscrambled her waking mind. It was Saturday. She was dealing with the Crop Circle Deaths and still no closer to getting a decent case against Rafe Campion since they'd found Linda Stewart's body on Monday.

It wasn't a fun way of ordering her mind and getting a grip, but it was better than where she had been a minute or two earlier. Because she'd been back again. Back in that quarry. No matter that she had never been there since the loss of Mabel and Zoe and could hardly remember it in any great detail. The director of her nocturnal inner horror movie had filled all the gaps in nicely, including the broken and bloodied bodies. She had been walking along the floor of the old chalk pit with Death at her side in his CSI suit, a clipboard in his hand, ticking off the corpses of first Mabel, then Zoe, then her mother and then Francis and finally, Lucas. Lucas was in a lower chamber of the quarry, which seemed to have been carved out like a roomy coffin. He had been lying on his side, wearing only a vest and shorts, and when she'd knelt down to touch his bare shoulder he'd suddenly sprung up, his face covered in blood and his eyes missing.

At which point she had woken up screaming.

There was a gentle knock at the door. 'You alright in there?'

Francis. She let out a long breath and called out: 'Yeah. Just a dream. Sorry... did I actually scream out loud?'

The door opened and he eased himself around it, checking she was decent, before padding across in his T-shirt and lounge pants and sitting on the end of the bed. 'Yeah,' he said. 'Thought you'd lost an earring or something.'

She laughed feebly.

'Nightmares not letting up then?' he asked, rubbing his messed up blond hair vigorously until it stood up on end in sympathy.

She shrugged. 'Some nights I sleep all the way through without them,' she said.

'Not many though, eh?' he said.

'How about you?' She squeezed his arm, well aware that he, too, had gone through a fair bit of trauma at their ill-fated weekend away back in May.

'I'm fine,' he said. 'I sleep like the dead.' He grimaced. 'Bad choice of phrase.'

'Way too many dead people in our lives,' said Kate, pulling the duvet back over her as a chill swept across her skin. 'Do you think we're cursed?'

He laughed quietly and shook his head. 'I think we'd be

a bit less cursed if you'd gone for that fashion model career instead of the police.'

'I'm too short,' she said. 'I would never have made it. And I would probably have found a dead photographer somewhere. Or an overdosed catwalk star. Or my own brain going terminal with boredom.'

'Well, it's definitely never been dull,' said Francis. 'This whole crop circles thing! Can't you just make do with everyday drug barons, bank robbers and people traffickers, like normal police?'

'Mum never wanted me to join the police,' said Kate, hugging her knees. 'She wanted me to stay away from the dark underbelly of humanity... I think that's how she put it. She thought we'd had enough of that after Mabel and Zoe.'

'She was probably right,' said Francis. 'She was all about helping us move on, wasn't she? She was so incredibly strong.'

'She was,' mused Kate. 'After those first few awful weeks of crying and waiting by the phone... she just seemed to snap out of it one day and make a decision to keep living her life for me and you. Like she got a new sense of purpose and just pushed away all the heartbreak... at least what we saw of it. Imagine how hard that was for her, accepting that her daughter was dead when so many people get eaten up with that awful hopeless hope for the rest of their lives. She just turned away from that and poured all her love into us — made us all look forward, not back. Moved us away, got a new house, new name, fresh start.'

'She was amazing,' said Francis. 'I miss her.' He sagged a little on the end of the bed and Kate reached out and squeezed his hand. He'd only been nineteen when their mum died. It was so much tougher for him.

'Hey... I meant to ask earlier... did she ever talk to you

about going off on a big trip around the world... after she was gone?' Kate asked. 'You know, when she knew she didn't have much time left.'

Francis wrinkled his brow. 'I don't think so. I mean... she might have but I don't remember. I was just trying to pretend it wasn't happening. I used to shut my ears when she talked to us about... after.'

'Yeah, I know what you mean,' said Kate. 'I don't think she ever talked about that to me, either. It's just something the solicitor said. I met her a couple of days ago, the one who dealt with all our legal stuff — Kirsty Pope — do you remember?'

He shrugged. Kate had dealt with all the funeral arrangements and the legal stuff, so she wasn't surprised he was largely oblivious to that, too.

'She said something about hoping Mum's money had been enough to fund a big trip somewhere — like a gap-year thing. Then she said she must have got Mum mixed up with another client.'

'I expect she did, then,' said Francis, with a shrug.

'Hmmm,' said Kate.

'Hmmm?'

'It's just that she looked really flustered when she realised what she'd said,' Kate explained. 'She was beetroot red and trying to hide it.'

'Well, she was probably—'

'Embarrassed... yes. But it seemed... anyway...' Kate yawned. 'This is not the time to be ferreting around for mysteries where there are none. I think my DI brain just won't switch off, that's the problem. I've only got to notice some guy looking at me in the street these days to think he's packing a gun and planning an abduction.'

'That can't be easy,' said Francis. 'They look at you a lot.

You could try wearing an orange anorak and some very thick-lensed glasses… and a *Frozen* T-shirt.'

She laughed and yawned again. 'OK — sleep! I've got to sleep and so have you… probably. Or are you on Japanese time or something?' Francis worked as some kind of IT genius for businesses all over the globe and kept very random hours.

'Nah — UK time right now. I'm for bed, too. Nanight.' He gave her hair an affectionate tug and left.

She settled down and drifted off at last. When her alarm went at six it felt as if she'd only closed her eyes for ten minutes, but she'd got another couple of hours, mercifully free of any dreaming.

'There's a parcel for you,' Francis called from the hall, while she was finishing her last bit of toast and dregs of coffee in her kitchen. 'It's on the shelf.' She heard his feet thud back up the stairs.

'Thanks,' she yelled back, her voice loud enough to travel through the thin partition wall they had created to keep their living spaces separate. She grabbed her satchel and her jacket and headed for the front door, keen to get into CID — even on a Saturday — and find out what news there was on the many lines of enquiry she'd set the team to all week.

The parcel was just a small padded envelope and she might have left it until later if she hadn't spotted the foreign stamps on it. She paused, dropping her bag, and stared at it. The name and address was printed onto a label and stuck on. The stamp and the franking mark were from… she peered closely… *Corfu?* Who the hell would be sending her something from Corfu?

She was suddenly very still, a wave of goosebumps washing over her. She reached down into her satchel and pulled out some latex gloves, putting them on before she picked up the padded envelope. It wasn't unheard of for harmful substances — or letter bombs — to be sent to police officers in the post... although this didn't seem bulky enough to be a bomb. She could feel something lumpy inside it, though.

Glancing up the stairs, she decided to leave Francis out of this, whatever it was. It was probably nothing. *Nothing.* A random free sample sent to her because she'd unwittingly subscribed to something online, that was the most likely explanation. But just in case she was about to unleash a cloud of anthrax in their hallway, she picked up the parcel and her bag and stepped outside, pulling the door firmly shut behind her.

She wandered across the small patch of dewy lawn beside the drive and took a deep breath. *Just open it!* The goosebumps weren't settling down and her imagination was going into overdrive. The knobbly thing under the padded paper... it could be a severed finger. *Oh for fuck's sake, Kate! Just open it and find out!*

She breathed out, breathed in again, held her breath and ripped the envelope open. Inside was a thin white plastic bag. As she withdrew it she realised it was spattered with red on the inside. *Oh god. Severed finger. She was right.*

But now that she had it in her palm she knew it wasn't that. The red almost certainly *was* blood — she'd seen enough of it to know — but there was no decaying digit inside that bag. The shape and the feel of it were instantly recognisable. A stab of shock went through her.

'Shit,' she breathed, swaying a little as she emptied the plastic bag and watched its contents slither and tumble into her hand. '*Sid!*'

Lucas's blue bottle glass pendulum lay cradled in her

palm, its steel chain crumpled around it. There was blood on the chain... and on the glass. Lucas's blood? Who knew? She felt a cold surge of fear for him. *Really? Really, Kate?* Yes — really! Because if Lucas Henry was dead and his pendulum had been sent to her as some sort of message, then she might never find out what he did to Mabel... and *why* he did it. And she needed to know that like she needed to *breathe.* She *had* to know.

So... what now? She should take this right in to work and get forensics all over it; verify it was Lucas's blood.

And what would that tell them? Nothing. Absolutely nothing. The only thing she had to go on was the stamp... Corfu. And that was a good fit with the CCTV footage Kapoor had shown her earlier that week. That image of a man who might be Lucas — it had been captured in an Italian port. Brindisi..? She feverishly pulled out her phone and entered the name into the maps app, locating the port on the heel of the boot of Italy and quickly spotting the ferry lines across the Ionian Sea to.... Corfu.

She felt a surge of adrenaline so strong it was all she could do to remain still and compose her thoughts. *Think!* If she handed this to Kapoor it would be acted upon, of course... Interpol would be all over it. She hoped. But how high Lucas Henry was on the priority list was anybody's guess. How many terrorists and murderers of unassailable guilt and serious potential threat were already occupying the time and resources of international police across the Mediterranean countries? People traffickers, drug smugglers, gun runners... It was hard to imagine that one wandering artist, wanted on a historic murder and abduction charge but still, technically, innocent until proven guilty, would create a storm of investigation overnight.

Lucas Henry was a giant in her life. Omnipresent. An

obsession. Apprehending him and forcing his full confession was the highest priority she had... but not even her own colleagues at Salisbury could truly share this priority. Not even DS Michaels, who ran a pretty close second. Michaels wanted to punch Lucas Henry from here to next week, and hear his confession spat out through broken teeth... but she knew this was the result of the young DC's wounded pride more than anything. Henry had worked alongside *his* partner and pulled off some impressive crime solving along the way, while Michaels had been lost in the wake. Lucas had also outwitted and embarrassed most of her colleagues in CID, Michaels among them.

So, it wasn't about finding out the truth of the Quarry Girls case. Everyone else would *want* to, of course, but the balance of their mental health did not rest on this the way hers did. She had to know what had happened. She *had* to.

With shaking hands, Kate put Sid back in the plastic wrapper and put that back into the envelope. She dropped the envelope inside an evidence bag, sealing it shut. Then she hid the whole package in a zip-up compartment of the satchel.

She was going to go to work today. She was going to carry on as normal. She was going to push on with these crop circle deaths and try to make sense of who was behind them.

But first she was going to book herself a flight to Corfu.

20

Brigitte Anderssen wiped a table top clean and smiled at a nearby customer, an old Greek gentleman who smiled back over his newspaper and sipped at his morning coffee. She didn't blink at the headline, even though she was mostly responsible for it.

She'd been in the job for less than twenty-four hours but felt that it was going well. It was high season and cafés and tavernas were usually in need of temporary staff to manage the influx of tourists. Early on Thursday evening she'd walked into the first taverna she'd found with a hiring notice in the window and picked up a job — immediate start. It helped that she knew her way around a bar and was able to slide in next to the owner instantly and prove that she could dispense drinks to the thirsty public at speed, with efficiency and charm. It didn't hurt that she spoke Greek *and* English… with an easily manufactured Swedish accent. It also didn't hurt that she was easy on the eye.

'You're hired!' Spiro, the stout, forty-something owner, had called across to her. 'Don't go anywhere!'

There was a room she could stay in — bingo! — and meals thrown in. She might not make much money — despite the very respectable tips she'd already picked up — but money wasn't her concern. She had fifty thousand euros weighing down her rucksack. What was more important was being able to vanish into the Corfu tourism industry while she decided what to do next.

Although she had toyed with waiting around for a while, she almost certainly would have boarded a ferry and got off the island two days ago if she hadn't happened to meet Lucas Henry. Who knew? On all the roads, on all the islands in all the countries of Mediterranean Europe, he had to come buzzing along hers. Of course, he'd had some help in tracking her down — his dowsing talents were the stuff of legend. She should know. By now she'd read all about his adventures with Kate Sparrow; how he'd managed to find Sparrow when she was about to be murdered in a cellar by a crazed artist obsessed with decay; how the pair of them had thwarted a psycho local radio manager and his PA before they could finish off their third victim; how they had ended the killing spree of a vengeful security guard at a holiday camp. All with the help of that sweet little bottle stopper pendulum.

Lucas Henry was quite the celebrity these days! But, more recently, for different reasons. Despite all his heroics, he still hadn't outrun the suspicion that he'd killed Zoe Taylor and Mabel Johanssen. Poor Lucas. He couldn't catch a break. She almost felt bad for him. Almost.

'Brigitte!' She looked around to see Spiro stacking glasses behind the bar. 'Take some time off today,' he said. 'It will be a quiet one, but this evening…' He gave a whistle and shook his head, rolling his dark eyes in wonder at the hordes he expected to come crashing through his doors later. It was half past ten and only three breakfasting customers were occupying the scrubbed wooden tables dotted across the flagstone floor. The taverna was more of an evening and late-night venue.

'Shall I come back at five... six?' she checked.

'Six,' he said. 'When the madness begins!'

'Thank you,' she said, taking off her apron and hanging it on a hook behind the bar. 'I'll see you then.'

'I can call you if I need you sooner,' he suggested.

She shook her head. 'I lost my phone. I have to buy a new one... with my first pay!'

He nodded. 'End of the week, OK? Cash in hand.'

'That'll be great,' she said, and wandered up to her room. She had returned Lucas's Vespa to the hire business on Thursday afternoon, dropping the keys back on the counter and then departing before anyone could have a conversation with her. She didn't want a police search triggered by a tourist who failed to come back after hiring a moped for only a day. The woman at the hire hut barely looked up as the moped key landed in front of her. There were no cameras that Brigitte could detect, but she'd pulled a sun hat on as soon as she'd removed the helmet and hung it on the Vespa's handlebar, to be sure her face wasn't on display to any covert lenses.

Five minutes' walk away was a different hire hut, where she rented another moped for a week, and rode back to Ipsos. There she had parked up and headed straight to its small post office counter at the back of a grocery and household store, and bought a padded envelope, dictating the name and address to the clerk so a label could be printed off and attached along with the stamps. Keeping her head

down and her sun hat brim shielding her face, she had laid
on a thick Italian accent as she'd paid for the fastest delivery
possible. No sense in delaying.

Not long after that she'd found her taverna and her
camouflaging job.

Now it was a sunny Saturday and she had some leisure
time. As she put on fresh shorts and a T-shirt, she was planning another little excursion. In her cramped accommoda-
tion up under the warm eaves of the taverna she leaned
close to the age-spotted mirror and checked that her artfully
applied moles were still intact. They were. She smiled at her
reflection, pleased with the contrast with her old self. The
brown eyes suited her — quite striking with the blonde hair.
She put a little smoky eyeliner on and a touch of gloss to
bring out her full lips. Then she giggled at herself. It wasn't
like it was a date, was it?

Then again... it could be. She felt familiar stirrings and
wondered about that for a while.

A few minutes later she headed out into the late afternoon, carrying a slightly bulky shoulder bag, and collected
her moped from the alleyway beside the taverna. Her rucksack full of money remained tucked under her bed, which
was chancey — but she had a very good instinct for people
and had trusted Spiro when he'd given her the key to her
room and assured her that it was the only one.

It was fun to ride around the island on two wheels and
she wondered why she hadn't done it before. Probably
because she'd had a Ferrari. While she would miss the
sports car, there was a simple pleasure to be had from a
moped — zooming along the country lanes with arms and
legs bare to the warm breeze and the smells of nature
wafting past you.

In fact, with her newly-dyed hair streaming out behind her from under the hired helmet and some temporary tattoos on her upper arms on display, she felt almost invincible. Her rational mind knew she was taking a huge risk. A police patrol car might come along at any time with a mission to pull over and question any attractive young woman travelling alone. But that same instinct, which had never yet let her down, told her she was free. The murders had been rash, but sending the *Contessa* out to sea with Christina Eliades' switched-on mobile phone and passport — that had been her masterstroke; a fabulous bit of misdirection which ought to keep her safe here for some time.

And that was good because she wasn't going anywhere just yet. She had things to do, places to go, people to meet. After half an hour of buzzing along the island's inland roads she found herself back at the cypress tree and the neglected corner of farmland. She pulled the Vespa in close to the wire fence and took off the helmet, resting it on the saddle. Then she dropped the weighty shoulder bag across first before climbing over the fence. It was hot and for a moment she worried about what she might find. Had she left enough water?

She walked quietly towards the rusting junk pile and then paused in front of the flat metal disc of the trap door. The silo had been empty when she'd first looked inside it. Now it had an occupant. She rolled a couple of tyres off it and heard a muffled groan beneath her feet. She smiled. This had all worked out so well. So easily. She'd had the element of surprise — and gravity — on her side as soon as Lucas Henry had looked up and seen her. She'd landed on him with no warning, knocking him to the ground and then whacking him across the head with a wooden stump lying nearby.

While he lay dazed and groaning she had pulled the most useful bracelets Stav had ever bought her out of her rucksack and put one end of them on Lucas's wrist before dragging him across the ground. When he had roused and tried to fight her she had deployed the wooden stump again. He had been unconscious while she lifted one side of the metal trap door and rolled him over the edge. He'd landed like a sack of shit, two metres down, and then she'd jumped in beside him and swiftly cuffed his left hand to one of the iron rungs.

By the time he'd come to, a couple of minutes later, he was completely at her mercy.

He had opened his eyes, groaning, and then stared around, face screwed up against the bright, hot light shining in from the semi-circle of sky above. He'd pulled his left hand and winced as the handcuff bit into his wrist.

'Sorry about that,' she'd said. 'But my late husband was kinky for bondage. I thought you might like it, too.'

He'd gaped at her, uncomprehending. She'd held out the pendulum. 'Was this what brought you to me?'

He closed his eyes and nodded.

'Well... I'm honoured! How many killers have you tracked with this so far..? I think it's...' She'd counted off on one hand. 'One nurse, two BBC employees and one security guard... yes? Quite a body count between them. And then there's little old me... and you have no idea of *my* body count, have you? You only know that I ended the lives of Zoe Taylor and Mabel Johanssen and left you behind to take the blame.'

'Why... why did you..?' he'd burbled.

She'd tilted her head, dangling the pendulum between her fingers. 'I've often asked myself that, Lucas... and honestly? I'm not sure. It was a long time ago. I've killed a few times since then, usually for money or convenience, but back then..? No. Neither of those things applied. I think it was genuinely... a crime of passion. Random but heartfelt. Maybe. But these days..? I guess I'm just...'

'A psychopath,' grunted Lucas Henry, and she couldn't argue with that.

She had put her flask of water in with him, and a couple of protein bars, a big bag of crisps and some satsumas she'd had with her. And a rusty bucket she found under a dead tractor, with an old bin lid to cover it. She might be a psychopath, but she wasn't a sadist. She took his rucksack, rifled through it for things of interest, before dropping it out of sight, into the pile of farm junk. And then she'd left. She'd needed time to think and plan her next move, and there had been a powerful force guiding her to that post office.

Now she was back with a much calmer state of mind, apart from the mild concern that he was dead from heat exhaustion. It had rained yesterday, though, so he was probably OK.

At the bottom of the silo she could hear the rattle of the cuffs as he tugged pointlessly against the metal rung.

'Hellooooo,' she called down, as soon as the half-moon of the door was flipped over. 'Mumma's bought you some lunch!' She took out a lump of bread and some smoked meat and tomatoes, wrapped in paper.

Lucas Henry lay propped against the wall, his left wrist still safely tethered. The skin was swollen and bleeding from his vain attempts to escape. There was a purple bruise on his left temple where the wooden stump had struck him.

'I hope you've not been too bored,' she said, easing herself over the edge of the metal well and dropping down inside, staying safely out of his reach. 'I left your right hand free in case you needed it, while you were thinking of me.'

He stared at her, dead-eyed.

'Oh come *on*, Lucas!' she chided. 'I think we both know you're quite partial to a blonde.'

'What did you do with Sid?' he croaked.

'Sent him on a little journey,' she said. 'Here you go.' She shoved the paper bag across to him and rolled the fresh bottle of water after it. She picked up the bucket and bin lid and climbed out, emptying its contents in some deep undergrowth, holding her breath, and leaving it to air for a while. Then she returned to sit with her arms around her knees and watch him eat and drink. He avoided looking at her, but she eyed him rapaciously the whole time. God, he was hot. Even sweaty and grimy, in a hole where he'd had to crap and piss in a bucket, he was really sexy. With the sun shining in, it was getting warm in here and the scent of him was thick in the air. His dark hair was falling in damp strands across his face and those green eyes were shadowed with... what? Anger? Violence? Lust? These could all look very similar, at certain times.

He finished the food and the water without a word or a look in her direction, giving her nothing.

'So... I looked through your things,' she said. 'You travel pretty light, don't you?'

He didn't say anything.

'No mobile phone... I'm guessing that's because they might track you through it. The police back in Wiltshire are really keen to catch up with you, aren't they?'

'You and me both,' he muttered.

'So... a bit of cash, a change of clothes, underwear, paints and brushes and watercolour pad. I like your work.' She pulled his pad from her shoulder bag and flicked through it, landing on a page with a watercolour sketch of what was undoubtedly Kate Sparrow. Sparrow wasn't looking at the painter but into the middle distance, her brows drawn down as if deep in thought and her chin resting in one palm. Strands of fair hair hung from an untidy attempt at a high ponytail. Her eyes were a silvery blue and her mouth a soft, natural pink.

Lucas glanced at the picture and looked quickly away. 'So... you've got a bit of a thing for Kate,' said Brigitte. 'What a great time for me to go blonde. I look a little bit like her, don't you think? Could you have a thing for me?"

He continued to look away from her, so she seized her moment, pulling another set of Stav's bracelets of fun from her back pocket, grabbing his right wrist and snapping the cuff shut around it. He fought back hard. She had known he would. But even after the food he was weakened and not really with it. Possibly concussed. She managed to clip the other cuff onto the rung behind him and secure both his arms up over his head.

He swore at her and tried to kick out, to head-butt, to knee upwards at her, but she scrabbled back out of his reach, laughing, and waited for him to subside. After a couple of minutes he lapsed into stillness, panting, staring at her wordlessly.

Brigitte took off her top and then undid her bra, dropping it to the floor behind her and watching his face the whole time. 'Is this what you picture when you think of Kate Sparrow?' she said. 'Even though she hates you for killing her sister? Even though she just wants to put the cuffs on you, just like me? Even though she wants to put you in prison and throw away the key? I don't want to do that to you.'

She crawled closer to him. 'You could still hurt me,' she said. 'Even with your hands cuffed. But if you do, I promise you this, I will close the lid on this silo and turn it into your personal circle of hell. I will walk away, and I will never come back.'

He flicked a glance at her.

'Read me,' she said. 'Even without your little pendulum pal, you can read me, can't you? Dowse my intentions. You know I mean what I say. Hurt me and I will leave you here to die in the dark. It'll be dehydration that gets you, before the hunger. It's not a nice way to go. Slow. Painful. Organs packing up one by one. Of course, you'll shout and scream, like you have no doubt shouted and screamed for the last 18 hours, on and off. Will anyone come? I don't think so. Not for a long time. Not in time to save you. I mean… maybe I'm wrong… Kate's pretty good, isn't she? And the clue I've sent her is probably enough for her to find you eventually, but even if you're still alive, you'll be a shrivelled-up thing, wallowing in your own shit and piss and barely recognisable.'

He stared at her, understanding settling across his features.

'So, think very carefully about how you react to me,' she said, reaching him and sitting astride his thighs. 'You might want to bite… but think hard about that first. You're not strong enough to take control of me. You might as well be nice.' She stroked his sweat-dampened beard and the fast-pulsing warm throat beneath it.

He gulped and closed his eyes.

'Are you going to hurt me, Lucas?' she asked, close to his ear, her fingers working down the buttons of his shirt.

'No,' he whispered.

'Good… then I won't hurt you,' she said, pressing her breasts against his bare skin with a long exhalation. God, this was intense. She hadn't felt pleasure like this in years.

'Why?' he breathed. 'Why are you doing this? To me...
and to her..?'

She thought about this question as she licked his lower
lip. Considered it as she opened his mouth with her fingers
and pushed her tongue inside. Gave it further pondering
while she fumbled with his belt buckle.

'Because,' she said, eventually, 'it's just who I am.'

21

K ate had never had the slightest problem focusing on a case. Certainly not a case like *this* one, with three suspicious deaths in one week. In so artful a setting, there could be no doubt that one sick mind was behind it all.

But one part of *her* mind seemed to have dislocated from the rest. As she sat in the staff canteen, waiting for Conrad Temple to bring over the coffees, a vital piece of evidence in the hunt for Lucas Henry sat in her satchel, unmolested by anyone in forensics. Unreported to Kapoor. Next to it lay her passport and a folded printout of her e-ticket for a flight from Heathrow to Corfu later that day. She was planning to fake a debilitating migraine and dump this case on Michaels and the rest of the team. She wished she hadn't taken the lead on it now. As SIO she had a responsibility to everyone working on the Crop Circles case — to say nothing of its victims. But Michaels could handle it, she was sure, along with backup from Kapoor and Sharpe and Mulligan, and all the rest. In fact, it was probably a great opportunity for him to prove himself and get that extra push towards taking his sergeant's exams.

All the justification she could muster didn't do much to assuage the guilt at lying to her colleagues. But far more intense than the guilt was the need to follow the clue sent to her. Who had sent it? Lucas? Why? Was it a message from him? But so bizarre and grim — Sid, spattered in blood — what was the point of that?

Someone else, then? Someone who had control of Lucas. Maybe this *real murderer* of Mabel and Zoe that he had vowed to find.

Except there *was* no real murderer, was there? There was just Lucas, trying to throw her off the scent and convince her he was innocent.

But then... why the message? To get her to meet him? And then what? Murder her too?

Or... what if she was wrong? This thought had chilled her heart more than once in the small hours when she couldn't sleep. His face, as she had wrestled him to the woodland floor and cuffed him. The horror on it. The shock. Except that's exactly how he *would* look as soon as he realised she no longer believed him. Because the game was over. He'd taken his twisted pantomime one step too far and blown it.

This vicious circle of thought could wrap itself around her mind for hours if she let it, which was why having this week's case had been such a blessed distraction. She had been feeling better as she focused on a crime which had *nothing to do with her*. If you excluded Reggie and Sally stumbling upon the body — which was random bad luck — it wasn't personal in any way.

'A penny for them,' said Temple, sitting down opposite

and depositing a tray of coffee and two chocolate brownies on the table.

She blinked and smiled at him, grateful, again, for the distraction, however temporary it had to be. 'Well,' she said, gathering her thoughts, 'the team's been hard at work and it looks like we'll be bringing Rafe Campion in again soon.'

'Nobody else in the frame?' asked Temple, stirring sugar into his coffee.

'Well, we took a look at Marcus and Diane Dundrill, Linda Stewart's son and daughter-in-law. If they knew the way the wind was blowing with her will and wanted to avoid losing sixty grand, they might have thought discrediting Campion could be useful. Or they might have thought she hadn't actually gone through with the will change and decided to bump her off before she could, and make it look like a Campion-inspired suicide. But...'

'...they probably wouldn't have stiffed two more of his followers as set dressing,' concluded Temple. 'Hey — eat a brownie. You look like you need it.'

'Thanks,' she said, taking an absent-minded bite. 'No... and they couldn't have done the next two anyway. Their alibis stack up.'

'Campion is a textbook narcissist,' said Temple. 'Loves the sound of his own voice, the glow of his publicity shots, the unquestioning belief of his followers. People like that can buy into their own mythology over time. Even if he set out to create a money-making scam, his ego is getting a massive kick out of all this. He's addicted to the buzz.'

'But is he a killer? Or some kind of lethal influencer?' Kate said, brushing crumbs from her chin.

'Well, in the pure sense of the word, yes, I think it's possible he's influenced this,' said Temple. 'Not in the social media sense... because they don't do that, do they, these Enlightened Energy guys? Bad juju, using Facebook.'

'So... he preaches the wonder of ending your days in a crop circle,' Kate ruminated, while Temple tackled his own brownie. 'Then... when three of his followers take him at his word and end their lives — *if* that's what they did — he just shrugs and says that's not what he meant... not what he meant at *all*...'

'TS Eliot,' said Temple.

'Umm..?' Kate raised an eyebrow.

'*The Lovesong of J. Alfred Prufrock*,' he went on. 'TS Eliot. *That is not what I meant at all... that is not it at all...* The classic line of someone who leads you up the garden path and then plays innocent.'

'Wasn't there something about mermaids singing in it..?' Kate wrinkled her brow, vaguely remembering GCSE English Lit.

'*I have heard the mermaids singing, each to each,*' he said.

She laughed. 'I never had you down as a poetry fan.'

'What *do* you have me down as?' he asked, cupping his mug and staring across the steam at her, smiling that charming Boston boy smile.

'*I'm running away on a flight to Corfu in about six hours,' she stated. In her head.* The compulsion to confess to him, here and now, was very strong. 'Well... you're a bit of mystery to me,' she said. 'And you're in good company, this week.'

'Well, any time you want me to demystify you,' he offered, stuffing in the last bit of brownie and giving her a wink.

She took her own last bite, laughing and shaking her head. 'When we're through all this,' she said. 'That might be fun.' She checked her watch. 'But it's briefing time now.'

'Then let us go, then, you and I,' said Temple.

———

'A CROP CIRCLE is more than an art form. A crop circle is the result of an intense energy vortex which has been created not by random chance... but as a message. To us. To all of us. A message from another dimension,' Kate looked up at the faces filling the briefing room. They ranged from perplexed to sceptical to highly amused. 'Some people believe this other dimension is a parallel universe, perhaps one of countless others in a multiverse,' she read on, Rafe Campion's photo smiling through a gap in her fingers as she held up the hardback. 'Or that each crop circle message has been delivered by aliens from a planet or planets beyond our galaxy.'

She paused. They all waited like a primary school class. Sharpe was even chewing gum. 'The truth may be all three but of one thing we may be sure — these beautiful patterns on the canvas of our fields *are* a message. And the circles themselves are possessed of an energy field like no other. It's an energy field which is a direct channel, for the enlightened, to connecting with the universe and the benevolent beings within it — beings who seek to ally themselves to the human race and offer guidance in our time of need. I have lain in a crop circle and experienced a transportation of the soul. I have astral projected from a wheat field in Wiltshire to a higher plane. I left my body and, had I chosen to do so, I could have remained in that higher plane, leaving my Earthly conveyance behind. Freed of its shackles. It's only because I was made aware of vital work I must do on Earth that I chose to return. You may make a different choice, but if you do depart this turn of your life in this manner, be sure that you will have embarked on the most extraordinary and privileged journey. Few are called.'

She put down the book. 'Well, I don't know about you,' she said, 'but *I'm* sold!'

There were muted chuckles around the room. Kate turned to the board and its images of Linda Stewart, Justine Patak and Callum Fanshaw, each lying in their artfully crushed circles of wheat. 'They were sold, too,' she said, as the humour drained from the room. "Section 2 of the Suicide Act 1961. Encouraging or assisting suicide. It's an offence. These people...' She tapped the board, turning back to face them. 'Ordinary people like your mum or your dad or your aunt or uncle... a bit lost and lonely, it seems. Vulnerable. Easy to manipulate. With some savings available to donate — or bequeath — to a shining cause offering hope and enlightenment and a way forward for mankind. Linda and Justine and Callum... all members of The Church of the Enlightened Energy... are all dead. Killed by poison, which they appear to have taken themselves, willingly. The path reports tell us that they were all unwell and perhaps this had some bearing on their decision to visit the crop circles. But did they expect to die there?'

She glanced around the room. 'I believe they were conned. All three of them left money to Rafe Campion's foundation.'

Sharpe waved a hand and butted in, furrowing his brow: 'But two of the suicide notes namecheck him,' he said. 'He'd have to be an idiot to think he wouldn't be investigated.'

Kate nodded and glanced over to Conrad Temple who gave a polite cough and then stood up from the table he'd been lounging against. 'Men like Rafe Campion are more complex than you'd think,' he said. 'We know from your work over the past couple of days that he's not short of money.'

'He's worth three point four million if you include the

family estate,' said DC Mulligan, consulting her notes. 'Not exactly small change, is it?'

'Doesn't mean the greedy bastard doesn't want more,' Sharpe pointed out.

'True,' said Temple. 'But men like Campion — narcissists and people manipulators — what they really get off on is the power trip. The sense that they are controlling the lives and the minds and the destinies of their followers. He's chosen a narrative that anyone can buy into — preservation of the planet with help from benign extra-terrestrials — and is wrapping it up in eco-friendly paper. But I believe, quite simply, that the few thousand followers he's got aren't enough. He doesn't want to use social media because — a. that messes with his whole low-tech vibe and — b. it exposes him to thousands of trolls and naysayers. This is not a man who likes to be argued with.'

He glanced around the assembled detectives and smiled ruefully. 'He wants the notoriety. He wants to spread his message. To get attention.'

'So getting followers to die for him — that's the way?' asked Mulligan, arms folded over her ample chest, looking deeply angry.

'It could be,' said Temple. 'I think the money from his followers, while important to keep the machinery of his foundation rolling... it's not his main goal. It's getting the world to listen to him — bumping his book up the bestseller list. Adding to his legend. All of this is catnip for a character like Rafe Campion.'

'But we can't do him for it,' said Kate. 'Not yet. We need more evidence and, despite all your very diligent work, we're not there yet. The press are all over us on this, I don't need to tell you. There's a lot riding on what you can dig up. Be in no doubt, the next time we see Campion in this building he's going to have a very expensive lawyer at his side, making sure nothing sticks — so everyone needs to step up and get something on him before the next interview. Let's find more followers and get them to talk about what goes on. Get them to tell us what they've contributed... whether they've been coaxed into giving up life savings or rewriting wills. Whether they're looking kindly on the idea of clocking out of this life in a crop circle some time soon... Let's get a shedload of witness statements. Let's find out who made those crop circles and whether Campion commissioned them. Let's astral project the manipulative shit right into a holding cell, yeah?'

Everyone returned to task with enthusiastic murmurs of agreement and Kate felt like a manipulative shit herself. She'd just pep-talked her team into doing a load of work that she had no intention of helping with, a couple of hours from now. She had already begun the deception, rubbing her head and grimacing. The migraine would kick in big time in a short while and, after struggling on for a bit, she would declare that she couldn't see properly and had no choice but to get to a darkened bedroom for the next twelve hours.

With the visual disturbance she would be unable to drive, so they'd call her a cab. And then, once in it, she would get home, grab her overnight bag and, if the cabbie was willing, get her taxi journey extended to Heathrow.

'Kate — can you step into my office?' Kapoor's cool voice cut across her furtive inner planning and she jumped guiltily. Christ... had he found the evidence in her bag? *Of course he hadn't!* Why on earth would he be rifling through her satchel? She rubbed her temples and followed him into the quiet office, where he slid a photograph across his desk towards her. Unlike most police evidence shots, it was framed in gold.

She picked it up, recognising a line-up of teenage boys in uniform. Gilt lettering at the base of the dark blue mount read *WINCHESTER COLLEGE — YEAR 10* and the year the photo was taken.

'Just thought you might like to see how our prime suspect looked in school uniform,' said Kapoor. 'Apropos of nothing, really.' He traced his finger along the back row of the thirty or so boys, lingering on a handsome Asian boy who could only be his son. 'That's Sami,' he said, with obvious pride. 'And next to him but one... the head boy.'

Kate spotted the self-satisfied smiled and the golden hair right away. Even the set of Rafe Campion's shoulders spoke of a massive ego. 'Have you spoken to Sami about him?' she asked.

'Not yet, but I may do, at an appropriate time. They weren't friends,' he said. 'I'm glad to tell you. Sami has good instincts for people. He would have been an excellent officer if he hadn't chosen medicine.'

'Handsome young bunch, aren't they?' Kate said, scanning the faces. She had noticed, before, that children in the country's top fee-paying schools had an unreasonable preponderance for beauty. Their fathers tended to attract beautiful women. The lucky dip of looks was genetically rigged for these kids. What often came in tandem was their fathers' confidence or, quite often, arrogance. Intelligence wasn't a done deal, that was for sure.

She paused and squinted at one of the young men a row down from Campion. 'Who's he?' she said. 'He looks familiar.'

'Probably a politician,' said Kapoor. 'Or perhaps a top barrister or successful actor. The alumni usually end up visibly successful.' She detected some conflict in him as he spoke.

'Did it work for you, sending Sami there?' she asked.

He pursed his lips. 'It did not sit well with me,' he said. 'My wife was keen and I... I didn't object. You have to do what you can for your children, and the local comprehensive would have been hard for him. Very few Pakistanis in the area we lived in. Not that paying fees spared him the racism... it just made it a more expensive brand.'

There was a knock at the door. Sharon Mulligan stood outside, bouncing on her heels. 'Guv,' she said, as soon as Kate got to it. 'Someone's come in... someone who thinks they saw something in the wheat field last night!'

22

'I heard about it on Radio Wessex,' said the man in the blue boiler suit, sitting on the edge of the couch in the little informal interview room off reception. 'These crop circles and dead folks and that.'

Robert Denny rubbed a grease-stained hand through his grey hair and furrowed his brow. 'I'd heard about the first one, too, start of the week. Stuck in my head, it did. I know a few farmers around here — I do maintenance on their tractors, see? I know what they think about all this crop circle bollocks. Sorry!' He flicked a guilty glance from Kate to Sharon, who had stayed put at Kate's side with her notebook, as Michaels was entrenched in phone calls upstairs.

'What do they think, Mr Denny?' Kate prompted.

'That it's a pain in the ar— neck,' he said. 'There they are, working all the hours God gives to get their crop in come autumn and some drunken students come down and mash up a load of it with a plank and make out it's aliens. Next thing they know there's a queue of dingbats in tinfoil hats stompin' across their land, messin' up more crop, and trying to lie down in it and get photos and the like — and then the media charges in.'

'We get your point,' said Kate. 'Farmers aren't keen. But what did you see on Tuesday night? And at what time?'

'I was drivin' home late after finishing a job up Marden way, would've been about... eleven thirty, I reckon. I was on the B-road, heading towards the A342 and I saw light in the field. Low down, movin'. Torchlight, I'd say.'

'Torchlight,' repeated Kate. 'OK... And you're sure it was at Chirton?'

'I am. I know my way around here. I ought to — I've lived here sixty-four years!' he said. 'I was thinkin' someone had maybe had a breakdown out in the field. If your tractor conks out on you in the middle of a field, you can be buggered. If you can't fix it there and then you've got to get a tow and those buggers don't tow easy through mud. I thought maybe some poor sod had been tinkerin' away on it all evenin'. So I pulled up, to see if I could help.'

'Go on,' said Kate, her excitement tempered only by remembering that she should be faking her migraine properly by now... definitely in the next half hour.

'Well, I got out and shouted through a gap in the hedge, in case he could hear me. Asked if he wanted any help.'

'He?' asked Kate. 'You saw a man?'

'I saw a figure which looked like a man, yes,' he said. 'And he was carryin' something long and heavy, I could tell that by the way he was movin'. But when he heard me — and he must have heard me because I've got a shout like a foghorn, my wife tells me — well, he started runnin'. The torchlight went bouncin' all over the place and then disappeared.'

Kate waited.

'So... I got back in the car and pulled on to the road

again,' he said. 'I did wonder if it was someone after sheep or the like, but there was no sheep in that field. Anyway, next thing I know this bloody car comes screechin' past, out of nowhere and damn near runs me into a ditch.'

'Out of nowhere?'

'Well, I didn't see any lights on the road and it was a clear view, so I reckon it must have come off a farm track — off that field. And there's no reason to be tearin' around like that in the dead of night if you haven't been up to no good, is there? So today, when I heard there'd been other crop circles with dead people in 'em... I mean I might be wastin' your time...'

Kate shook her head. 'Not at all. We really appreciate you coming in to talk to us. I... don't suppose you happened to notice the make of the car? A colour? A registration number..?'

'It was dark and I didn't have my glasses on,' he said. 'Although I'm perfectly legal,' he added hurriedly. 'I just can't see that kind of detail in the dark, at speed.'

'Oh,' said Kate.

'But the dash cam caught a bit of it,' he said, proudly pulling a small black unit from his overalls pocket and waving it in the air. 'How's that for you?'

Kate took it from him with a grin. 'Bravo!' she said, a note of admiration in her voice.

'I bet you thought an old duffer like me wouldn't have tech like this,' he said, grinning back. 'My boy gave it to me for Christmas after someone cut me up on the A36 and tried to say it was my fault. Been runnin' it ever since. Here you are...' He reached over and pressed a button to set the video rolling.

'It's not totally clear,' he said. 'But I thought your IT guys could probably expand it or sharpen it up, like. I can let you have that, if you want it.'

Kate stared at the image of a car flashing by, its driver side headlamp flaring across the screen. She was pretty sure the make of the car could be identified, maybe the colour too — and that definitely looked like partial on the plate.

'Mr Denny, you are a star!' she said. 'Now... I'm going to leave you, and DC Mulligan here will get your details and make sure your dash cam is returned to you later on. I'm taking it off for our IT guys to work on right away. Thank you!'

Mr Denny was pink with delight — not something Kate saw often at Salisbury nick. 'Thanks Sharon,' she said, more quietly, massaging her left temple. 'Sheesh — all this excitement. I need paracetamol!'

She ran the dash cam upstairs and dropped into Kapoor's office to show him before taking it to Nick and Derek in IT forensics. 'Excellent,' said Kapoor. 'We need a break... this could be it. Are you OK?'

Kate leaned in the doorway, screwing her eyes shut for a moment and then holding out her left hand, scrutinising her fingers. 'Bugger,' she said. 'I hoped it was just a bit of low blood sugar.'

'And..?'

'I'm getting a migraine,' she said, massaging her left temple again. She got a migraine once or twice a year and they were always grim and knocked her out for at least a day — sometimes two or three. So she knew exactly how to fake this. 'Can't see properly.' She let out a long exhalation. 'Just half a hand right now... But it'll pass.'

'Yes, in a day or two, if I recall,' said Kapoor. 'You need to go home.'

'But... this!' She waved the dash cam in frustration.

'Can be handled by someone else,' said Kapoor, holding out his hand for it. 'Get yourself home. Call a cab. You're not driving.'

'It's just a migraine,' she insisted, shielding her eyes from the afternoon sun shafting through his window.

'The last time you said that and tried to stay at work, you ended up projectile vomiting all over DS Sharpe,' said Kapoor. 'Or was that just a reaction to his choice of tie?'

Kate snorted. Sharpe *was* renowned for some pretty dreadful ties. 'OK,' she sighed, reluctantly dropping the dash cam into Kapoor's open palm. 'I'll call a cab and get home to bed. But *please* keep me in the loop. I can check texts... probably'.

'Kate — you won't be checking texts,' said Kapoor. 'You'll be asleep. I'm appointing Michaels as SIO on this for the next 48 hours.'

She groaned, masking her eyes with her palm.

'Is your policy book up to date?'

She nodded.

'Good — then he can pick up where you've left off. Now go,' he said, getting up to take the evidence through. She nodded, a swell of emotion closing her throat. He was a great boss. The best. And she was deceiving him to his face. He would find out about it later and she cringed to think of the next conversation they would have. Christ, he might even be firing her.

Kapoor left her leaning in his doorway. She glanced at that school photo on his desk and felt a tickle of... *something*. Something other than jangling guilt about what she was doing today. She couldn't work out what it was in the photo that was tickling, and she might never know... but before she called her cab she took a quick snap of it. She might get time to look at it later and see what it was.

Then she wandered back into CID, self-consciously using voice recognition to call up her usual cab contact and keeping her eyes shielded with one hand as she went to collect her bag. 'Good news and bad news, Ben,' she said to Michaels as she passed him.

'Yeah — the dash cam — I just heard!' said Michaels.

'Bad news is I can't see it,' said Kate. 'Migraine incoming. Have to get to bed for the rest of the day. Maybe two days. Sorry. Chief Super says you'll be carrying on as SIO though, at least until I'm back, so hey...'

His face was an entertaining mix of sympathy, worry and delight. 'Bad luck, boss,' he said, biting back an excited grin. 'You want me to get you a lift home with Traffic?'

'No — I've got a cab coming. I'll pick up my car tomorrow. See you...'

She got away fast, not wanting to lie to anyone else's face.

23

Brigitte pressed the binoculars to her eyes and studied the exit doors of Corfu International Airport. She'd watched the British Airways turbo prop glide in over the sea towards the narrow peninsula airstrip nearly an hour ago, but Corfu was legendary for its delays through passport control and baggage collection. Any minute now, though, a stream of tourists would emerge onto Greece's jewel island.

Of course, she had no idea whether Kate Sparrow was on the flight, but she had calculated the three o'clock was the first possible landing that *could* contain the detective. The package would either have arrived yesterday or today — and if it was yesterday, this was the first workable flight in from Heathrow. Not that Kate was definitely coming. She might simply have handed Lucas's bloodied pendulum over to her forensics team. Maybe a whole squad of Interpol officers was just about to descend on Corfu. She doubted it, though, on two levels. Lucas really wasn't big enough fry for more than a couple of visiting officers, and Kate — she was sure Kate would come alone. Probably

without the permission of her boss; one Chief Superintendent Rav Kapoor, according to the online research Brigitte
had done.

She'd read a lot about Kate, accessing the public
computers under the cool arched brick ceilings of Corfu
library earlier that day, because she still didn't have a smartphone — and didn't dare to get one just yet. The three cases
Kate Sparrow had cracked with Lucas Henry were reported
widely. The first — the Runner Grabber case, as it had been
dubbed by the media — wasn't as juicily detailed as it might
have been had it made it to crown court. Because the serial
killer they'd hunted down was dead before arrest, there was
only an inquest. It was enough, though, for Brigitte to glean
what had happened from thorough court reporter write-ups
in the *Salisbury Journal* — and the sensationalised versions
of the story which had ended up in the national press.

Kate had been hunting a killer who specialised in trap-
ping attractive young female runners in order to use them in
some bizarre Art of Decay project, stringing them up,
drugged and naked, and then photographing them as they
slowly starved and dehydrated to death. Sick with a capital
S! Brigitte was impressed with the clever MO of the killer:
digging a pit in the woods and then applying chloroform
and diazepam to knock the victims out as they struggled to
escape. She was also fascinated to learn that Kate herself
had been on the victim list and actually ended up getting
caught. Kate had been bound, hand and foot, naked and
drugged, and only escaped thanks to the broken leg of a
Barbie doll she'd managed to use to cut through her bind-
ings. She'd seriously injured her captor with that same doll's
leg — something which made Brigitte laugh and clap her
hands in delight as she'd read it — but even so, Kate was
very likely about to be the next dead exhibit until Lucas

Henry came crashing in, having dowsed his path to the killer's lair.

It was a brilliant story! Who'd have thought Mabel's little sister would get up to all this drama?

The next case — the Gaffer Tape Killers — had seen Kate and Lucas partnering up again to track down the murderers of two local radio presenters, killed in a bizarre, ritualistic way. Both had been choked with their own microphone socks and then gaffer-taped to a transmitter mast. This time, Kate and Lucas had managed to prevent the death of a fan of the station by electrocution. He had been taped to the top of a radio car, the mast ascending to overhead power lines by remote control with seconds left to spare! Such drama! This one had come close to ending both Kate and Lucas's lives, with Kate shot in the shoulder and Lucas badly beaten. At least they managed to get *one* of the killers to court this time, although the surviving murderer got off with a plea of insanity — or whatever politically correct term they used for a *batshit psychobitch* these days — and ended up in Broadmoor.

Brigitte rested the binoculars for a while, still keeping her eyes on the exit as she relaxed on the wooden bench. It wouldn't be long now. She often pondered on her own psychopathic traits. A hallmark of psychopathy was a failure to empathise with the pain of others and she wasn't sure that was quite right. She *understood* the pain and suffering she caused, and she didn't do any of it lightly. She wasn't particularly into torture — sadism wasn't her thing — but she did *love* taking control; making life or death decisions; watching her victims' faces closely while she toyed with them. Observing the moment when their lifeforce finally fled their bodies, leaving their eyes dull and empty. And, afterwards, she didn't do guilt. What was the point of it? So, yes, she probably did fit the bill for being a psychopath. She wouldn't have it any other way. Imagine feeling other people's pain? Who'd want that?

But she didn't actually *set out* to kill people. It wasn't an obsession or an addiction — just a byproduct of getting what she wanted, where she wanted and, sometimes, *who* she wanted. She could even be kind at times, when she chose. When she'd killed Claudine in France a couple of years ago, she'd made sure her family found her in a nice state, dressed beautifully, her bashed-in cranium resting on a pillow and not uppermost for them to see as soon as they arrived, like a split melon. Because she had been fond of Claudine. And the sex they'd had was really good — memorable. It was only Claudine finding out a bit too much about her that had ended it, really. A shame.

Kate's latest case with Lucas hadn't really hit the press yet, because it hadn't yet come to court, but the reports which had got out told a tale of some kind of revenge spree in a Buntin's holiday camp, of all places. A security guard had cracked after his sister died and killed three people, badly injured one, and nearly crushed Kate and two of her friends to death in a concrete World War Two bunker on a Suffolk beach. Poor cow couldn't catch a break, could she? It was meant to be a relaxing weekend away.

Brigitte didn't yet know how much Lucas had done to save lives at Buntin's, but it looked like he'd shown up again, just in the nick of time. Kate's brother Francis had been there, too. Brigitte paused, remembering the recent photo of Francis, tall and fair and slightly awkward. Sweet.

Ah. People. She snapped the binoculars back into action and studied everyone departing the airport, almost all of them queuing for taxis, giving her ample opportunity to check their faces. Ten minutes passed and she put the binoculars away. No Kate this time. She might be on the midnight landing, but Brigitte would still be working at the taverna, so she couldn't be here to watch her arrive.

She checked her watch. It was just after four. Lucas could probably do with a wash. She liked a bit of sweat on a man but yes... a little soaping down would be nice. She licked her lips, remembering how deeply her pleasure had run earlier; how intensely she had peaked before climbing off him. Lucas had done a sterling job of pretending to be immune to her, but some responses you just couldn't hide. She wasn't fooled.

She walked back through town to where she'd left the Vespa. Passing a store she saw newspapers and glanced at the headlines. BODIES FOUND IN CAVE CONFIRMED AS MAINLAND POLICE read one, while another went for HEIRESS SOUGHT FOR POLICE MURDER AND DEATH OF HUSBAND. The photo on both front pages was pretty good — Christina Eliades looked very Hollywood in it, her red hair gleaming against an emerald green dress; a shot she recognised from a gala business dinner she and Stav had attended last year. Happily, with her new blonde locks, carefully applied moles and brown contacts, as well as her authentic Swedish accent, there was very little chance she was going to be found. Policing on Corfu was about as efficient as its airport.

A frisson went through her, not of fear, but excitement. She decided to pop into the store and buy some luxury shower gel and a sponge — maybe a soft new towel if they had one. Thinking about washing Lucas was getting her hot again already. She had just enough time before starting her evening shift. She honestly couldn't remember when she'd last had this much fun.

Going through passport control, Kate felt like a criminal. She was perfectly entitled to catch a flight to Corfu any time she liked. She had paid in full for her one-way ticket and her passport was up-to-date. But every time she thought of her colleagues back in Salisbury, toiling on with the crop circles case, assuming she was at home, sick, and leaving her in peace to recover, her insides crunched. She *hated* deceiving them, but she really didn't have any choice. She *had* to do this.

Trying to breathe normally, she shoved her rucksack into the plastic tray on the roller belt, along with her trainers, wallet and iPhone. Just before she'd got here she had realised, with a stab of shock, that the security staff would almost certainly spot the metal chain of the dowsing pendulum in her bag and pull it out to check it. If she'd had a case to check into the hold she could have avoided that by packing Sid inside it, but she was travelling light.

So she had detoured to the disabled cubicle in the nearest ladies' toilets, which had its own small sink set low into the tiles. Inside, she had tipped the bag from the padded envelope and carefully peeled Sid from it. She'd tucked the blood-smeared plastic back into the package and shoved it right to the bottom of her bundle of clothes, deep inside the rucksack. If she later needed to test the DNA she still had plenty to work with. Then she crouched down by the low sink to rinse Sid clean. The pinkish tinge to the water as it drained away made her shiver. She couldn't be sure the blood was Lucas's, but her instinct told her that it was... and that he was in trouble. Was she picking this up from the pendulum... doing her own spot of dowsing?

Don't be ridiculous, Kate! She scowled at her reflection in the mirror. *He's probably just reeling you in... or trying to.* But what if he wasn't? And if he *was* bleeding out somewhere, should she even care, given what he was guilty of?

Except you DON'T KNOW, do you, Kate? Not for absolute, one hundred per cent certain!

Once again she reran her last moments with him — the struggle in the woods after he'd unearthed Mabel's earth-sodden bra and pants, shaking and wretched. Why couldn't she have talked to him instead of losing it completely and trying to single-handedly arrest him? She had been tired and stressed and utterly freaked out, and she hadn't been making good decisions.

But it was on him that he had run. He hadn't given her a chance to calm down and talk to him rationally — *he had run*. If he'd had a good explanation for taking her into the woods and digging up her dead sister's underwear, he should have let himself be arrested and then explained it all to her in the interview room.

Kate dried Sid and his now slightly less suspect-looking chain with loo roll and then slipped him into the pocket of her light denim jacket. At security, she put the jacket into the tray with her other stuff. She could have pulled the pendulum out and put it on display, but she didn't want to look *that* keen for the security guys. She hoped they weren't going to have an issue with it. The chain, arguably, could be used to choke a passing stewardess. But then, so could a lot of neck chains worn by passengers and dumped into the Plastic Trays of Scrutiny.

As it turned out, she got lucky. Nobody seemed bothered by a chain and a blue glass bottle stopper and she wasn't even required to tip it out of her pocket. Her tray rolled right through the X-ray machinery and out the other side without getting diverted for a rummage. She collected it at the other end, lightheaded with relief as she slipped her trainers back on.

The wait on airside was surreal. She couldn't settle. She tried to read a book she'd picked up in WHSmith, but even one of her favourite authors couldn't distract her. She checked her watch. The flight left at seven and would get in around midnight, Corfu time. She had booked a hotel room within walking distance of the airport and planned to grab what sleep she could before dawn. And then what?

All she had was Sid and the envelope with its DNA heavy contents — and the franking mark which identified the precise post office it had been sent from. Earlier that day, while nobody in CID was close enough to look over her shoulder, she had messaged a friend in Sweden who worked for Europol and asked for a favour. The friend kindly tapped into the international franking location system and revealed the starting point for Sid's journey — a general store with a post office counter in the small coastal resort of Ipsos on Corfu's north-east coast. So, tomorrow, that's where she would go.

As she glanced up at the departures board and saw her flight was boarding, Kate realised this plan was as good as it was going to be for now. She just had to get to Corfu, get some sleep, get breakfast and get going.

If all else failed she could always ask Sid. *'Where's your master, boy? Go fetch him... take me to him, Sid, there's a good stopper!'* She chuckled to herself, shaking her head.

There was a buzz in her pocket and she palmed out her phone, spotting a text from Conrad Temple. **Heard you went home sick. Hope it's nothing too bad. See you in a day or two. :)**

As a spike of guilt stabbed through her the phone buzzed again. This time it was from Michaels.

Don't worry about responding. Get your rest. But the partial came back on that plate. It's HO something 6. That's all they could get. Looks like a Ford but we're not sure. Def not a vintage Jag. :-/ No colour discernible. See you tomorrow if you're up to it.

She paused before texting back: **Check what other vehicles Campion has on his property. He wouldn't use his Jag to go off crop circle-making. Thanks, Ben. Going back to sleep now.** She got to her feet, grabbed her rucksack and headed off to leave the country.

The flight was uneventful. At any other time she would have been thrilled by it; she didn't fly often but whenever she did she loved to get a window seat and stare down at the world below, visible through tufts of cloud and shafts of sun. Google Earth live-streaming. She did what she could, though, to distract herself a little with this before dusk crept over the eastern horizon and dimmed the view.

Kate arrived in Corfu airport exhausted. She had been in a constant state of high alert ever since she'd found that package first thing in the morning and it was relentlessly sapping her energy. Part of her wished she really *was* lying in bed at home, battling something as simple as a migraine rather than the emotional tangle of doubt and guilt and desperation currently seething in the pit of her belly. She walked the twenty minutes from the airport exit to the hotel in half the time it had taken her to get through border control. The Corfu night was as warm as a Wiltshire afternoon and full of chirruping insect song. The air was scented with sea salt and lush greenery — the perfume of holidays. It was all at extreme odds with her reason for being here.

She found the small hotel on a quiet street. Inside it was clean and pleasant, and its owners solicitous and unfazed by her early hours arrival. By 1am she was in bed, a cotton sheet over her shoulders, convinced there was absolutely no way she could sleep.

Ten minutes later, it seemed she was right. She got up and took Sid from her jacket pocket. Sitting at the small dressing table, she rested her elbows, steepled her hands together as she'd seen Lucas do, and allowed the pendulum to hang quite still on its chain between her laced fingers.

'Sid,' she said. 'I'm going to ask you something.'

The pendulum began to mark a slight circle over the dressing table.

'Right, I see you're listening,' she said, faintly aware of how ridiculous she sounded. 'So, I'm only going to ask you this once and if the answer is no, please stop. If it's yes, please go into a figure of eight.'

Sid continued to move in a tiny circle, no more than a pencil's head in diameter.

'Am I going to find Lucas Henry on this island?'

Sid spun wider. Then he tipped a whole cascade of goosebumps across her neck and shoulders by moving into a figure of eight and repeating it with no sign of slowing.

'This is bollocks,' said Kate, snapping the stopper into her palm and dropping it back into her jacket pocket.

She fell asleep five minutes later.

25

R ecent events in Lucas Henry's life had made certain rather excitable people talk about him as if he was a superhero.

As HE LAY SHIVERING in the dark, on the compacted earth floor of the sunken silo, his shackled left wrist swollen and aching and his hand numb, he realised, with shame, that he had bought in to his own publicity. His mission to find and bring down Zoe and Mabel's killer had been nothing more than hubris. Sure, nobody he'd ever met could dowse as well as he could. Yes, there were many times when his ability bordered on the supernatural. And yes again, he had undoubtedly saved lives with that ability — but considerably fewer lives than were saved every day by paramedics, doctors, nurses, firefighters. None of *them* claimed demi-god status, did they? None of *them* assumed they could outwit a psychopath.

. . .

FOR HE *HAD* ASSUMED THAT, and *he* had been the one outwitted. He had dowsed his way right into a spider's web and now he was effectively wrapped up in silk, getting slowly devoured. Only, so far, this spider was keeping him alive, so she could enjoy his torment for a while. The food and water she'd given him was just enough to keep him going — not enough to build up his energy reserves to the level where he might be more of a threat.

NOT THAT SHE really needed to do this. When she had told him she'd leave him to die here if he hurt her, he didn't, for a moment, doubt her. He knew his captor was deadly, coldly, serious about that. Right now he was entertainment for her, and she was excited to keep coming back to check on him.

A FEW HOURS after her first special visit she had come back with some more bottles of water, some shower gel, a small natural sponge and a clean towel. She had cuffed his other wrist again, attaching it once more to the rungs above his head, peeled off his clothes (his shirt snagged up on the cuffs above him) and washed him. She'd started at the dried blood matting his hair on the side of his head where she'd clubbed him with that chunk of wood — and soaped steadily down his body with great concentration. She'd rinsed him and dried him. Then she'd stripped herself again, too, and washing wasn't all she'd done with him. He felt sick whenever he thought of it, but he had known better, at the time, than to complain or resist. If she stopped getting turned on by her captive, she was likely to grow bored and not bother herself with returning.

There was always a chance someone might pass by and

rescue him. And he still shouted occasionally, when his diminished senses picked up a human being somewhere nearby. But the patterns were fleeting and weak, indicative of passing travellers up on the road. He had been dragged a good thirty or forty metres before she'd dumped him down into this pit and the soil that surrounded the silo dampened his shouts. If someone came within ten metres they might hear him. But nobody had. This was an overgrown, neglected corner of some farm — way out on its boundary where things were left to rust and decay. There was nothing here to tend or harvest. It could be weeks before the landowner came by.

AND IT WOULD ONLY TAKE days to die if she stopped bringing water.

HE PICKED up plenty of different energy patterns... foxes, rodents, owls, bats and other nocturnal creatures. If the lid of the silo had been left more ajar he might have had bigger company but as it was, all he had were spiders, flies and the occasional mouse or vole, squeezing in through the finger-width crack where she had kept one of the metal trapdoors very slightly propped apart by a stick at one end. This, presumably, was so he wouldn't suffocate in the heat of the day.

THE LIDDED BUCKET she had left for him had been emptied again after her last visit. He guessed even psychopaths would struggle to get horny with the stench of human waste in close proximity. Since she'd left and night had robbed him of the last narrow sliver of light, he'd barely needed to pass anything, which was both convenient and worrying. He was dehydrated and ravenously hungry again, and he really needed to sharpen up and think of a way out of this.

BUT SHARP WAS the last thing he felt. Woolly and confused and in a state of constant ache, his only release came with fitful, dream-filled sleep. And even there, he was tormented by the usual nightmares of the quarry, now with a whole new dimension to them.

THE HORROR of his current situation was palpable throughout and the only break he ever got was when Kate made a guest appearance. Sometimes she was fighting him to the ground and screaming at him, trying to get the cuffs on his wrists. Other times she lay on his chest, warm and calm, and slept with him like he was something she loved.

HE WASN'T sure whether it was better or worse to wake up from that one.

THERE WAS nothing he could use to work at the handcuff. His captor had taken his rucksack and everything in his pockets. No handy bit of metal lay on the floor, nothing he might use to pick at the lock.

HIS ONLY HOPE now was random luck. And luck hadn't really been on his side for the past seventeen years, had it? Not like it had for *her*. It looked like luck had served Brigitte, or whatever she called herself, extremely well — right up to the point he had wandered to the base of that tree and looked up at her, offering himself like a sacrificial lamb.

No, as far as he could tell, from any angle, he was royally fucked.

26

There's something weird going on.

A text from Francis was the last thing Kate had expected to wake her up. It was 5.13am Corfu time, which meant it had to be 3.13am back home. She sat up under the thin quilt and reached for her bedside glass of water, woozy and trying to get her bearings.

Where did Francis think she was..? Had she even told him..? No. She had left a note on his door, saying she'd be off the radar for two or three days and not to worry. He *would* worry, of course, and she couldn't blame him for that. His sister had a habit of throwing herself in the path of maniacs.

What's weird? she texted back.

Can I call?

On surveillance. Can't talk. Text instead. She could have talked to him but she felt freaked out and scared and guilty — and she knew if she heard his voice she might tip over. Also, the ring tone would instantly give away that she was outside the UK.

OK. I've been thinking about what that solicitor said. About us going off on a trip. I wondered if Mum had left

something extra for us that we didn't find. Something in one of her investments or bonds. So I got in and had a look around.

You hacked our late mother's archived accounts? Kate added a gaping emoticon and some exclamation marks.

Yes. Arrest me. He added an eye-rolling emoticon.

OK... so what's weird? Kate had another long draught of the water and felt a little better. She would make tea shortly; have a shower.

There's no extra money hiding anywhere, BUT... there was some weird stuff going on in her deposit account. Payments going out to a numbered account that don't make sense.

Kate peered at the screen, baffled. A numbered account? she thumbed back. Where? To whom?!

Francis's reply was dry. A NUMBERED account. That means there's no NAME on it, Sherlock!

Kate blinked. She had known this, of course, but she couldn't make sense of what her brother was telling her. Eventually she replied: As in a Swiss bank account?!

Exactly that, came back the reply.

How much?

Two or three thousand. Every four or five months. As far back as the archives go — which is five years before she died. I'm going to go through everything in the loft to see if there are paper statements that go back further.

Kate shook her head, baffled. What the hell? she texted. What was she doing? Their mother had been a warm and loving woman, and apparently an open book... but, after losing Mabel, there had always been a sense of some part of her locked away. It was understandable, Kate guessed, but maybe there had been something *other* than pain and grief behind that human edifice? Was she being blackmailed by someone? Supporting a foreign lover..? Sponsoring a child in memory of Mabel..?

No idea what she was up to, texted back Francis. **Does that remind you of anyone?**

She smiled at the phone and nodded. Francis was way too sharp. **Sorry. I will see you soon and explain everything**, she tapped out. **Have a dig around and let me know what you find. Take care and GET SOME SLEEP. xxx**

She got into the shower, now fully awake, and freshened up. The fizz of adrenaline from the strange revelations in her brother's texts eased away in the hot water and then returned two-fold as her mind came to rest on what she was doing here, nearly two thousand miles from home. It got fizzier still as the guilt at leaving her colleagues to crack the crop circle case without her hit home.

What was she hoping to achieve today? Find Lucas. And then what? Arrest him and force him to come back to the UK and get charged with murder? Alone? Was he likely to come meekly with her after weeks on the run?

She knew she had behaved rashly. She should have spoken to Kapoor and requested a proper leave of absence from her workload — and maybe DC Michaels to accompany her out here as backup. But she *knew* Kapoor would have grounded her. She couldn't blame him for that. No detective should be investigating their own sister's murder — it broke every rule in the book.

There was no use agonising about it. She got out of the shower, dried her hair and dressed in shorts and a T-shirt. Then she made for the small reception area at the foot of the stairs, her satchel — retrieved from the rucksack and filled with essentials — slung over her shoulder. She would have slipped straight out into the sunlight, but she was intercepted and forced to sit down.

'You are still tired and hungry,' the lady proprietor pointed out, concern wrinkling her brow. 'You cannot be good like this. You must have your breakfast.'

Kate found it strangely touching that this matronly Greek woman was so worried about her. She suddenly missed her mother and felt a wave of sadness that there was so much about Emily Sparrow that she would never get to understand. So much had happened in that strong, determined and brave woman's life that she was never going to fathom. The middle-aged man on the table opposite smiled at her over his newspaper and she smiled back, her eyes drifting to the headline: EE KLIRONOMOS KATAZI-TEETAI YIA THIPLEE DOLOFONIA ASTINOMIKON

The image that went with it was of a beautiful red-haired woman — clearly not a Greek — with a cold smirk of a smile. Kate's instincts prickled. She recognised ASTINO-MIKON as "police" and checked DOLOFONIA on her phone and wasn't surprised to see it meant MURDER. The woman could be the victim but something in that smile told her otherwise... it was familiar, that look. She'd seen it before. The last time was on the face of Donna Wilson, who'd very nearly killed her. Before that... Wendy Morris, who had also very nearly killed her. And before that..? There was someone else... The waiter arrived with a tray of breakfast and Kate put down her phone and decided to focus on the simple task of fuelling herself for the day ahead.

Twenty minutes later she finally stepped out into the soft morning breeze, fuelled with honey and nut filled pastries, fresh figs and coffee, which had all gone down surprisingly easily. She checked the tourist map Mrs Papadopulous, her kindly hotelier, had given her, with an X marking the spot of a local car hire firm, and set out to get herself some wheels. Within an hour she had temporary custody of a bright red Kia Picanto and a detailed motoring atlas of the island. Now all she had to do was remember to drive on the right side of the road and wrangle the map. She could have used her mobile SatNav but now that she had fully embraced her rogue status, she knew it was wise to keep the phone switched off. Any texts from her colleagues she could still pick up occasionally, but it was safer, regarding her whereabouts, if any calls went direct to voicemail.

But just before she set out to Ipsos she took a breath and texted more subterfuge to Michaels. **Having a heavy time with this head of mine. Will be clocking out for another day. Please let Kapoor and the team know. Sorry.**

It wasn't entirely a lie. She *was* having a heavy time with her head. In another country, though, not in Salisbury, which she had failed to mention. She hoped asking forgiveness would turn out to be a better option than asking permission. She switched off the phone and shoved it deep into the pocket of her shorts, double-checked the map route she had worked out, and started up the car. The alien road system took a little getting used to — there wasn't actually much opportunity to drive on the right as most roads seemed to be single-track with passing points. Just travelling along the winding country lanes, a china blue sky above her, idyllic views of countryside to her left and gleaming ocean to the right, took up a lot of her attention. And this was a good thing because whenever her mind drifted away from the road ahead and the negotiation of junctions, she could only wonder what the hell she was driving into.

———

BRIGITTE ANDERSSEN GOT UP EARLY. She was frustrated that she had not managed to watch the last flight in from the UK last night, but her shift at the taverna had run on too late. She had been tempted to simply leave. It wasn't as if she was going to need a reference.

But the sensible voice inside her head — which always sounded like her mother's — had reminded her that she needed to stay under the radar while she remained on Corfu. Any odd behaviour — like vanishing in the middle of her shift without explanation — might stick in somebody's mind if the police came looking for a single white female wanted for murder. And a description of Christina wouldn't put off the more focused detectives. They weren't completely stupid. They had *heard* of hair dye, make-up and coloured contact lenses.

So she hadn't made the midnight flight arrivals, but she could think a bit further down the line and visit the next place Kate might be if she *had* arrived on the red eye. Because without any doubt, the Detective Inspector would have checked the franking mark on that package. She would have worked out where it had been sent from and she would be going straight to it, maybe as soon as it opened.

So Brigitte got up at six, despite only flopping into her narrow attic bed at 1am, got a notepad from her bag and started playing with letters and numbers. At seven, she showered and blow-dried her hair. She put on white capri pants, a red slash-neck top, strappy flat sandals and a head-scarf, Greek-style. With her Ray-Ban sunglasses it all looked quite Audrey Hepburn.

She applied red lipstick, black eyeliner and mascara, and winked at her reflection as she gathered her bag and her delicious plans.

She stopped by the darkened, empty kitchen to collect a

fresh flask of water and a stick of bread. A small tub of olives, too, and a peach. She didn't want Lucas getting scurvy. Those lips were getting a little cracked and dry. She wrapped the food up in a paper parcel and dropped it, and the flask, into her bag. She should eat breakfast before she left, but she was too excited. She'd get something on her return to Ipsos. Nobody stirred as she let herself out onto the street and went to find the hired Vespa tucked around the side of the taverna.

It was just a twenty-minute ride to the field, and she was relieved to find it looking exactly the same as she'd left it. The only movement was the occasional flitting bird and, among the tangle of junk metal, the slow turning of a bike wheel on its bent frame, clicking gently as the breeze took it. The round trap door was still ajar at the centre and she could smell the essence of the man trapped under it. God — she was hot for him again — immediately. She was very, very tempted to get down into the warm, musky fug of his prison and lick the sweat off his skin... but she had work to do, so instead she opened one side of the semi-circle of iron and stared down at him. He lay flat on the earth, his left arm still hanging from the cuff. The skin around his wrist was bleeding. Damn. He was going to get infected if he kept on pulling against it. Maybe she should change the cuff to the other wrist.

'Wake up, Sleeping Beauty,' she called. His eyes opened slowly, squinting against the shaft of sun.

She leaned over the edge and dropped in the paper packet and the flask of water.

'How long?' he said.

'How long, what?' she asked, getting to her knees and resting on her hands as she gazed down at him. It was *so* tempting to go down, but she didn't want to mess up her white capri pants... well, not on the *outside,* anyway... and she really needed to be back in Ipsos before nine.

'How long are you going keep me here?' he said.

'Do you know?' she said. 'I haven't really decided. I mean... aren't we just fine as we are? Why complicate things?'

'It won't work,' he said.

She narrowed her eyes at him. 'What won't work?'

'Whatever you're planning... with Kate... it won't work. She's smarter than you think. You'd do well to leave her out of it altogether. Leave me the key and go. Get off the island. Away from the police... they're closing in on you.'

'Lucas... what makes you think I'm planning anything for Kate..? Or that the police are after me? Have you been *dowsing* me?' she asked, fascinated.

'I didn't need to,' he grunted, sitting up and reaching for the water flask. 'I heard the news report about the dead Athens detectives... and the missing woman suspected of killing them. It's you, isn't it? You're lying low, waiting for the best time to get off the island and run.'

'Well, well, you *are* a surprise. But you worked all that out while you still had your little friendly pendulum. How are you managing without Sid?'

'Well enough,' he said. 'Sid was only ever a prop. No dowser actually believes their rods or pendulums are magic, you know. They're just tools. It's quite possible to do without. That's how I can read your plans right now. You're thinking of bringing Kate to you. I bet you sent Sid to her, didn't you?'

She grinned, delighted with him. 'Yes! I did. With some of your blood on him. And the franking mark on the package. Easy to trace it back to Corfu with that. She's probably already here. I'll find out soon. Or maybe you can tell me. Can you sense Kate here?'

'No,' said Lucas. 'She won't come. She'll pass the evidence to her team and someone else will come. Probably teaming up with local cops. Not Kate. You don't know her like I do. She follows procedure whenever she can.'

'Like she followed it with you?' Brigitte laughed. 'Riding around like a pair of superheroes — the lady detective and the rebel dowser? That's not by the book, is it? Not when you're around. I don't blame her.'

'She won't come. You're wasting your time.'

'Well,' said Brigitte. 'We'll see.' And she stood up and kicked the trapdoor flat with a muffled clang. 'Enjoy your breakfast. I might see you later. Or I might just take your advice and get off the island, in which case, I hope your death's not too painful.'

She walked away, grinning. Oh, Lucas thought he had all the answers, didn't he? But he was wrong. *She* was the one tracking a lost person this time. Because Kate Sparrow *was* lost, wasn't she? On so many levels. She'd lost a sister and then a mother... a father long before... she was searching for the truth about Mabel's death, with absolutely no regard for how much the truth would hurt. It would be fascinating to watch her face as the layers of self-delusion were stripped away. Are you *sure* you want the details, Kate? Are you *sure?*

She got back on the moped and headed back to the resort, thinking about Lucas's warning. Maybe he was right. Kate might turn out to be her nemesis — who knew? It was a whole new level of fascination. A thrilling step-up in the game. She hadn't really thought through her actions a few weeks ago, when she'd first recklessly picked up the phone. It had all been impulse and devilment after seeing fresh news reports surfacing, triggering her memories about the

Quarry Girls. She had wanted to stir the pot; see what floated up to the surface.

But then she had been distracted by planning the end of Stavros and getting a taste of wealthy widowhood. She might never have done anything else regarding the Quarry Girls if Lucas Henry — the Quarry *Boy* — hadn't come for her. Now she was being forced to think and plan extremely fast and it was exhilarating. She had almost forgotten the dead Athens police and the ongoing womanhunt for Christina Eliades. She mustn't get complacent about that and she wouldn't — which was why she'd stayed at the taverna, keeping her head down, last night.

But her attention was utterly swept up now in this grand new project. She *couldn't wait* to meet Kate.

27

I t took Kate thirty minutes to get from the town of Corfu to the seaside resort of Ipsos. It might have been faster if she hadn't stuck to driving like a granny, eyes riveted on the road to be sure she didn't drift instinctively to the left. She was on one of the main tourist routes on the island and it was well marked out on her map. She knew other routes inland were often single-track and you could get stuck behind a goat truck for half an hour. There was no reason to be rushing, though. The shop with the post office counter wasn't going anywhere.

She eventually reached a wide stretch of main road, topped with cracked tarmac in need of resurfacing, which led past a series of single-storey shops, tavernas and businesses, painted in Corfu's trademark shades of yellow, salmon pink and pale orange. There was no tourist car park that she could see, but plenty of spaces at the kerbside, so she pulled in and consulted her map. The temptation to briefly switch on her phone and locate Danny's Supermarket on Google maps was very strong, but fear of the texts and voicemails she might find restrained her.

So, she did it the old fashioned way. She got out, locked up the car, walked a few paces, and *asked someone*. 'I'm looking for Danny's Supermarket..?' she said to a nut-brown old man, leaning against a wall, having a smoke. She wished she had even a smattering of Greek but there was no point pretending she wasn't another dumb English tourist. She half expected the man to screw up his face and respond in an unintelligible stream of words, but he just smiled and said, in careful English: 'It is down here, you see. A five-minute walk.'

'Thank you!' she said and left him still smiling after her. The directions were sound. She did indeed find Danny's Supermarket a five-minute walk away, sandwiched between a taverna and a cafe bar, a bright blue ATM standing outside it like a TARDIS. It wasn't yet nine but plenty of people were enjoying breakfast in the taverna's street-facing courtyard, and the smell of coffee and warm baked bread drifted from it.

Kate stepped up to the entrance of the supermarket and saw, with relief, a small sticker on the glass door, indicating that parcels and letters could be sent from here. Although Sid and his chain were pushed deep into her shorts pocket, she had brought the packaging with her, now containing only the blood-smeared plastic. She pulled it from her satchel as she approached a single tiny glass window right at the back of the store. Behind it sat a dark-haired young woman, checking through some folders of stamps.

'Excuse me,' said Kate, as she reached the small counter. 'Do you speak English?'

The young woman nodded. 'Yes. How can I help you?'

Kate presented the package. 'Can you tell me if this is your franking mark? I mean... was this package sent from here?'

The young woman scrutinised the mark and then nodded. 'Yes. That is us.'

'Do you see the date?' Kate pressed on, glad that there wasn't currently a queue behind her. The clerk nodded. 'Were you working that day?'

The clerk blew out some air and thought for a moment. 'Yes. I think so.'

Kate took a deep breath, counting on Lucas to have made a lasting impression. 'Do you remember a man coming in to send this? A good-looking man... dark hair... a bit of a beard... green eyes?'

The young woman smirked. 'There are many good-looking men in Corfu,' she said, shrugging. Kate sighed in defeat and reached for her phone. She switched it on and pulled up an image of Lucas, stored there for some weeks. It was a publicity shot taken by Mariam, Lucas's art gallery-owning friend, and it was beautifully lit to show off all the angles and planes of his face, the pleasing hang of his wild dark hair and the intense dark green of his eyes. 'This man,' she said.

The clerk leaned forward and raised her eyebrows approvingly. 'He *is* good-looking,' she agreed. 'I would remember him.'

'So..?' Kate prompted.

She shook her head. 'No. Sorry. I hope he *does* come in.'

'I know this is ridiculous to even ask,' added Kate, clutching at straws. 'But do you remember who *did* send this package?'

The clerk laughed. 'I send hundreds of parcels every week.'

Kate closed her eyes, swept with the mortifying realisation that she was on a wild goose chase.

'But is your name Kate?'

Her eyes shot wide open. 'I'm sorry? What?'

'Is your name Kate? Kate Sparrow?'

'Yes,' said Kate, her plummeting hopes bouncing back up in a second. 'That's me. How on earth do you—?'

'I was asked to give you this.' The clerk slid a red envelope under the glass partition with KATE SPARROW inked on it in bold black letters.

Kate picked it up, adrenaline spiking through her. 'So... do you know who left *this?*'

The clerk smirked again. 'I promised I would not say.'

Kate reached instinctively for her warrant card. 'I'm police,' she said, holding up the wallet and hoping the English lettering on the badge wouldn't be too obvious. And then remembered that she was *speaking* English and looking English and just about doing everything but singing the National Anthem.

The clerk didn't look impressed. 'I cannot say.'

'Are there security cameras?' asked Kate. 'Could you show me?'

The clerk glanced over Kate's shoulder. 'No cameras,' she said, stonily. 'And you are not police to *me.* You would need to come with Corfu police to ask this. Now... there is a queue. Please...'

Kate realised three people were now waiting behind her. She nodded and left, the red envelope in her hand — not a bad result after a pretty inept investigation on her part. But what the hell..? Someone was playing games. Was this Lucas at work?

She wandered along the pavement and found an unoccupied bench. The red envelope looked like the kind that might contain a birthday card — and it did feel as if there was a card inside. What *else* might be inside? Given her last mystery package had contained blood, as well as Sid, it was entirely possible there was something unpleasant in this one, too — although she couldn't detect any lumps or ridges through the paper. She instinctively dug out some latex gloves from the supply in a pocket of her satchel and put them on.

She took a deep breath and held it as she tore the envelope open. Inside was nothing but a postcard of assorted Corfu attractions. On the back, written in the same black ink, were numbers. Grouped together.

8-21-19-8-9-14-7

5-22-5-14-9-14-7

4-9-19-13-9-19-19-9-14-7

A cipher? She blinked and shook her head. Then she stood up and slowly turned around, taking in everyone within her sightline. She had a distinct impression that whoever had left this for her was watching right now. She stared at a dark-haired man apparently enjoying a coffee in the nearby taverna courtyard, but when he glanced up, catching her and offering a smile and a wink, she turned away again. Not Lucas. And anyway — she didn't think this was his style. Or maybe it *was* his style if he had some reason to play this stupid cat-and-mouse game with her. After all, she had already come to accept that she *didn't know him.* Even though a part of her kept insisting that there was a connection between them — something intuitive and unspoken — the truth was she didn't know him at all. How could she *know* the man who'd killed her sister and not pick up that small, important fact about him..?

There were other people who might be watching from a distance. A middle-aged couple with a white poodle were constantly sweeping the street view with their gaze, as if expecting someone. A black guy listening to something through his earbuds, drumming his fingers on the table while he waited to be served, definitely eyeing her up. The stylish blonde woman in a red top and a headscarf, finishing a pastry and a cool drink, could be looking right at her now, through the mirror lenses of her expensive looking sunglasses.

Kate went back to the numbers, getting a pen and notebook from her satchel. OK. The simplest cipher was just alphabetical. So, that would mean the number 8 stood for H. Then the number 21... U. She worked on with increasing confidence, jotting the figures and letters down in her notebook until the first word was done. HUSHING.

Well. It *was* a word, but it didn't make much sense. She pressed on with the next one.

EVENING.

And then the third.... DISMISSING.

After a few seconds of incomprehension, it quickly dawned. Of course. It was a *What3Words* location. Sighing, she went back to her phone, and switched on ROAMING, doing her best to shut out the little red icons which immediately flashed up — three texts and two voicemails awaiting her attention. She resolutely called up *what3words.com* instead and entered the words, lower case, a dot between them.

A moment later a location flashed up... three square metres of land on what looked like a ragged promontory jutting east into the sea, with a single-track road or footpath running to its tip. It was a short drive back down the coast road. Kate stood up and looked around again. The black guy with the earbuds was now eating his late breakfast with gusto, still plugged in and nodding to his music. The man with vague similarities to Lucas now had female company and was flirting for gold. The poodle couple were waving at friends coming their way. The woman in the headscarf and sunglasses had gone. Nobody else was paying her the slightest bit of attention.

Kate hit NAVIGATE on the site and connected to Google. She was done with the paper map. She would ignore all texts and voicemails for now, hope to god nobody in the UK phoned her, and just focus on getting to this spot. It occurred to her that she was doing exactly as this anonymous puppet master was expecting. That grated on her. A lot. Whether it was Lucas, or someone involved with Lucas, she didn't want to give them the satisfaction.

But what else could she do?

28

'Here you go, lovey — you try it!'

Lucas took the pendulum from his Aunty Janine. It felt stupid. He was ten now — in Year Six at school — and he didn't believe in magic.

'Just hold it between your knuckles, see? Like that. Now... rest your elbows on the table.' Aunty Janine, wearing a purple dress and matching purple sandals, settled back onto her old leather sofa and nodded at him. 'Now let it hang still...'

'Oh for god's sake, Jan!' muttered Mum, taking a sip of her third glass of wine. 'You're filling his head with nonsense.'

'It is not nonsense,' said Aunty Janine, as Lucas rested his elbows on her coffee table; the one with inlaid mother of pearl which smelt sort of smoky and sweet. There were always interesting, exotic smells in Aunty Janine's bungalow. She travelled a lot and brought stuff home from all over the world. 'Now — Lucas — keep perfectly still. Make the pendulum hang quite motionless. Can you do that?'

'Yeah,' said Lucas, focusing hard now and finding a stillness inside him that he'd not noticed before. The blue glass bottle stopper hung in the air like a freeze-frame.

'Now,' said Aunty Janine. 'Do not move a muscle. But, with your mind, tell it to spin.'

Mum snorted again, refilling her glass.

Lucas told the stopper to spin. At first nothing happened and he was about to give up... but then it moved. Just a bit. In a circle. Then the circle got a little wider.

'There you are — you're doing it!' said Aunty Janine.

'Of course he's doing it!' said Mum. 'He's holding the bloody thing!'

'Sssshhh! Pay her no attention, Lucas. Keep it spinning... and now... ask it to do a figure of eight.'

Lucas did. And a thrill rose up through the hairs on the back of his neck as the pendulum adjusted from a circle to a figure of eight. He knew he wasn't moving it. His fingers were frozen; his steepled hands like steel, his resting elbows like concrete. But the pendulum was moving!

'There — you have it,' said Aunty Janine. 'You have the gift. Now let's test it. You can make it rock back and forth, and you can make it circle... and you can make it do a figure of eight. So... now you ask it some questions. Or rather, I will ask the questions. Right. What colour bra have I got on today?'

'Janine!' protested Mum. 'For god's sake!'

'Ssshhh. Is it black or white? Spin for black — rock back and forth for white.'

Lucas kept his focus on the stopper. It dropped out of its figure of eight and marked a circle again. 'Black,' he said.

'Correct!' said Aunty Janine.

'It was a fifty-fifty chance!' spluttered Mum.

'OK — here's another one. When I went into Salisbury today, did I go to the delicatessen? Yes or no? Yes — circle, and no — rock back and forth.'

'No,' said Lucas, as the pendulum dropped back into a rocking motion.

'Correct,' said Aunty Janine. 'Now — let's go three ways. My maths teacher when I was at school... was he called Mr Hansen, Mr Collier or Mr Lopez? Circle for Hansen, rock to and fro for Collier and figure of eight for Mr Lopez.'

It took a few seconds to settle into the pattern but eventually Lucas said: 'Mr Lopez.'

'Correct!' cried Aunty Janine, jubilantly.

'Oh, this is bullshit,' muttered Mum.

'Language, Joanna!' admonished her sister.

'Well... you've probably told him about your teachers. You're always gassing on about your schooldays to him, aren't you?' Mum grabbed a copy of the Salisbury Journal and opened it at a random page. 'Right — let's try this. Who's just been elected to City Mayor? Mike Gardener, Bob Knowles or Chris Judd? Circle for Gardener, swing back and forth for Knowles, figure of eight for Judd.'

Lucas felt a prickle of unease. His Mum's testing wasn't the nurturing kind. Mum wanted to prove him wrong; to belittle him — and her sister — and make herself feel better.

He took a deep breath and focused hard. The pendulum stopped dead. It didn't move at all.

'Mum...' he said, that prickling sensation across his neck again. 'You're not telling me the right name. I don't think any of them are going to be mayor.'

Mum didn't say anything for several seconds. Then she gave a sharp exhalation of annoyance, gave the newspaper a shake and read out three other names. 'Spin for David McCarthy, rock for Olwen Tanner, figure of eight for Steve Fear.'

The pendulum started to move. A few seconds later it was a pronounced figure of eight. 'Steve Fear,' said Lucas.

Mum put down the paper with a slap and picked up her bag. 'He's heard it on the radio or something,' she muttered, getting up *and flouncing out through the kitchen to light up in the back garden.*

But Aunty Janine looked at him in a different way, narrowing her eyes as if seeing him as a completely new species. 'Lucas Henry,' she said. 'You really do have the gift.'

'The only gift he's got...' Mum called in, on a draught of cigarette smoke from the open back door. '...is for being a pain in the arse.'

Lucas opened his eyes and felt, appropriately, a pain in his arse. He had dropped into a doze while propped against the side of the silo wall and the hard-packed earth was digging into his tail bone. This drifting back into the past through dreams was happening more and more. He didn't know how much time had elapsed since he'd been imprisoned — she'd taken his watch along with everything else — and his mind had taken to periodically swooping him away to revisit various events in his personal history, just to save his sanity.

He wriggled into a different sitting position, flapping a whining mosquito away from his face with his free hand. He'd already been bitten three or four times. He felt around beneath him to shift the bit of sharp stone out of the way and his fingers closed on the edge of it, but it wasn't moving. It must be buried in the ground. He worked at it again and realised it wasn't a stone. It seemed like years since he had been at Alberto's farm, sensing all those coins buried beneath and beyond the boundary... but it was just a few days. And the patterns were still fresh in his mind... metal in soil made for very distinctive patterns. Looking around the empty silo, with only the bucket, the water flask and the paper left over from his meagre breakfast on the floor, he had allowed himself to assume there was nothing here. And there *was* nothing here... on the *surface*.

But there were things that lay beneath...

29

K ate did not drive directly to the location pinpointed on her map. She navigated to a beach road about a kilometre away, parked the car in the shade of a large tree, and walked towards the small peninsular instead. There was some kind of hotel complex occupying the spur of land, which reached out into the turquoise sea like a curved finger. She could see woodland behind the hotel and decided to approach *hushing.evening.dismissing* through the trees, remaining unseen if she possibly could and making use of the small pair of binoculars in her satchel.

If someone was waiting for her, she might even get the drop on them. Although how she was going to know, she couldn't guess. If it *wasn't* Lucas... and she was getting a growing instinct that it wasn't... then she reckoned it was unlikely they'd be standing around, holding up her name on a placard.

The walk along the tree side of the coast was cool, green and would almost have been soothing if she hadn't been seeing shadows and stalkers behind every trunk and in every patch of undergrowth. Two people wandered through in the distance — both with dogs — and she thought fondly of Reggie, back home in Salisbury, his life uncomplicated by anything. He certainly wouldn't be agonising about that corpse he'd found. She wished she had time for a dog of her own... some sweet, simple, furry friend. Mum had never allowed them to have anything else after Kate's third hamster died. Her pets never seemed to last more than a few months despite her every effort to keep them clean, well-fed and happy. Mabel, with her trademark big sister smirk, said they just hadn't wanted to live, and neither would she if she had to share a room with someone with such stinky pits. Mum told them she wasn't going to risk a puppy, too... that there'd been enough death in the household. That was a grim bit of foreshadowing, wasn't it?

Kate reached into her bag and pulled out the binoculars as she saw bright daylight saturating the trees at the edge of the woodland, making out the sea, surging and sparkling, just beyond. She turned a full circle, watching carefully for any movement and seeing none. Edging onward she spotted a pair of wrought iron benches. The grassy outlook, above a rocky outcrop over the sea, was deserted, despite its pretty view. The way the woodland hemmed it offered almost complete seclusion. It was off the beaten track. She guessed the riddler who'd left the envelope for her was watching it, too — waiting for her to sit down in the sun. She settled low against the trunk of a tree, trained her binoculars on the spot and waited. Half an hour passed. Nothing moved except seabirds and a distant jogger, who ran past without a glance.

So... was she going to sit down and wait? She felt a twist of anger. Well fuck that. She was not going to play along like this. She'd come all the way from England in response to that package and then obediently followed a second clue from Ipsos... now it was time to play her own hand. She knelt down and pulled out her notebook, marking out a cipher of her own. She'd noticed a café close to where she'd parked. That would do. She wrote a series of numbers and checked back what they read.

Then she stepped out into the light, picked up a rock, and pinned the note to the grass under the closest seat. She turned around once more, to check whether anyone was approaching. Saw nobody. Fine. There was no timescale in the cipher she'd been given. No instruction. She might wait for hours for nothing.

'Bollocks to this,' she said, aloud, and walked around the headland to the open area of the hotel resort.

The note, should anyone decipher it, read: **The Oyster Shell at midday. Or you can just fuck off.**

———

BRIGITTE WAITED for another ten minutes after the figure of Kate Sparrow departed from the clearing above the rocky inlet. She *had* been about to descend from her vantage point in the hotel's penthouse suite, booked and paid for by phone yesterday, and then she saw the note being left and decided *not* to run down like an excited child on Christmas Day morning. There was time for more play yet.

She followed Kate's progress along the hotel complex driveway until she was certain the detective wasn't doubling back, and then went swiftly down to the bench and retrieved the note. Oho! *This* was *good!* A cipher for a cipher. She took it back to her suite and quickly deciphered it.

The Oyster Shell at midday. Or you can just fuck off.

She laughed out loud and literally punched the air. This was SO much fun.

But. She couldn't let Kate take control. She would have to play this carefully. If Kate had this cafe location staked out in some way, Brigitte would be at a severe disadvantage. She was pretty sure Kate was travelling alone and not, as Lucas had tried to suggest, accompanied by any other police colleagues. There were other ways, though, to catch a person out, if you had the lie of the land before they arrived. No. The location would have to change.

She considered the beach front area. There was a fairground set along it — a permanent amusements area with a small Ferris wheel, a water slide, various little kid rides and a carousel. It was busy and noisy. She narrowed her eyes as she watched the carousel. *What goes around comes around.*

She called for room service and a young man came up, neatly turned out in his white shirt and tight black trousers. 'I wonder if you would help me with something!' she asked, remembering to accent her Greek with Swedish. She looked at him in her *special* way and enjoyed the sight of his smooth cheeks flushing. 'Can you take a gift to a friend for me? Down to a cafe on the waterfront... It shouldn't take you more than ten or twenty minutes.'

'I...um...' he looked awkward, no doubt wondering whether leaving the complex would get him into trouble.

She sidled up to him, a fifty euro note in her fingers and her mouth close to his ear. 'I will make it worth your while.'

———

ON THE DOT of midday a good-looking young man who looked like a waiter came into the Oyster Shell Cafe, glanced around it impatiently, and spotted Kate sitting with her coffee. He stepped quickly across and dropped a white envelope on the table. Then he gave her a nod and turned around.

'Wait!" Kate called after him. 'Who sent you?'

He shrugged, said: 'Sorry... no English!' and hurried back out into the street.

Kate could have gone after him but she felt it would be time wasted. Whoever was messing with her clearly *wanted* to meet at some point. She got the disposable gloves on again before taking the envelope. Old habits die hard. Also, for all she knew, this head case might have dusted the thing with a toxic substance. Glancing around to check she wasn't being watched and surmising that she wasn't, she gently opened the envelope. There was a note... but there was something else that caught her attention first. Held together with a small rubber band... a lock of dark hair. She gulped, suddenly assailed by a very bad feeling. She carefully pulled it out and cradled it in her latex-covered palm. It could be *anyone's* hair. Plenty of lustrous dark locks available on Corfu. But she knew whose hair this was. She lifted her cupped palm to her nose and caught the scent of him, which sent a stab of adrenaline through her. And not only adrenaline. Somewhere in her base level olfactory system, a shameful connection flickered straight to the desire centre of her brain.

She stuffed the hair back into the envelope and found another simple cipher. It took a couple of minutes to write it out in her notebook. **Unicorns. Carousel. Fairground. Right now or fuck you too.**

Kate didn't bother to look up the three words on the app. It was plain what was meant. There was a fairground right opposite this cafe and a carousel visible from here. She would probably have to ride a bloody unicorn on it. Was she

going to play along? The "**or fuck you too**" comment might
mean this was the end of the road if her tormentor got
annoyed enough. She doubted that, but it was too big a risk
to take. She sighed and drained her coffee. Time to go
hunting unicorns. It seemed apt.

———————

BRIGITTE WAS FEELING exhilarated but also nervous. She was
playing this *really* close to the wire. If she was honest with
herself, she didn't really have an endgame in place and this
was almost unheard of for her. Of course she *had* acted recklessly before — the broken bodies of two Greek detectives in
a Corfu cave were testament to that — and she sometimes
took actions that were driven purely by fascination or desire
which, she later had to own to herself, were unwise. But
when it came to laying out her life plans or her long cons,
she usually had it all worked out in fine detail. That was
part of the pleasure of it — making a plan and then seeing it
all come together. She rarely had a misstep.

But Lucas... that had just been idle play. She had wound
him up because he'd been on her mind. She'd had some
dreams about him... probably triggered by the news reports
she'd first picked up on the BBC World news channel after
the Runner Grabber case. It was fascinating to see pictures
of the poor boy who had so nearly gone to prison for her
crimes... all grown up and so sexy. Once she'd realised who
he was — and who his detective buddy was — she was
hooked. She'd put an alert onto her laptop and phone,
which picked up subsequent news stories featuring the
names Lucas Henry or Kate Sparrow... the Gaffer Tape
Killers came next. Shortly before the Buntin's Murders had
hit the headlines she'd managed to track down his mobile

phone number. She had spoken to a dimwit assistant —
with no clue about personal privacy — at the Salisbury
gallery his art collection had been showcased in. She'd said
she had a high net worth client who wanted to commission
Lucas Henry and she needed to get in touch with him as
soon as possible. Bingo!

Once she had the number she did nothing with it for
some time. Just having it was a tremendous thrill; knowing
she possessed, in the palm of her hand, a device and a series
of digits which could enable her to totally mess with the
mind of a man in another country, whenever she felt the
urge. Would he know who she was? Would his dowsing
talent speak to him of the murderer breathing at the end of
the phone..?

She waited several months — busy being the perfect
wife to Stav — before she finally made some calls. Silent...
and then gently breathing... and then speaking a few soft
words. Hearing his reaction was an incredible turn on. She
wondered if he could pick up the patterns of what she was
doing while he held the line..?

Some part of her had always known he would come
looking but, honestly, when he had burst back into her
world, staring up at her in the tree, she hadn't really been
ready. Somewhat busy evading capture for her most recent
kills. Still, she'd got on top of the situation fast and decided
if she was going to play out this game properly, it might as
well be now. She honestly didn't know yet whether Lucas
would live or die. What she would do with Kate once she
had her was also all to play for. So much would depend on
them.

So yes. She was busking this. But busking with style. She
idled in the shade of an ice cream kiosk, pretending to be
absorbed in her mobile while in fact training its camera on

the ever-turning carousel ahead of her. Three or four
minutes after Juan the room service guy had delivered the
envelope to her, Kate arrived, glancing around suspiciously
and eyeing the carousel. The ride was slowing down to take
on a fresh batch of fun-seekers and the sleigh seat, with a
garishly painted unicorn at either side of it, remained
empty. Kate looked around again, scanning everyone getting
off, and then shook her head and got on, handing some
euros to the ride runner and settling into the unicorn sleigh.

Excellent. Brigitte tucked her phone away and boarded
the ride, too. She had chosen the unicorn sleigh for Kate
because its high back seat meant anyone in it couldn't see
behind them. Also because there was a useful gap in its
fibreglass build. How did she know this? Because yesterday,
while she was planning all this, she had weighed up using
the carousel as a meeting place and taken that sleigh ride
herself, before abandoning it in favour of the benches on
the overlook. But since Kate had decided to be difficult, she
had called it up as a plan B.

Brigitte got astride an ostrich and rode up and down as
the old oily mechanics rose and fell. She waited until the
ride was up to full speed and then pulled another envelope
from her bag. Any moment now, Kate was going to grow
weary and maybe get out of the sleigh and stare around the
carousel, and she didn't want that — not yet. Checking that
the operator wasn't watching and about to give a warning
shout about getting off the saddle, she slid down and
approached the sleigh, holding on to a barley-sugar twist of
painted post. Readying herself to depart, with her spare
hand she posted the envelope through the gap in the curved
hood of the sleigh. It would slide down onto Kate's head or
shoulders and the detective would no doubt spring out as

soon as she found it, so Brigitte lost no time in leaping from the ride.

She nearly ended up on all fours as she hit the ground but managed to save herself and break into a run, then get around the side of the kiosk before turning to peer through the lower branches of a small kumquat tree. Kate was on her feet, hanging on a unicorn and scanning the fairground like a hawk. She also jumped off the ride, landing better than Brigitte had, and then stood still while she ripped open the envelope. She read the contents and then raised her eyes, staring around from person to person, frustration and anger on her face.

Then she theatrically screwed up the note and dropped it into a bin before raising her arms and dropping them to her sides, shaking her head. *Forget it. I'm out.*

She won't. She won't just walk away. She's come too far for this. She wants to find Lucas. She wants to find ME. Brigitte told herself this as she watched Kate walk away through the small fair. She checked her watch. The timing was still right. She'd told the guy to wait at least fifteen minutes. Told him to be clear. Paid him triple, up front. As she followed the retreating figure of Kate Sparrow she had to acknowledge a frisson of fear that her plan might not work. *No. It'll work. Watch... and wait.*

She should have been more direct. Shouldn't have buggered about with all this cipher bollocks. Ah, but where was the fun in directness?

As Kate reached the road, the car was waiting. What would she do..?

30

As Kate reached the road, the car was waiting. What should she do..?

The taxi driver got out and called: 'Taxi for Kate Sparrow..?' He was glancing at what looked like her photo on his phone.

She scanned his face for evil intent and found none. He was most likely just a cabbie, paid to do a pick-up. 'Where have you been told to go?' she asked. Regardless of what the latest note had suggested, she had no intention of getting into the car when she could perfectly easily drive to the location instead.

He shrugged. 'It's not a place,' he said.

'What?' Kate felt a tension headache building. This whole day was turning into a ridiculous game of cat and mouse, and she was close to calling a halt to it all and phoning for that back-up. She didn't relish confessing to Kapoor and begging for help after running out on the job back in Wiltshire, but it was probably the sensible thing to do.

'I take you north,' said the driver, looking as bemused as she felt. 'Then I get call with details.'

Kate blew out a long breath, weighing it all up. If she didn't get into the car, the driver would depart and that might be the end of it. By the time she'd got help, via Kapoor and Interpol and the local guys — who would need a lot of briefing — it could be hours... a day even. She'd heard that life was pretty slow moving on Corfu and the police might be no exception. Also, they had their hands full with this double police murder, if the papers were anything to go by. Helping her to track down Lucas Henry wasn't going to be high on their list of priorities. She cursed, screwing up her eyes and shaking her head as she gave herself up to the inevitable, and then got into the car. She could always get the driver to stop and let her out as soon as he'd got the details of the drop-off — after getting those details out of him first, of course...

'Who booked you?' she said, pulling the rear door shut and then winding the window down and resting an arm on it. If he threw the central locking system on, she would have a chance of escaping through it. Glancing around she found a metal water flask tucked into the pocket behind the front passenger seat. She wedged that in the window space too, to prevent the glass from sliding up and cutting off that option.

'I don't know,' he said. 'It was a booking on the app. To pick up Kate Sparrow by the fair.' He shrugged. 'All paid. Good money.'

'But there must be a phone number, yes?'

'Of course,' he said.

'Will you give it to me?'

His glance at her via his rear-view mirror, was anxious. 'I'm not supposed to do this.'

She held up her badge, hoping for the best. 'I'm police...

astinomikon… from England. I need to contact the person who booked you to pick me up.'

He looked rattled and handed back his mobile, showing a number on the app booking page. Kate copied it quickly into her own phone and handed his back while the driver took them away from the coast and up into the hills.

Kate texted: **Who are you?**

There was no reply.

Answer me or I'm out of this car and that's it.

There was a long pause and she nearly went through with her ultimatum, opening her mouth to tell the driver to pull over. But then the phone buzzed in her palm and a message came back.

I just want to meet you, Kate.

Kate rang the number but it went straight to voicemail — an automated response offering no clues. Her mobile buzzed again.

Be patient. It's only ten minutes away. We will meet and talk very soon.

There was a *bing* in the front of the car and the driver picked up a message. 'I know where you go now,' he said, glancing back at her. 'It's OK. You will be there soon.'

'Where? Where is it?' she demanded.

'It is no place,' he said. 'It's just a road… a track… in the country. I have… what… numbers?'

'Coordinates?'

'Yes.'

'Show me!'

He sighed and handed the phone back to her. She entered the coordinates into her map app and saw that he was right. It *was* the middle of nowhere. Not something that sat well with her *at all*.

'Look… what's your name?' she asked.

'Yiannis,' he answered, with a watery smile. It was clear he was regretting picking up this fare.

'OK, Yiannis... I'd like to get out before we get there. I want to walk some of the way, OK? Can you take me close to it but not actually to the exact coordinates?'

'Sure, no problem,' he said.

'When we're a couple of minutes away from it... OK?' she said. 'This person I'm meeting... I'd like to see who they are before I show myself, do you understand?'

He nodded. 'Yes.'

'And... I'd like you to park up and wait for me, OK? Can you do that?'

He didn't look happy. He clearly wished to be moving on with his day just as soon as he'd dropped off this awkward customer.

'I will pay,' she said. 'Double your usual rate. For all the time you're waiting. OK?'

'OK,' he said, unhappily.

Silence reigned for a few minutes as they travelled narrow lanes and moved further inland, pausing several times to allow tractors or farm trucks to pass them. The day was getting hot and Kate realised it was well past noon. Going by the soupy breeze blowing in through her open window, she knew she would miss the aircon in the Merc as soon as she stepped outside. At any other time she would have been charmed by the vistas of olive groves, vineyards and kumquat orchards patterning the hills and valleys on this picturesque island. But all she could focus on was a meeting up ahead, with someone who might or might not be Lucas Henry. Someone who might or might not have dark plans for her.

She glanced at her phone, weighing up a call to Kapoor. But what could he really do for her, here and now? Ignoring the five text messages now blinking on her home screen she shoved it deep into her pocket.

'We stop here,' said the driver, pulling onto a dusty verge at the side of what was now little more than a farm track.

'Thanks,' said Kate, getting out. She leaned back in and pressed a fifty euro note into his hand. 'Stay and wait for me, please,' she said, giving him her most winning smile. He nodded, switching off his engine.

Kate stood and surveyed the dusty track. She was deep in the most rural part of the island — and clueless. How could she hide herself and get the advantage of her opponent if she had no idea what they looked like or where they were? Creeping up on them would be a grand plan if it weren't for these small details.

'Fuck it,' she muttered, and set off along the verge, tall hedgerows blocking much of her view on either side. She pulled out her phone again and stared at the location on her map app, her own position signalled by a red arrow as she converted it to walking directions. She was five minutes from her destination, but as far as she could fathom there was no way of coming at it under cover. She couldn't hack her way through these bloody hedgerows, could she? Where was her opponent?

Kate stopped, the Mercedes now out of sight behind her. She dug into the zip-up inner pocket of her satchel and closed her hand around the cool chain and bottle glass pendulum. Well... it was as good an idea as any, right now. She stood as still as she could, bracing her elbows against her chest to create a steady crane for Sid to dangle from. She allowed him to come to a rest, as still as he could be while she still had to breathe. She remembered Lucas telling her that rods were better for a walking dowse, but she didn't have rods. She had Sid.

'Sid,' she said. 'Is the person I am looking for within five minutes' walk of here? Circle for yes. Rock for no.'

She watched as Sid began to circle. 'Is there a way to get closer without being seen?'

Sid rocked. *Shit.*

'Am I in danger?'

Sid circled.

'You're not really building my confidence up here, Sid,' she said. There was nothing else for it. She just had to keep walking.

The hedgerow thinned out and revealed some wire fencing which ran along some overgrown and neglected looking land. A pile of rusting farm machinery rose high enough to be seen above the snaking weeds which engulfed much of the wire fence. Glancing at her phone, Kate saw her red arrow converge with the dot of her destination. She was here.

There was nothing to see. Just the junk — a tangle of dull red struts, dented chassis and skinny wheels — a couple of trees and a sloping meadow, with wildflowers and patches of weedy thicket growing to waist height. She could hear nothing but the breeze in the trees and the buzz of insects, interspersed with the occasional whine of mosquitoes. She rummaged in her bag, brought out a can of repellent and liberally sprayed her bare arms, legs, neck and — eyes screwed up — her face. The smell was acrid. She wafted it away and approached the wire fence. She could get over it. Hide among the weeds, maybe, while she waited for another car to pull up and spill out her mystery date.

She slung the satchel over first and then followed it, wobbling erratically on the thin lines of wire, and then landing with a thump on the other side. Sid, his chain now over her neck, seemed to vibrate a little within her sweaty cleavage. Oh nonsense. He was a *bit of glass.*

'Come on, then,' Kate called out, spinning slowly around, in case this person was already here, watching her. 'I'm here. Out you come.'

Nothing. OK. So maybe she was the first on the scene. She might as well get the lie of the land. She wandered around the biggest of the trees — a cypress, she guessed — noting that she could probably get up into it and wait there with a decent view below and around her. Yes. She could do that. She grabbed hold of a lower branch and clambered up into it. From here she could see further down the road in both directions, but nothing was approaching. The Merc wasn't visible. Of course, Yiannis might well have just turned around and buggered off with his fifty euro note. She wouldn't be surprised.

Kate scanned the farmland and felt a slight sense of deja vu as she spotted a perfect circle in it. *Shit.* Not a crop circle, this time, but a round rust-red plate amid the dust and weeds close to the farm junk. At least there wasn't a body in white lying in the middle of it. She felt that sense of vibration again, down by her heart. And it wasn't just nerves. Surely. It was coming from Sid. Or from her own fevered head. Maybe both. Kate glanced around again. She felt safer up here, able to scan what was going on below... but that metal circle on the farmland...

'Everything you do in this world is *part* of a circle.' Rafe Campion's voice went through her mind, as if he was sitting on the neighbouring branch, offering up a little live commentary. 'Fuck off, Rafe,' she muttered. 'I'll get to you soon enough, you smarmy shit.'

And then she was down again, and walking towards it. It was the covering to some kind of pit... an underground silo or something. It was too big to be a well or a drain. As she got closer she could feel the heat radiating from the aged iron, which was hinged on two sides and designed to open up in two semi-circular parts. She slowed down, suddenly scared. *Really* scared. This was like one of her nightmares... those dreams where she was approaching something horrible... like the quarry her sister had been taken from, or the cellar where women had been strung up like dolls and starved to death... or the collapsing concrete bunker that had nearly crushed her.

In those dreams she knew something awful lay ahead and yet she could never stop herself walking straight towards it. Opening it up. Inviting the horror to engulf her.

Kate heard another mosquito whine past. She took hold of the drop ring on the straight edge of one of the iron trap doors, and hauled it up. It was heavy and awkward, and the ring slipped through her sweaty fingers twice before she could drag the cover perpendicular. Beneath it lay a dark stillness.

She let the half-moon of metal drop open to the ground side and stared down into the cavern below.

She had been wrong about the body in the circle. There *was* a body here. A dead man lay in the pit below her.

Her knees gave way as she realised it was Lucas Henry.

31

'**E**verything has its own frequency. Its own pattern. Earth, air, fire, water... metal, rock, animals, water, trees...'

'Oh for god's sake, Jan, do you know how happy-clappy-hippy you sound? Could you BE more tie dye and lentil bake?!'

Lucas looked from his aunt to his mother and back again. This was the fourth visit to Aunty Janine's where she'd got out the pendulum and played the Find Me game with him. He looked forward to it more and more, even though Mum was scathing and dismissive whenever it was mentioned. In fact, back at home he'd learned not to mention it at all.

He knew he should defer to his mother first... not his aunt, with her hippy, tie-dye, lentil bake ways... but he understood Aunty Janine and was certain she understood him. Mum didn't understand him at all. She told him so often enough.

'You're putting all kinds of daft ideas into his head,' Mum went on, taking another drag from her cigarette as she lay back in the sun lounger in her sister's garden. On the fold-out table next to her, the glass of wine was already empty and Janine would *have to drive them home, because it was the fourth glass his mother had drained. She'd brought the bottle herself.*

'These ideas aren't daft,' argued Janine. 'Dowsing is an ancient art and a very useful tool. My pendulums and rods have helped me make many decisions and they've never steered me wrong.'

Mum snorted. 'They're just trinkets. You're having a conversation with your own brain, that's all. And making your own decisions.'

'You're not far off,' Janine said. 'The pendulums and rods ARE only tools... but they help me to access a part of the mind that most people never use. They can help you, too, Lucas,' she said, turning back to him. 'Now... there's something buried in the garden. Find me.... a metal thing.'

And, doing his best to ignore Mum's rolling eyes and aggressive stubbing out of the last inch of ciggie, he set out with Aunty Janine's hazel twigs resting loosely in his fingers. He didn't overthink it, just as she'd advised, but let his mind float around the idea of the metal in the garden... it was long and thin... it was buried... close to brick...

A minute later he was on his knees, twigs laid down, digging into the soft earth of the flower bed that ran along the base of the red brick wall. He pushed aside gangly flowers of blue, surrounded with a kind of green spiky lace, which Aunty Janine called Love In The Mist, and plunged his fingers deep into the soil. And deeper. And deeper, ignoring the scrapes and scratches of stones. He became aware of his aunt standing over him, watching in silence as he unearthed a key with a long shaft and a curly design at the turning end.

'Lucas... you are something quite extraordinary,' she said, touching his head with proud fingers.

'His fingers are bleeding,' pointed out Mum, standing next to her. 'If he gets tetanus it'll be your fault!'

Lucas drove his fingers deep into the soil and worked at the metal thing. It wasn't a key. It was just a bit of iron... a nail perhaps... something thrown away long ago, but well preserved in the soil. Like the ancient coins on Alberto's boundary but more valuable to him right now than any gold. His fingers were bleeding again, from the hours of digging, one-handed. He couldn't remember the last time he'd had a tetanus booster but that was the least of his problems. He *had* to get out of here.

He was sweating heavily, which was not good. He'd finished the last of the water she'd left him hours ago and could ill afford any further dehydration as the warmth of the day began to permeate into the pit. The sliver of light shafting in from the crack between the trap door panels cut the floor in two and threw the rest of it into deeper shadow. He was working blind... but he could sense the shape and the depth of the long, bent nail with surprising clarity, given the poor shape he was in. Desperation sharpened the mind, he guessed.

He had dug down far enough that he could feel just a bit of give around the base of the nail. He worked at it with his sore fingers... converting the give to a shift and then the shift to a tilt and then... one... more... tug... yesss! It came away. He squeezed it weakly in his fist and lay back to rest, chuckling drily at his small success. The nail was too thick to pick the lock of the cuff, even if he knew how to do that. But it might be strong enough to lever apart one of the metal links on the connecting chain. And it still had a point.

After some time on his back, recovering from his exertions, he dragged himself up into a sitting position and, ignoring the searing sting around his cuffed wrist — now raw and bleeding after so long in the metal bracelet — began to work at the chain. He had to feel his way and brace the short length of metal links against the rung, pulling it taut while levering the nail through it. His senses told him the link could be broken. The cuffs, while strong, were not police issue. They weren't fur-lined and flimsy either, but they *could* be broken if he just stayed focused long enough.

It was impossible to know how long he worked at it. Twice he gave up and slumped into a dreamless doze before forcing himself awake and back to the task. When the link finally gave he dropped to the floor, dazed and spent. His head raged with pain and the laser thin light dissecting the pit cut across his left eye, dazzling him. He knew he had to get up and get out of there... right now, before she came back. Because she was coming back soon... he could sense a female presence getting closer.

His problem, though, was that his battery was flatlining. He stared up at the heavy metal doors and tried to convince himself that he could stand up, climb the rungs and, with one hand clinging on, use the other to shove the iron lid up and over and escape. Even if he hadn't been half-starved and dehydrated to the threshold of stroke, it would have been bloody hard. The trap doors were designed to be opened from above, not below. It was going to take every last shred of willpower to overcome the terrible weakness now assailing him.

Right. Time to get up and escape. A surge of adrenaline got him up onto his elbows and then a wave of nausea and a belt of pain through his head felled him again and he slumped back down. Shit. Was this it..? Was his life really about to end in a pit in an abandoned corner of a farm on Corfu? Would she even bother to hide his body once she found him dead? Probably not. Why bother? His decaying remains might lie here for months... years... Who would come looking for him? His aunt, who had genuinely loved him, was dead. His mother, who barely cared about him, was in Spain with her new man and hadn't even sent him a birthday card in three years.

Mariam, like every other friend or lover he had known, understood that he was a drifter. It could take *years* for her to wonder what had happened to Lucas Henry... that guy who used to paint... and find bodies...

Which left only Kate. Who was seeking him in anger and revenge.

Lucas pictured Kate, shoving aside the last few seconds he'd seen her and remembering instead the time shortly before when they'd stood on a hillside, in a riptide of conflicting emotions, close enough to touch, close enough to kiss... He realised tears were leaking from his eyes. They might be the last water he could spare...

And then the lid was lifted and sunlight flooded in and that familiar female silhouette looked down on him. A surge of fury smashed through him as she leapt into the pit and, dredging up one final belt of energy, he launched himself across at the bitch and stabbed her in the throat with the nail.

———

KATE SCREAMED in shock and relief as Lucas rose from the dead in a split second and launched an attack on her. How it was possible to feel both shock *and* relief, whilst being mortally attacked, was something she would have to revisit later. Right now she reacted on instinct, blocking his fist and the glint of metal in it as it drove towards her throat.

The nail pierced her skin... but it was the skin on the side of her bunched right fist that took the puncture and then her attacker was knocked back again, gasping and moaning 'You *bitch!* Get off me, you fucking *bitch!*' His eyes weren't focused and the pupils were pinhead small.

'LUCAS!' Kate threw aside the bent nail he'd come at her with and leaned over him, appalled. He was thin and dirty and dishevelled, and a cuff with a trailing broken chain hung from his left wrist, which was rubbed raw and bleeding. 'LUCAS! Look at me! It's me — KATE!'

He babbled something incoherent and tried to get up again. She pushed him into a sitting position against the pit, which was hot and stinking. 'Jesus Christ, Lucas! Who did this to you?' She touched his face, appalled.

'Coming back,' he rasped. 'She's coming back... get away...'

Kate dug into her bag, pulled out her flask of water and, undoing the lid, held it to his lips. He put a shaking hand to the flask and she steadied it with her own, acutely aware of her fingers touching his even here, even now. 'Steady,' she said as he gulped. 'Easy does it.'

She pulled the flask away and his eyes rested on hers, some recognition now in them.

'Lucas,' she said. '*Who* is coming back?'

'The murderer,' he said.

Kate gulped. 'The murderer... you mean... the one who killed Zoe? And Mabel..?'

'Got to get away,' he said. 'Before she comes back.'

'Too late.... she's baa-aack!'

Kate spun around at the sound of a light, teasing, female voice. A woman, carrying a can, stared down at them both. The sun was behind her, so her features were in shadow, but something about the voice rang a bell with Kate. Maybe she was losing her mind alongside Lucas because it sounded weirdly like her late mother.

Kate pulled out her warrant card and waved it. 'Police. Stand back!'

'Oh my! You are *so* commanding, DI Sparrow!' laughed the woman.

'I said, stand *back,*' snapped Kate, a burst of hot fury driving her to her feet. *This* was the person behind all the cipher crap and mystery packages.

The woman just laughed again and then splashed something from the can. It hit the compacted earth floor in front of Kate and gave off an instant, acrid stink. It was petrol.

'What the hell?' Kate made for the rungs, reaching down to drag Lucas up with her.

'Oh no no no,' sang out the woman, kneeling above them, still in silhouette. A little burst of flame leapt from her hand as she slopped more fuel out of the can and across the pit. It splashed coldly against Kate's bare legs. 'This is the kind of lighter that burns on when you drop it. Ever heard a pig go *woof?!*'

Kate froze while Lucas struggled up next to her, panting hard. 'What do you want?' Kate asked, marshalling her panic and clicking into DI mode. She sounded calm. Professional.

'A little time to talk,' said the woman. 'First — hand me your bag. Just in case you're carrying.'

Kate silently threw the satchel up to the woman, who caught it, tossed it aside and then sat down, cross-legged, emptying more fuel into the pit, still holding the flame aloft. 'I won't set you both on fire,' she said. 'As long as you do as you're told. Relax, Kate. Take it easy. We've got so much to catch up on.'

'Who the hell are you?' said Kate, the hair prickling on the back of her neck while the petrol vapours tickled her nose and throat. Her heart was pounding but she was determined that it wouldn't affect her voice.

'Don't you recognise me?' asked the woman. She took off her cotton sun hat, revealing long blonde hair in bunches and an arrogant smirk.

Kate felt Lucas grab her hand and squeeze it.

'I'm sorry,' he said. 'I cocked up. Thought I could handle it on my own and bring her back. I never meant to get you caught up in this. Shit... I'm so sorry, Kate.'

Kate glanced at him, baffled, and then back at their captor. 'You're the woman in the news, aren't you? The one wanted for killing two police officers! You've dyed your hair but I can see it's you.'

'Bravo!' The woman clapped her hands. 'What amazing powers of deduction you have! I'm *the woman in the news!*'

That voice. THAT VOICE.

Kate found herself turning to look at Lucas. He seemed revived, probably thanks to the water — and the threat of being burnt alive at any moment. He also seemed... desolate... He reached out his good hand, nails caked with dirt, and cupped the side of her face. 'Kate...' he said. 'Oh Kate... I'm so sorry. It would have been better if you'd been right. If *I'd* killed her.'

It was his welling eyes and the raw compassion in his voice that finally gave her the answer.

Kate turned back and stared up into the face of her sister.

32

I f anyone had turned her into a killer, it was Lucas Henry. If she hadn't watched him kissing Zoe, Mabel might never have reached the boiling point necessary for a true-blue psychopath to be born.

Of course, she realised now, nearly seventeen years later, that psychopathy was pretty much in the DNA. It was rarely a question of nurture — nearly always nature. After all, there was nothing terrible about her life. No abuse or neglect. Even her father had had the good grace to be absent for most of her early years — working away — until he died when she was seven. She barely remembered him. And her mother, widowed while pregnant with her third child, had done a first-class job of single parenthood. Honestly, Mabel had nothing to complain of.

Apart from boredom. Oh god, but she was bored. Living that small town existence almost crushed her to death. For as far back as she could remember she had known she was extraordinary — set apart from others. At school she was clever and pretty and got plenty of attention, but absolutely hated having to kowtow to the teachers, especially the stupid and ugly ones, and there were plenty of those. She couldn't wait to get away. She thought she might be an actress. Modelling was too dull, although she'd had offers. With her late father's Swedish colouring and her own sense of style, she turned heads. Her mother said little Kate was just as pretty, but it was obvious that her sister was a very humdrum, everyday kind of pretty. And so *fucking annoying*. Endlessly sweet and nice and correct. Even killing three of her hamsters in a row didn't wipe the stupid Pollyanna grin off her face for long.

And the little brother? Jesus! What a whiner. There were times when she'd seriously considered taking him for a walk to the lake and 'losing' him in it.

Yeah. All the signs had been there. She knew this now. But even so, she might have held it all in; become a common-or-garden kind of psychopath instead. The kind that ends up running a massive conglomerate or getting to high office in politics, largely because they just don't give a shit about the people it's necessary to tread on to get there.

Killing Zoe hadn't exactly been planned. She'd thought about it, true, but until the day it happened, she hadn't really believed it *would* happen. Until she actually saw Zoe with Lucas, running her fingers through his hair, sticking her tongue in his mouth. That had triggered absolute RAGE inside her. She had — only that day — suggested that Zoe *could* do this with Lucas, and more. As long as it was a three-way thing. Mabel was fascinated by sex and frustrated that Lucas was so crap at it. But maybe he'd up his game if he had *both* of them at once. And she could find out what it felt like to kiss a girl too. And do other stuff. With Lucas watching.

But when she'd outlined this to her two so-called best friends it was like she'd suggested shooting a puppy in the head. They had stormed off and left her alone. Furious, she had followed them both and, lurking by a hedge, had watched the sweet little love scene between them on Lucas's doorstep.

So... she had texted Zoe and apologised. Said they should talk it through. They met up on the edge of the plains and then walked down to the quarry. Zoe could have saved herself. She could have been nicer. Maybe even admitted to the kiss on the doorstep and said she was up for a three-way after all. It could have been very different, but instead she was snotty and uptight and ready to abandon their lifelong friendship over a *boy*.

So Mabel checked there was nobody else about and then smashed Zoe's head in with a rock.

———

KATE STAGGERED BACK against Lucas and felt him wrap his arms around her, steadying her from behind. Her sister's cold, amused monologue was far, far worse than anything which had haunted her nightmares.

'You... *you* killed Zoe?' she whispered.

'Yes, I did,' said Mabel, nodding slowly. 'It was fascinating to watch her crumple onto the ground and bleed out. I watched her face very closely, trying to see that moment when they say the spirit leaves the body. I knew she was dying — there was a fucking great chunk of her skull missing and you could actually see the brain. So... I looked into her eyes... but it was disappointing in the end. No last words. Just burbling, really. No death rattle. No rapture. After a couple of minutes her eyes went fixed and dull and that was it. All over with. A bit like your hamsters, really, after I sprayed aerosol glue into their cages until they suffocated.'

Kate gulped, fearing she was going to throw up.

'You never did ask what the funny smell was,' Mabel laughed. 'God, so *thick*!'

'Your mother knew, though, didn't she?' said Lucas, his words rumbling through his chest, into her shoulders. Kate realised she was leaning her back against him, literally using him as her support.

'She guessed I was a little... different,' admitted Mabel. 'She took me to the doctor after the hamsters. I was referred to a psychotherapist. They did tests to check my brain, but I aced them all and really charmed that letchy old shrink, so nothing came of it.'

Kate suddenly felt a thud of awful realisation. 'She... she knew about you? About Zoe?!'

Mabel clapped her hands again, blinking the brown eyes which were, she had explained, contact lenses to throw any passing police off the scent. 'You're so on it, little sis! Yeah — Mum was brilliant. I ran, after I'd buried Zoe. I thought I might just hitch rides and travel the world until I made my fortune. And I did for a while. I had quite a fun time across the UK for a few weeks, travelling in disguise, picking up men and getting them to pay my way in return for sex. But then I realised I was *properly* screwed because I wanted to travel the world and I had no passport... so I had to call Mum.'

'And... she helped you...' Kate said, feeling faint as seventeen years of her life flew around like playing cards scattered to the wind. She was going to have to re-order everything in her world. It was already starting to make sense; the way her mother, after a few weeks, had suddenly seemed to click into another gear and move on from the loss of her daughter. The way she had firmly killed all hope and insisted that Kate and Francis must move on, too. The "gap year" money mentioned by the solicitor and the regular payments to a numbered account. It was all to support the daughter she could never risk revealing as alive and well. Because Mum had *known* what Mabel had done. Kate felt her knees giving way and Lucas's arms tightening around her.

'Don't give Mum a hard time,' Mabel went on. 'She didn't know the half of it. I told her we'd had a fight and Zoe had fallen and it was an accident. I said I couldn't come back because nobody would ever believe me after I'd run away. I made her promise to keep me dead and gone so you and Francis would never be dragged into the mess I'd made. All I needed was a bit of money and maybe some help getting out of the country.'

'And she did that,' said Kate, dully. 'She got you out.'

'She had some helpful contacts through her job,' said Mabel. 'Social workers meet some useful people; some helpful lowlife... I got a new passport. First of many. And regular money I could pick up in Switzerland. And a nice lump sum when she died. Sorry about that, by the way. You must miss her.'

'And you?' said Kate, watching her sister closely for any sign of sadness.

Mabel shrugged. 'It was a shame,' she said. 'But... when you've got to go, you've got to go. And maybe she was smarter than she let on. Maybe she knew I was... what I am. Mother's instinct and all that. That can't have helped. But she must have loved me a lot. She even buried my bra and pants and some blood and DNA at Pepperbox Hill for me, in case we ever needed to convince the police. She was a diamond!' She flicked the flame thoughtfully. 'And I made the most of my inheritance. Climbed the social ladder with it and got myself a rich, fat husband. Shame about the drowning...' She smirked.

Kate took a breath. 'Mabel... why tell me this? Why now? And why do what you did to Lucas? What is that... revenge?'

'Look, little sis, Lucas came for *me!* I didn't invite him.'

'Didn't you?' grunted Lucas. 'What about the phone calls?'

'Oh my god — yes — I *did* call you, didn't I?' she giggled. 'In the middle of the night. Oh, you're so sexy when you're freaked out!'

Kate felt a flicker of rage amid the sick horror.

'I was just bored,' Mabel said. 'Did I tell you I get bored? Really quickly. I saw you both all over the news and I was *fascinated.* I wanted to find out more. But even so, all I did was look you both up online and then make a few calls in the night to Lucas. *You* did all the rest, Lucas, coming for me with your little pendulum buddy. And once you got here and made me jump you and imprison you, I thought, well, in for a penny — in for a pound. Might as well get Kate to the party, too. I mean, you always did want to be included, didn't you, Katie? Always *whining* to be taken along with the big kids.'

'You're having the time of your life,' stated Kate, shaking her head in appalled wonder.

Mabel smiled down at her in a way that made her blood run cold even in the heat of the afternoon sun. 'You know what? I *am!* The most frustrating thing about being a successful murderer is that you're really not meant to ever tell anyone about it. Which is a shame because, oh, the stories I could tell you!'

'Like how you pushed those detectives off a cliff?' Kate asked.

'Oh — yes. Well, that wasn't very exciting, really. Just barged them through the railings before they knew what had happened. Means to an end.' She shrugged. 'I may tell you more stories one day... now that we're back in touch.'

Kate raised her eyebrows. 'So you're not going to add *us* to your killing spree?'

Mabel stood and picked up the petrol can, beaming. 'Look... you're my sister. And you, Lucas, you're just too sexy to torch. Probably.' She held up the lighter with its flickering flame and tilted her head, thoughtfully. 'So... here's the way I see it. If you chase me and try to arrest me, Kate, what good is it going to do you? Imagine what's going to happen to you and Francis when this all comes out in the press? I mean... your career is going to tank isn't it? A police inspector with a banged-up psychopath for a sister? And what about Mum's reputation? Shot to pieces. Aiding and abetting a murderer. Perverting the course of justice. Would you do that to her memory, Kate? Would you? And imagine what Zoe's family will have to say to you when it all comes out...'

Kate felt winded. Dear god, the mind behind that pretty smile.

'If you just go home and forget to mention that you met anyone here except your bestest dowsing buddy, then you could even keep Francis happily in the dark, couldn't you?'

'But that will leave Lucas in the shit,' said Kate. 'The police would still be after him. I couldn't do anything about that if I didn't mention you.'

'It's a tricky one,' admitted Mabel, getting to her feet. 'What are you going to do? Who are you going to betray? Our mother and brother or Mr Pendulum here?'

Kate was silent. She could think of no answer.

'So... me and my petrol can are going to take a walk now,' said Mabel. 'And dribble our way back to the roadside.

I emptied another can all the way down here, too, by the way. Do you know how fast a flame can travel across a trail of petrol? It takes a second... maybe two. How long do you think it would take you and poor, knackered Lucas to clamber up out of that fire pit? So. Don't go anywhere. Stay put and stay calm. When I've been gone five minutes you can get out and return to your lives. If I see you move before then... WOOF! You *might* survive, but you'll be pretty crispy.'

Kate and Lucas said nothing.

'Oh and don't be *sad*,' said Mabel. 'Now that we've been reunited I know it'll tear you apart to lose me again. So... I might drop you a line once in a while. Ciao!'

She walked away, humming a tune. Kate stood motion-less, her mind beginning to buffer with all the horrific intel it had to process. She felt Lucas turn her around and press her head against his chest, and she let herself be pressed, breathing in his scent and taking from him the comfort she would have been repulsed by only a day ago. 'I'm sorry,' she mumbled, as he stroked her hair. 'I'm so, so sorry.'

33

Despite the danger they were in, Lucas felt his spirit stagger to its feet and then take flight as he held Kate Sparrow close against him.

'I'm sorry,' she sobbed. 'I'm so, so sorry...'

'It's OK,' he said, stroking her hair.

'It's not,' she said. 'I shouldn't have accused you. I should never have let myself be convinced you'd killed her. That you could kill *anyone*.'

'No... you shouldn't,' he acknowledged, 'but if I had managed it all a bit better, it would never have come to that scene at Pepperbox Hill. I don't know what the hell I was thinking of, taking you there alone and then leading you into the trees and digging up your long-lost sister's bra and knickers. What the hell would *anyone* think? I should have told you about the calls and the patterns I was picking up over a cup of coffee in Salisbury — and then taken you there with your police colleagues and directed the forensics guys. I know that now, but I think I was a bit too strung out at the time. So were you. We'd had a tough few days.'

She sniffed and looked up. 'So... you're saying we're both not guilty?' She gave him a watery smile.

'We're both fucking idiots,' he said, grinning back at her. 'After all, we're standing in a barbecue pit, possibly about to die in flames.'

He heard the buzzing sound he now recognised and let out a sigh of relief. That was Mabel heading away on a moped. 'She's gone,' he said. 'Let's get out of here.'

Kate had to help him up the rungs, he was still so weak. At the top she grabbed her satchel, led him away into safe, clean grass, and pulled out a bar of chocolate. 'Eat,' she said.

He stuffed the bar in his mouth, sending spasms of sugar-induced pain through the glands under his tongue. The intense sweetness boosted him in seconds. He held out his wrist with its cuff and dangling chain. 'Any chance you can do your lock-picking trick?'

She nodded and pulled a skinny bit of metal from another part of her satchel, working at the lock for several seconds before clicking it open.

'Have you ever considered a career in safe-breaking?' he asked.

'Come on,' she said, instinctively depositing the handcuff in a plastic bag and dropping that into her satchel. 'We've got to get you to a hospital. You need that wrist sorting out and you should probably be on a drip for a day or two. Christ... I can't believe she did that to you. My sister...'

'I told you,' said Lucas. 'You might look similar but you're nothing like her. Hang on...' He walked stiffly over to the heap of junk, dug under a bent wheel, and retrieved his rucksack. Everything except his watercolour pad was still in it.

They reached the fence and it took some doing,

climbing back over it, but the sugar hit helped and soon they were walking back down the dusty road, Kate offering her shoulder for support, and her arm around his waist. He had no idea what direction they were going but Kate seemed to have some plan.

'Well, bloody hell!' she said, four or five minutes later. 'He waited. He actually *waited.*'

And there at the roadside was a silver Mercedes with taxi plates and an anxious looking local driver getting out of it.

'Yiannos!' Kate called. 'You bloody hero! Thank you so much for waiting!'

Yiannos nodded back at them. He looked up and down the road and then at the mobile phone he was holding. His anxiety sent spiky frequencies through the hot air. 'Kate,' said Lucas. 'Something's not right here.'

'Do you think *anything's* been right today?' she said.

There was a whoop of a siren and a Corfu police patrol car was suddenly belting up the track towards them. Lucas flinched out of pure habit — he had been expecting arrest at any moment for weeks and weeks. Another siren carolled up the hill from the other direction and thirty seconds later they were blocked in.

'It's OK,' said Kate, reaching for her ID. 'It was just a matter of time.'

But she couldn't find her ID and now there was no time because the taxi driver had dived back inside his Merc and slammed the door and firearms officers were out on the road and aiming at them both, shouting something in Greek which could only have been '*Get your hands up in the air and freeze!*'

'Oh bugger,' said Kate.

THE DARK FURY in the officers was palpable as they aimed their guns at her. And although Lucas wasn't outside the crosshairs, she realised it was very much *her* they were aiming at. And she knew why. While her treacherous sister had cleverly changed her appearance with hair dye, fake moles and brown contact lenses, Kate had been skipping around the island looking very much like a woman who had murdered two cops. If they had factored in a change of hair colour... and that wasn't a stretch... they would have only facial features and eye colour to go by. She realised now that the face on the front of this morning's newspaper had seemed familiar to her mainly because it *looked like her*.

She held her hands up high. 'Do exactly as I say, Lucas,' she said, under her breath. 'Hold up your hands and make some distance between us. Slowly. Do not get close to me.'

Lucas glanced across at her, hands already rising. 'Why?'

'Because they think they're arresting a cop killer. They won't mind at all if someone shoots me dead — DON'T move closer! Stay cool and we'll both get out of this.'

'Where's your warrant card?' he hissed.

'Probably still in the pit. Think I dropped it around the time I realised my sister was alive. And a murdering psychobitch.'

The armed officers were getting closer and they did not look friendly.

'Christina Eliades!' one of them called out.

'NO!' she called out, clearly but not aggressively, her hands over her head. 'I am NOT Christina. I am Detective Inspector Kate Sparrow of the British police. I am unarmed.'

Lucas translated into Greek in real time, just in case any

of the officers didn't understand English. That man never stopped surprising her.

'Tell them to look for my ID in the pit,' she said. 'Just in case it helps.'

But before Lucas could say anything else they were both slammed to the floor, their hands behind their backs, cuffs snapping shut, Lucas gasping in pain as his raw wrist wound was shoved roughly back into metal bondage. 'It'll be OK,' she said, struggling to turn her face towards him. 'Lucas, I promise you... it'll be OK.'

34

OK was a relative term. Kate wasn't sure she would ever be OK again. It took the rest of the day to convince the Greek police that she wasn't Christina Eliades. It didn't help that her DNA was a partial match for what had been found on the broken bodies of the dead detectives. It was hard to explain that the woman who had coldly murdered two of her European colleagues was in fact her sister, born Mabel Johanssen and missing, presumed dead, for nearly seventeen years.

It was going to be harder still to return to England and tell Francis and Kapoor and Michaels and Sally next door and Zoe's devastated family and... god, how many people would she have to pour this poison onto?

The only bright spot in all of this was that Lucas was vindicated at last. Although, until they caught and convicted Mabel, would he ever truly be off the hook? She could see already the way the press might twist the tale... that she had fallen for the prime suspect accused of killing her sister and had hatched a story to convince the world he was innocent.

Shit. There would be no option but to open up her late

mother's financial history to the investigation. It was crucial evidence. There might even be, somewhere, some CCTV evidence of Mabel entering a bank to access her money. Except, given it was a secure numbered account in a Swiss Bank, the odds were there would be nothing at all. Wasn't that the *point* of numbered accounts? Anonymity?

'Your boss has come through for you,' said the SIO who went by the name of Karras, coming into the interview room where she was slumped, exhausted, in her seat, resting her head and arms on the table. 'You are booked onto a flight first thing tomorrow, to return to England. So is Mr Henry. Your colleagues want to talk to him on his return about outstanding offences.'

She nodded. She guessed Lucas would have to go through the process like anyone else who'd absconded while under arrest.

'But we will be expecting your help in the coming weeks,' Karras went on. 'You will need to make yourself available for further interviews via livestream and possibly come back here for court hearings, once we apprehend your sister.'

'Of course,' she said. She looked at the man, levelly. 'I want you to catch her,' she said. 'She's my sister but she's done terrible things. To a lot of people. She needs to answer for it. I will do all I can to help you.'

'Good,' said Karras, nodding his head slowly. 'I knew Ben Adamos, one of the detectives she murdered. He was a good man... he had a ten-year-old son.' He gulped and sniffed hard and Kate felt familial shame steal across her. She knew it wouldn't be the last time she felt it.

There was another two-hour session of statement making. It was complicated and they brought in a female officer called Maria Hatzis, who was the most fluent in

English and about Kate's age. Maria brought English Breakfast tea and biscuits and made sure her witness had the time
and space to tell everything she knew. She understood that
this story went back a long, long way, to a girl of ten who
had lost her sister and, in truth, half of her mother. Kate
cried at times, brusquely wiping away the tears and pressing
on. Hatzis patted her hand and said: 'I would cry, too. I
would cry like I was broken. Take your time. Let it out.'

She was released around nine in the evening and found
Lucas waiting for her on the steps of the Corfu Town police
station. His wrist was bandaged and he looked better than
the last time she'd seen him. He wordlessly took her hand
and they walked towards the waterfront.

'I left my hire car on a coast road somewhere in Limni,'
she said. 'I gave the key to the Corfu police. They're going to
send someone to pick it up and deliver it back to the rental
place. My hotel is only a short walk from here. You're going
to have to come with me... Kapoor sent an order. You're in
my custody until we get back to the UK where you can hand
yourself in for evading arrest, absconding from the country
without a valid passport and generally embarrassing and
pissing off most of Wiltshire Police.'

'Do you need to cuff me to you?' he said. 'Because can I
ask you to use the right wrist?'

She laughed and shook her head. 'This time last week I
was ready to lock you up for life. Jeezuz. Who knew, just a
few days later, we'd be strolling through Corfu, chatting like
mates?'

'Mates, are we?'

The silence between them was heavy. They both quick-
ened their pace towards the hotel, passing holidaymakers
spilling out of tavernas, the scent of the sea carrying up from
the shore on the warm evening air. In the distance, through

a green park, the town's Venetian fort could be seen, uplit as summer dusk turned the blue sky to orange and peach on the horizon.

'No,' said Lucas.

'No what?'

'Can't wait,' he said, and pulled her into the shadow of a eucalyptus tree, pressing her against its smooth trunk and finding her mouth with his. She had little time to process the shock before the desire took over and her arms were snaking around his neck, her fingers finding his hair and the warmth of his skin. She felt a thrilling surge of long-delayed pleasure as he pressed against her, his heart thudding at the same quick pace as her own.

At length he broke off to beam widely at her and mutter 'I think there's something of mine in here,' before slipping his fingers down her top. She was taken aback for a moment, staring up at him, open-mouthed and laughing at his audacity. He *was* right... anything down her top pretty much *was* his now — there wasn't much point in arguing with that. He didn't need to be a world-class dowser to read the patterns from *her* right now.

Lucas tugged Sid from her cleavage, one eyebrow raised. 'I didn't know we had a threesome going on.'

She pulled the chain over her head. 'He's back where he belongs, now,' she said, looping Sid around Lucas's neck.

Lucas froze. His eyes seemed to cloud. He suddenly turned away, scanning left and right and then stared back at her. 'She's here,' he breathed. 'She's *right here*!'

Kate felt a jolt. She went to move into the street but he held her back in the shadow. 'Ssshhh. She doesn't know *we're* here. Wait. Watch.'

Kate stared at the people wandering past — most of them young, slightly drunk tourists, some older locals on a late shopping mission or heading for home, three women in dark clothing and headscarves, two of them stooped and elderly — Greek orthodox nuns, perhaps — a couple sharing the same moped, helmets obscuring their faces.

'Where is she?' Kate whispered, her pulse, already pounding, picking up faster still. The figure on the back of the moped glanced around for a moment, a lock of fair hair blowing back as the bike buzzed on past. 'Shit! That's her!' Kate took to her feet and ran along in the wake of the moped, committing the number plate to memory. The surge of fury that drove her on was so intense it almost stopped her breathing, but she mastered it, put it to use and picked up speed. The moped couldn't go too fast, here in the centre of town where pedestrians freely wandered the roads and precincts — it could only weave through them. She might be able to catch it if she ran fast enough and she *could* run. She had run marathons. Nothing was going to stop her.

A hand grabbed her shoulder and spun her around. Lucas stared into her face, panting. 'STOP! That's not her!'

'But I saw her!' Kate yelled, turning back and trying to race on.

'NO... you... didn't!' He held her fast by the arm, slowing her steps. When she looked back at him she saw how tired he still was — bruised, bandaged and exhausted — and felt a stab of guilt. 'It's not her,' he said. 'Do you trust me?'

She nodded slowly, breathing hard and wiping her brow as he led her down a side street, clutching Sid in one fist. Ahead she saw three dark figures... the women in black clothing and headscarves. *No! Seriously?*

'Are you sure?' she hissed. 'I mean... god... dressing up as a nun. That's a bit James Bond, isn't it?'

'And you think Mabel doesn't know that?' he said. 'Isn't it just her style?'

He was right. As the three women approached a T junction in the paths ahead, Kate saw one of them peel away from the other two with no comment or wave. She realised then that the two older women had been largely unaware of their shadow, caught up in conversation as they were. The person following them had been using their slipstream to hide in; pretending to be part of a group.

Could that really be Mabel? She was carrying a black shoulder bag and keeping her head well down. But as her foot kicked up the back of the long black skirt, Kate saw a flash of silver sandal. She noted the signpost ahead of them as the lane wound around towards the sea. 'She's heading for the marina,' she said. 'She's going to get a boat away from here... and show up in Italy or Greece with some new identity. Fuck this! That's not happening! Lucas — call the police — tell them our location.'

'I haven't got a phone,' he said. She flung her mobile at him, chanting the unlock code, and then took off, ignoring his plea to wait and let the police take care of this. She felt bad that she had to abandon him. He was too knackered and she knew his knee injury would slow them down if he came, too. And anyway, this was *her* sister. She had to take responsibility before the bitch got away and murdered someone else.

She pounded along the streets, weaving in and out of tourists as cleanly as she could, hoping not to create a stir which would cause her quarry to turn around and realise she was being chased down. But it seemed Mabel had a sixth sense for she was definitely speeding up, even though she hadn't glanced back once. Kate cut across a stretch of turf as Mabel took a turn into the park area, still heading for the marina. There were fewer people around here — most of them now in the town for the evening's food and drink sessions. Good. Easier to keep tabs on that shadowy figure now disappearing beyond some kind of monument — a limestone rotunda with Corinthian pillars, surrounded by a wrought iron fence.

Kate sprinted for it, wishing she had some kind of weapon in the satchel banging on her hip. While her black-belt in Taekwondo gave her confidence, she'd prefer to keep her sister at a distance, ideally at gunpoint, until Lucas brought in the cavalry. Mabel was too snaky, too oily and unpredictable. Kate also feared that some latent sisterly weakness might pull her punches and soften her kicks. She'd had only hours, after all, to process loss and love into betrayal and bitterness. It was going to be hard to attack Mabel in the way she would attack any other cold-blooded killer. Even Mabel had been affected by the sibling connection... she hadn't murdered her little sister when she easily could have.

Kate ran through an opening in the ring of railings and leapt up onto the circular stone platform, dodging between two pillars. She saw a dark movement off to her left and then went sprawling as a foot shot out of a door alcove.

'Fuck's sake, Kate,' said a voice above her. 'Let it go.'

She was up in a second while her sister bore down on her. Mabel's headscarf was knocked back, revealing newly cropped dark hair and a newly arrived port wine birthmark across half her face. She was holding a glinting knife. Her hand was steady. 'Don't make me regret not making a flambé of you and lover boy today. I let you go. You should return the favour.'

'Oh no,' said Kate, calculating the angle of her kick and wishing her sandals were less flimsy. 'You don't just walk away from what you've done, you sick bitch.'

Mabel rolled her eyes in just the way she always had

when Kate had gone into her room or borrowed something without asking. 'You don't even *know* the people I've killed. Apart from Zoe and you hardly knew her, either. She was *my* friend, not yours.'

'So that made it OK to smash her head in, did it?' spat Kate. 'In a fit of jealous rage. Because Lucas preferred her to you. And she preferred Lucas to you. You're nothing but a spoilt brat with a fucked-up brain.'

Mabel laughed and shook her head. 'Lucas did *not* prefer her to me. He couldn't get enough of me. I drove him wild. I drove him wild just yesterday. And the day before. Did he tell you what we did together, down in that pit? He might have been afraid, but you should have seen the hard on! I rode him 'til he screamed.'

'Cheap shot, Mabel — not going to work,' said Kate, gulping down the acid rising in her throat. 'I am not letting you go.'

'Come on then,' said Mabel, backing away with her knife hand still steady and ready. 'I didn't want to kill you in that pit. I was feeling sentimental and thinking of Mum. But Mum's dead and I have no problem with sending you to join her if you take a step closer.'

Kate launched her kick and sent the knife spinning up into an arc as she landed on Mabel, crashing her backwards into the foot of a pillar. Mabel shrieked and rolled away under her, slick and strong as an eel, sending an elbow crashing up into Kate's jaw and seizing the blade as it spun on the stone rotunda floor. She rolled back as Kate made to dive on her and brought up the knife, slashing through her sister's left forearm, sending a scarlet arc through the air in its wake.

Kate fell sideways, clutching the wound which was deep and spurting. *Fuck.* It looked like a severed artery.

Mabel was back on her feet, a slight shake now in her knife hand. 'You made me do this,' she hissed. 'I warned you not to. Like I always warned you not to do things I didn't like. And you always had to do them anyway. If you can't do as you're told, Kate, I can't be held resp—'

The wind was knocked out of her as Kate propelled herself forward head-first, a human battering ram right to the centre of her sister's torso. The blade zig-zagged in the air as Mabel staggered backwards, gasping. Then Kate was upon her again, knocking her off the circle of stone and onto the paving around it, grabbing for her knife hand and seizing her wrist. Mabel snatched a handful of Kate's hair and tore at it brutally while wrestling her weapon arm away. Kate smashed Mabel's hand down against the stone, again and again, hearing the knuckles crunch, until at last the knife shot from her sister's fingers and skittered away out of reach.

She was dimly aware of people nearby, watching this appalling scene in shock. 'CALL THE POLICE!' she screamed. 'ASTINOMIKON!'

Mabel stared up at her, gleaming blood spattered across her face from the deep knife wound she'd inflicted on her sibling. 'No way,' she grunted, her eyes glittering. 'This is NOT the way it ends!' And she sank her teeth into the wounded arm.

The bite was merciless. The knife wound was bad enough but adrenaline had distracted Kate from the pain. This though, was indescribable agony and she felt herself begin to black out as she tried to stay on top of Mabel, pinning her down. Black bloomed around the edges of her vision as she screamed and lost her grip for just a moment. Just long enough.

A second later Mabel was on her feet and leaping over

the railings, flapping away like a crow startled from carrion, the black dress lifting in the air behind her.

And then her ludicrous costume did what Kate and Lucas and the whole of the British and the Greek police force had failed to.

It stopped her.

As she threw herself across the top of the railing the billowing black cloth caught on a spike and snagged her backwards. She landed with the full force of both gravity and velocity, hitting the top of the railing with a sound like the puncture of a leather football.

The scream was sickening. From her position, bleeding copiously on the ground, Kate could see what had finally brought her sister to the end of her long, deadly career. Three spikes had disappeared into her torso, just beneath the shoulder blades. A rivulet of blood was already dripping down each of them.

Kate staggered to her feet, struggling not to vomit. 'Mabel..?' She hardly dared to look as she stumbled to the railing.

Her sister lay in an awkward backward arch, her feet not quite reaching the grass and her arms limp. She made a wet, sucking sound, but said nothing. Her eyes were open. So was her mouth. Footsteps and shouts permeated through the hissing shock in Kate's head. Flashing lights and sirens were approaching. Lucas — or one of the bystanders — had called the police in at last.

'K...K...K...'

Kate leaned in closer to her sister's mouth, which was drooling strings of crimson. 'What?' she croaked. 'What do you want to say?'

'K...K...' Mabel's eyes swivelled, one of the brown

contact lenses dislodged, revealing half a glassy silver-blue iris beneath it. 'K...come... come... for... you...'

Kate realised that even now — right up to the moment when her sister had tried to kill her — she had still hoped there might be a whispered apology.

'No, Mabel,' she said, dully. 'I came for *you*.'

35

K ate and Lucas did not make their early morning flight, British Airways tending to have issues with passengers in need of a blood transfusion.

Lucas stayed in her hotel room for two nights while she was in the hospital. He needed a little recovery time himself. By the time he'd arrived on the scene of Kate and Mabel's deadly fight paramedics were working on both sisters and neither victim was conscious. He literally dropped to his knees on the grass, fear taking the air from his lungs. When he had learned how to breathe again, he'd tried to run across to Kate but there were already police cordoning the area and he was stopped.

In the end he was found by the detective who had interviewed him earlier that day, who allowed him to sit with Kate in the ambulance as she was rushed in. Kate was ghostly white, blood blooming constantly through the bandage on her arm. She did not respond when he called her name, and he did not dare to let his thoughts stray to Sid and the question he most longed — and dreaded — to get answered.

His relief when she woke up, two units into a four-unit transfusion, was beyond measure. He was allowed to stay at her bedside, her arm now stitched and cleanly bandaged and antibiotics coursing through her to fight infection in her deep bite wound. She was too tired to talk to him, fading in and out of consciousness and pale as the sheets. And when she did finally have the strength to speak, he was swiftly elbowed aside by the Greek police who had descended on the small island en masse, to clear up the Christina Eliades murders. By the time they'd squeezed out every last detail of the chase and the fight and Mabel's final fling on the spikes of the celebrated Maitland Monument, Kate was too exhausted to open her mouth again that day.

He was back first thing the next morning. Sitting and gazing at her for so long was like a meditation. He was lost in the shape of her patterns, the frequencies her physical and electrical form existed on, as they rose and fell and eddied and rallied while she slowly regained her strength and awareness.

At one point he brought Sid out and tried to divine his future as it related to Kate Sparrow... but as was often the case when asking questions which were just too close to home, he couldn't get much sense from the pendulum or any of the readings he was picking up through his own body, heart, soul... whatever it was. All he could read was the unbreakable bond he had with Kate. But that didn't confer a happy ever after, did it?

There were newspapers lying around the hospital visitors' cafe which he visited from time to time. Mabel — alias Christina Eliades — was all over them. MURDER SUSPECT SKEWERED he slowly translated, featuring a shot of the railings Mabel had eventually been lifted from, sand blotting up the blood on the grass and stone, crime scene tape fluttering in the foreground. Alongside it was another glamorous photo of Mabel, dressed like Audrey Hepburn in a black and white dress and hat, with that sultry smile she had perfected back when she was fifteen.

He was glad he couldn't read much Greek. He didn't want to pick over the details of his first girlfriend's brutal crimes. So he was happy to find an earlier paper, stuffed at the back of the rack, its front page featuring the photo of four happy men on an Italian tomato farm who had dug up a treasure trove of ancient gold coins, reportedly worth millions. Alberto, Gino, Pepe and Farid posed with spades and huge grins at the pit they had all dug, well inside Alberto's boundaries. Lucas beamed at his old friends and hoped he would be able to call Alberto in the coming weeks and cash in his five per cent. He was going to need it.

He took the front page, folded it carefully, and tucked it into his shirt pocket to share with Kate some time. He finished his coffee and headed back to her bedside where he sensed she was close to resurfacing. A nurse came in and checked her blood pressure and at last she opened her eyes fully and stared across at him.

'Is Mabel..?' she breathed.

'She's on life support,' he said. 'She should be dead. She might die yet. They're not telling me much.'

Her eyes filled with tears. 'Shit,' she murmured. 'Francis.'

'It's OK. I called him,' said Lucas, holding up her phone. 'He's worried about you but I convinced him not to fly out. I... I didn't tell him about Mabel. I thought you'd want to. Although I can... if that would be easier for you.'

She shook her head. 'No. I'll tell him in person as soon as I get back. I don't think it'll get out before then. Thank god it all happened in another country...'

He took her hand. 'How are you feeling?'

'Better,' she said. 'I just want to get home. Find out if I've still got a job...'

'I think you have,' said Lucas. 'I've been on the phone to your boss, too. Kapoor called your mobile and I picked up. Filled him in with a bit more detail than the Greek police had offered up. He was going to fly out, too, but I convinced him to just meet us at Heathrow tomorrow. If anyone's going to arrest me, I think I'd prefer it to be Kapoor. He *probably* won't taser me.' Lucas grinned. He had dowsed a tumour in Kapoor's left kidney last year, getting him to seek treatment while it was still early and operable. He hoped he could cash in that favour in the next couple of days.

Kate's fingers closed around his. 'What if I'd never got you into any of this?' she murmured.

'Hey — I wouldn't have missed it for the world,' he chuckled, drily.

'You've got a lot of texts and messages,' he told her later, when she was sitting up and eating breakfast. 'Lots from Francis, of course, and loads from Salisbury CID. Your mate Ben Michaels seems to have found it quite amusing that you nearly died in the middle of a stone circle. What's that about?'

'Oh god,' she said, through a mouthful of toast. 'I left him high and dry to solve the crop circle murders... or suicides... probably murders.' She sighed. 'I really could have used your help on that one.'

'Well, it's not too late,' he said. 'Michaels doesn't seem to have got very far, judging by his messages.' He thumbed through them, biting his lip. 'He's really pissed off you didn't take him to Corfu with you. Fences to mend, I think...'

'That's the least of my worries,' she said. 'The first of them is Francis. What the hell am I going to say to Francis?'

———

IT WAS on the flight home that Kate told Lucas about the crop circle case. She was remarkably revived, thanks to the assorted Greeks who had kindly donated about half the blood currently in her veins. She'd decided she would donate to the National Blood Bank in the UK as soon as she was able, by way of appreciation.

'Rafe Campion is the obvious suspect,' she told Lucas, resting her arm, in its white calico sling close to his, and glancing down at the Italian Alps through white tufts of cloud. 'He's a narcissist who's built his own religion and really bought in to his own demigod status. He may not have poisoned them himself, but it looks like he brainwashed them into doing it.'

'For their money?' asked Lucas.

'Maybe... partly... but also because... because he could,' she said.

After a while he said: 'You don't think that, though, do you?'

She sighed and frowned. 'It makes sense. He's the obvious suspect, like I said, and there's motive — and definitely opportunity. The MO would fit — the ritual nature of it, the crop circles setting, the sense of sacrifice...'

'But..?'

'I don't know,' she said. 'And anyway, I don't have to know now. I'm suspended pending a disciplinary. Michaels is running it with Sharpe and Mulligan.'

'Shit — sorry about that,' said Lucas.

She shrugged. 'It's no less than I deserve, running out on them all and lying about being ill. It wasn't like I didn't know the penalty. I just... didn't care enough to stop myself.

There was literally nothing more important to me than tracking you down — not even keeping my job.'

'Kapoor won't fire you,' said Lucas. 'He's on your side.'

'Maybe, but he's got no choice about what happens next. I've got it coming. Still, at least he'll be happy to nail Campion, as soon as they've pulled together enough evidence. Campion was head boy at his son's school. Kapoor did *not* take to him.'

She called up the school photo she had taken a snap of, on a whim, and showed it to Lucas, pointing out first Sami Kapoor and then Rafe Campion.

'Looks like a smarmy little shit, doesn't he?' said Lucas.

'Yes... but is he a *murdering* smarmy little shit?'

'Well, let's see,' said Lucas. He pulled Sid out from his shirt. Pushing his tray table down, he put Kate's phone with the picture on it, flat on the tray and rested his elbows on either side, dropping the pendulum between his steepled hands.

'Lucas — you're twenty thousand feet up on a frigging plane!' Kate pointed out. 'How the hell can you dowse like that?'

'Shhh,' he said. 'Let me focus.'

The pendulum wasn't exactly steady but he pressed on regardless. 'Is the crop circle killer in this photograph?' he muttered, as Kate leaned in, fascinated and sceptical.

The pendulum spun. 'Apparently yes,' said Lucas. 'You have your man.'

Kate pointed to Rafe Campion. 'Is it this smarmy little shit?' she asked.

Lucas focused again and they both watched as Sid began to rock.

'That could just be turbulence,' said Kate.

Lucas said: 'It's not. Your hunch is right. It isn't him.'

Kate felt a tingle pass through her. She reached across and rested her finger on that other face... the one she vaguely recognised. The one Kapoor thought might be an actor or politician or some other high-profile person. 'Is it him?' she asked.

Sid spun. Kate sat back in her seat, stunned.

'So... who is it?' asked Lucas.

'I don't know,' she murmured.

'You do know,' he said. 'That's why you made a connection. You just need to focus.'

Kate closed her eyes. She left herself drift. She could feel Lucas's bare right upper arm close against her left upper arm, touching the skin above her bandage. The contact was both distracting and calming. She breathed deeply and dropped down a layer.

Then she shocked nearby passengers by shouting: 'Fucking hell! It's HIM!'

36

'He was a swindler, a cheat... a self-anointed messiah, brainwashing his followers. He needed to be taught a lesson.'

Kate leant forward, staring at the feed from the Salisbury CID interview room. Kapoor had somehow delayed the process of suspending her. So from the comfort of her own sofa, Francis plying her with meals and drinks as she recovered her strength, she had helped to mastermind bringing their prime suspect in. Kapoor had agreed to allow her to watch the bodycam feed as Michaels and a team of officers went in for the arrest.

Earlier, Michaels had briefed her on the investigation's progress over the phone — but not before he'd vented. He was, as Lucas had warned her, seriously pissed off with her for running off to Corfu alone.

'I thought we were a team!' he'd said. 'You should have taken me as backup.'

'We were in the middle of a murder case!' she had argued. 'We couldn't both cut and run, and you know it. And as soon as I'd said anything, Kapoor would have grounded me and handed it all over to Interpol.'

'So... you should have let him!' She couldn't see him but she knew he was swiping his hand through his neatly waxed dark hair, the way he always did when he was frustrated.

'Ben, I know,' she said. 'I'm sorry. It was all just too... too personal. Do you understand?'

There was a pause and then he grunted: 'Yeah. I suppose so.'

Then he'd filled her in on what had been uncovered while she was away. Following an anonymous tip-off on the CrimeStoppers line, he and his team had tracked down three geometry students from Bournemouth University who'd confessed to making the first crop circle — and filming it at dusk on the eve of the discovery of Linda Stewart's body. They all seemed, Michaels said, to be genuinely freaked out about the body found in their artwork the next morning. They also had good alibis for the next couple of days, meaning they could not have made the subsequent circles.

'And you can see it when you look,' Michaels had told her. 'The second and third circles are smaller and not as precise. Whoever made them is an amateur compared to the students.'

'So we're ruling out aliens, then,' she'd said, eliciting a snort from her DC. Then she'd told him her own theory and hours later she was watching live as Michaels and three backup officers first identified the Ford Focus sitting outside an address in Burchfont and then went in to make the arrest.

And now here he sat, his handsome face wearing a noble expression as he justified his actions.

'Five members of my congregation had defected to the

so-called Church of the Enlightened Energy,' said the Reverend Jason Bennet, his words dripping with scorn. 'And more would have followed. Campion was targeting them, the worthless shit, just to piss me off. Just to prove that he could. I tried to reason with them — tried to convince them he was a fake and only after their money. But they wouldn't be told.'

It had taken a few days to make the connection between the three victims — all of them were, until recent months, attendees of Burchfont Parish Church. Kate had known about Linda's connection, of course. She remembered the vicar telling her about the artistic order of service Linda had done for the church at Christmas. There were many examples of her handwriting for Bennet to copy when he made the suicide note — but they were all neat and calligraphic, rather than the woman's natural script. This explained the odd disconnect Kate had felt when she had seen that note fished from Linda's silver slipper.

'So, rather than let them go,' Michaels said, 'you preferred to poison them and frame Rafe Campion for it.'

'For influencing their suicides... or murdering them himself... yes,' said Bennet, whose shift into confessional mode was quite breathtaking. He had the air of a man who believed God was entirely on his side. 'I want you to know that I made sure they did not suffer at all. And they were all ill and not likely to live for very long anyway. I made their deaths painless and meaningful.'

'Meaningful,' repeated DS Sharpe, staring the man down and bouncing the point of his pen on his notepad as if he'd rather stab it in the vicar's eye. Kate wouldn't blame him if he did.

'Their deaths will stop many hundreds of others

following a false idol and losing their life savings, their homes, their dignity...' Bennet went on, loftily.

'How did you get them to the crop circles?' asked Michaels.

'I sent them a note, in a good copy of Campion's handwriting. I've been an excellent forger since school. The other boys used to pay me to make sick notes for them when they bunked off. I got him to sign and dedicate his nauseating book so I could copy it, and then I sent them a note from their idol, with coordinates, telling them a new crop circle had arrived and they should find it and transcend with the help of a mind-opening elixir. I left the little flasks of elixir waiting for them, along with a lantern, and they all arrived and did the rest for me. None of them was forced to do it. They went willingly, even the second two, knowing about Linda's death.'

He paused and shook his head, smiling to himself. 'It's hard to believe they were so idiotic, but that's the effect Campion has on weak-minded people. Of course, I needed to plant their goodbye notes, but again, that was easy. I had writing samples from all of them, in Christmas cards and other such things. I watched from the shadows and then set the scene once I was sure they'd... transcended. The only difficult part was making the bloody circles. It's not as easy as you're led to believe. Took me a lot of sweat and toil. But I did it.' He beamed around at them all as if expecting congratulations.

Michaels and Sharpe looked at each other and then pressed on, drawing out the detail of the confession, including the confirmation that Bennet had been out driving in his Ford on the night the tractor mechanic had seen the light in the field and then been nearly blindsided by it. The matching plate, along with the thick red mud on the tyres, was confirmation, even if it wasn't needed.

Bennet seemed almost lit up, as if he was delivering his most inspired sermon. It emerged that his brother was a local vet, which was where the Rev had sourced the Pentobarbital. It also emerged that he and Campion had been deadly rivals throughout their time at school together — a feud that had spilled over into their adult lives.

Kate wondered if Campion had come back to the area and pulled his Church of Enlightenment stunts in the locality purely to piss Bennet off. It was entirely possible. Kate's satisfaction in getting Bennet arrested was dulled only by the sadness at what he had done and for such puerile reasons. The more he talked, the more it became obvious that this was less about his Godly mission than about point-scoring with Campion. Two entitled, upper-class public schoolboys had grown up allowing their petty rivalries to follow them into adulthood and blight the innocent in appalling ways.

As the interview was wrapped up and Bennet returned to his cell to await remand, Kate's energy deserted her and she closed the laptop and slumped onto the sofa.

'You need a break,' Francis said to her, arriving with more tea and sitting down next to her.

'We both do,' she said. 'And look how well *that* went last time we tried.'

'I want to see her,' he said.

Kate gulped. She had been expecting this.

'I want to look her in the eye and ask why,' said Francis.

Kate wished her sister had died. First, she wished she had died seventeen years ago, victim of a random, senseless murder. Then she wished she had died a few days ago, on those spikes.

But Mabel had pulled through and was now under police guard in a Greek prison hospital. Months — years, even — of court cases would follow. The details would slowly be picked open, like a suppurating scab wound, and she and Francis would be caught up in the evil outpouring, like it or not.

She squeezed her brother's hand and nodded. 'I understand. But let's wait, yeah? Until we both feel strong enough. You can come with me when I have to go back to Corfu — or Athens, most likely — and testify. You'll be able to see her in court, I guess.'

'Well,' said Francis, getting up and stretching. 'At least Lucas is finally in the clear.'

'Yeah,' she said. 'He could still be charged for absconding... perverting the course of justice... but Kapoor doesn't want to charge him with anything. He's... quite taken with Lucas.'

'Well, Kapoor's not alone in that, is he?' Francis raised an eyebrow at her. 'When are you seeing him again?'

Kate sighed. 'Tomorrow, maybe. I don't know. It's all so... I mean, I don't know if we can be...'

'Oh for fuck's sake — when the hell are you two going to just shag each other into next week and get it out of your system?' said Francis, encapsulating it all rather well.

37

'Larry — it's worth five million euros!' Alberto whispered down the phone, as if someone was listening in. 'That is what they tell me! *Five million!*'

Lucas sat on the step of his back terrace, watching the insects dart around the wildly overgrown garden. The scent of wild mint and lemon verbena was drifting through the warm late summer air. He smiled at Alberto's happy voice. 'How much does the Italian government get of that?' he asked.

'About a quarter,' sighed Alberto. 'But that's still three million, seven hundred and fifty thousand, my friend. And your five per cent will be... one hundred and eighty-seven thousand, five hundred euros. Give or take. How does that sound?'

'It sounds amazing,' said Lucas.

'And the other thing,' said Alberto, his tone shifting to a loftier pitch. 'As we speak, the police are holding one Lazlo Palari in custody, while they investigate the bodies found on his land this week.'

'Shit! No! Really?!' Lucas thumped his left fist on his

knee and then winced as the bandaged wrist howled. 'You got the spaniel?!'

'We did,' said Alberto. 'She's a rescue dog and she has the best nose in the business. We went walking right past a certain foxhole in the boundary and...'

'That is just brilliant, Alberto!'

'Watch the news channels,' Alberto said, not quite able to keep the glee out of his voice. 'It will all come out now, you'll see. And in the meantime, my workforce is up to twenty! They're getting out of Palari's farm while they can.'

He concluded with promises to let Lucas know as soon as the auction date for the coins was set. 'Come out and stay with us!' he said. 'We will all go to watch the bidding!'

'I will,' said Lucas and then ended the call, tucking his new smartphone back into his pocket. It was still a novelty to be connected again after so long off the network.

He felt Kate arrive before she rang the doorbell. He found her on the doorstep and led her around to the garden. 'The house is damp and smells like a crypt,' he said. 'You can come in when I've fixed it all up.'

She nodded and followed him, her fingers lacing into his.

'Did you get your guy?' he asked, turning to face her and trying to behave as if his heart wasn't currently trying to smash its way right out of his ribcage. This was the first time — ever — that they were together simply because they wanted to be. She was wearing a blue denim button-up dress, flat strappy sandals and an expression that mirrored his own.

She smiled, raising a bandaged forearm to push a strand of hair off her face. 'Yup. We were right. The *Salisbury Journal* is going to be in meltdown about this when it gets out. REVENGE-CRAZED VICAR KILLS RIVAL'S FOLLOWERS! But hey... how are you?'

'No,' he said.

'No... what?'

'Can't do the talk,' he said. 'Shut up.' And he pulled her to him to continue with a kiss which had started a week ago in Corfu. They connected effortlessly, moving together with a physical fluency he'd never encountered with anyone else. No awkwardness. No bumped noses. No stumbles of any kind.

It was as they found a dry, nettle-free patch in the wild grass, fusing into each other with the relief of water meeting a parched riverbed, that Kate's phone went off.

She ignored it. As did he.

It went off again. And again.

———

'OH FOR GOD'S SAKE!' Kate rolled away from Lucas, laughing, and made as if to hurl her bloody mobile into the bushes. But she caught the name on the call. Kapoor.

There was very little — with Lucas Henry lying back on his elbows, shirt undone, tangled hair full of grass seed and eyes full of delirious intent — that could induce her to pull away. But this was Kapoor's personal number.

Lucas caught her expression. He sat up and picked some seed from her own hair. 'Go on,' he said. 'We've waited nearly a year. I can stand another few minutes.'

She sighed and picked up the call.

'Kate.' The sound of his voice clamped some part of her into a tight ball.

'What is it?' she asked. 'Are you suspending me now?'

'I wanted you to hear this from me first,' he said, in a voice which told her he was very much off duty.

She gulped. 'Tell me what?'

'It's about Lucas. And Mabel...'

Kate stared up at Lucas, watching his face slowly crease with concern as he read her expression... her patterns.

'The Greeks... they want him back in Athens for questioning. Mabel is claiming...' Kapoor took a breath. 'She's claiming he was part of it all. The murder of Zoe.'

'That's just bullshit!' Kate burst out. 'She confessed everything to me! She has no proof he was involved!'

'And you have no proof of her confession,' he said. 'And Mabel is claiming she *does* have proof relating to Lucas. Somewhere. Kate... I'm so sorry. I don't believe this either. I think she's just going to put you both through it because she can. I'm so, so sorry...'

Lucas gazed at her as she ended the call. His expression told her he knew exactly what was coming.

She got to her feet, sick to her heart. 'I have to go,' she said. 'But... I'll be back. You might want to... go away somewhere for a while. Maybe today.'

38

H er sister smiled at her beyond the screen. Even now, on a drip, sagging in a wheelchair, and facing life in prison, she had the look of a winner.

After casually implicating Lucas in her first ever murder, Mabel had shut down. She had insisted she would say nothing more. Not to anyone. Not before she had spoken to her sister, alone. Once she had done that she would waive her right to silence and cooperate fully. The Athens police, frustrated, had agreed to her demand. Kate had flown to Greece the same day Kapoor had called her.

'He's mine,' Mabel said, her smile spreading lazily. 'He was mine at the start and he was mine when he came to me on Corfu and he will be mine to the end. You do see that, don't you?'

Kate shook her head. 'He hates you,' she said. 'He told me what you did in that pit. You revolt him.'

'There's no happy ever after for you two,' said Mabel. 'I'm about to give my evidence to the police.'

'*What* evidence?' Kate wanted to break down the plexi-glass barrier and smash her sister to the floor.

'DNA, fingerprints, semen... I have it all,' said Mabel, smiling. 'On Zoe's knickers... I kept those, you know. I bet they didn't tell you that she wasn't wearing any when they found her, did they? I took them and I messed them up with what Lucas spilled on my skirt when he couldn't control himself. And then I buried them... or rather, *Lucas* buried them, somewhere in Wiltshire. I'm going to tell them we killed her together... a sex game gone wrong.'

Kate gulped back nausea. She gripped the table and swayed. This was the time to reveal she had a recording device on her... but all phones and gadgets had to be surrendered before she could enter the prisoner contact area.

'Why are you doing this? What the hell do you *want*?' she hissed.

'Not much,' Mabel said. 'I want to be in a prison in England. Close to my family.'

Kate gaped at her.

'And I want to see you from time to time.'

'You're joking.'

'Not at all. I am very interested in your life. I want to stay in touch.'

'You think I can make that happen?'

'Yes — I think you can.'

'And that's it?' Kate gritted her teeth.

'No,' said Mabel. 'You'll have to leave Lucas alone. Remember? I have never liked sharing my things with you. If you take my stuff, you get payback. He was mine first. He can't be yours. Leave him alone and I will never speak of the *terrible* things he did to Zoe.' She shrugged and tilted her head. 'Of course, it's your choice, little sis. Your choice...'

———

SHE WAS BLUFFING. She had to be. Kate knew this. *Knew it.* But there would always be a seed of doubt, now, wouldn't there? Not that Lucas had done any of the appalling things Mabel was concocting in the many hours of downtime she now had. But that she had got something which might pass for evidence buried somewhere in England.

Another bluff. And yet, Kate had to admit, Mabel *had* persuaded their mother to bury her own underwear and DNA evidence, just in case. What else had Mum done to protect her first born?

Kate could ignore the threats. She go back to Lucas. Give in to everything she wanted. Give him everything he wanted.

But how could she ever be sure someone as clever as Mabel wouldn't find out? How could she know she wasn't condemning him?

Like her twisted sister said... there could be no happy ever after.

As she waited in the airport, grappling with hardest decision of her life, Lucas Henry called.

'When are you back?' he said. 'Kate — I have to see you.'

Kate sank to a bench.

She ended the call.

And switched off her phone.

ACKNOWLEDGMENTS

Massive thanks to Beverly Sanford (editing), Nicola Sparkes (vital insights), Sarah Bodell (police procedure guidance) and Neville Dalton (fine-tuning).

To The Collective and my core ARC reader crew - Pippa, Mary, Deb, Julie, Maureen, Carrie and Carol - whose help and enthusiasm has topped up my tank.

To Meg Jolly for superb cover art and big support, to Debbie & Alex Scarrow for accommodating my whimpering over Zoom and to William Ware for vital legalese tweaks (and not laughing outright at my first draft).

And, finally, to Simon Tilley, for late night wisdom and laughing/sharply inhaling in all the right places.

ALSO BY A D FOX

available now on Amazon

HENRY & SPARROW book 1:

THE DYING DOLLS

HENRY & SPARROW book 2:

DEAD AIR

HENRY & SPARROW book 3:

SEVEN DEADLY THINGS

and for a free copy

of the Henry & Sparrow prequel novella

UNDERTOW

go to www.adfoxfiction.com

ABOUT THE AUTHOR

AD Fox is an award winning author who lives in Hampshire, England, with a significant other, boomerang offspring and a large, highly porous labradoodle.

With a background in newspaper and broadcast journalism, AD once interviewed the late great Reg Presley of The Troggs, a Wiltshire man whose belief in alien-delivered crop circles was passionate and absolute. She has never forgotten it and, honestly, doesn't entirely rule the aliens out...

Younger readers will know the AD alter ego as Ali Sparkes, author of more than fifty titles for children and young adults including the Blue Peter Award winning Frozen In Time, the bestselling Shapeshifter series and Car-Jacked, finalist in the national UK Children's Book of the Year awards.

For more on AD Fox, including blogs and updates, visit www.adfoxfiction.com

Printed in Great Britain
by Amazon